AN INNOCENT HEART

VIKKI MOUNT

Diamond Tiger Publishing

An Innocent Heart

Copyright © 2023 by Vikki Louise Mount

Book Cover by Vikki Louise Mount

ISBN 978-0-6459899-1-5

www.vikkimount.com

For my parents,
Sheila and Chas Mount.
Gone but never forgotten
and forever loved.

CONTENTS

PREFACE

This book has been 15 years in the making, with countless hours of research and consideration.

Although I am a proudly Australian author, I have used U.S. spelling in deference to the setting of this book—Houston, Texas.

This story is fictional, but some locations and businesses mentioned are real to add local flavor.

The U.S. government and military, along with 27 states, still have the death penalty, with Texas leading the nation in the number of executions.

The Death Penalty Information Center states: -

> The death penalty carries the inherent risk of executing an innocent person. Since 1973, at least 190 people who had been wrongly convicted and sentenced to death in the U.S. have been exonerated.

That is an average of nearly four people yearly for the last 50 years. And those are only the ones they have identified. There are probably many more.

U.S. death row conditions are dire. Inmates typically spend twenty-three hours each day enduring solitary confinement in a small cell, denied any loving human contact as they await the inevitable, which, most times, is more than a decade. More than half of all prisoners currently sentenced to death in the U.S. have been on death row for over 18 years. Imagine suffering this psychological torture as an innocent person.

Often, inmates go insane from the isolation. Many turn to God for salvation. Some want permission to donate their organs after the state executes them to make their death meaningful and perhaps, if guilty, to seek redemption.

As not all my readers are U.S. citizens, I feel it is important to state that the death row donor (D.R.D.) program and the execution device (the Boltinator), first mentioned in chapter 12 of this book, are fictional.

At the time of this book's creation, although no law specifically forbids death row inmates from donating organs postmortem, the states with the death penalty have denied all requests by death row inmates to donate their organs after execution. There are inmates on death row fighting for that right as you read this.

Thus, my tale was born.

This story is for those innocents on death row—past and present—and for the people who loved them.

Chapter 1

Devastating Sentence

J on Kingsley felt like he was drowning, and no one seemed willing to throw him a life ring.

Judge McIntyre, a bespectacled, silver-haired woman in her sixties clad in a plain black robe, turned to the jury box, which comprised seven men and five women. "Members of the jury panel, I realize what a lengthy process this has been. We appreciate the time you've taken to make this decision today. You're now excused and are free to leave the courtroom."

As the twelve departed, Jon swiveled around in his seat to watch them leave and wondered what sentence they had given him. He suspected it wouldn't be good since no one seemed willing to make eye contact.

Jon could see his wife, Sarah, wasn't coping. Her long blond hair, usually a well-cared-for shining glory, hung in stringy clumps around her pale face and needed a wash. The weight had fallen off her from months of worry, making her appear fragile and childlike.

Her cornflower blue eyes locked with his. She looked scared and on the verge of tears.

Jon mouthed, "I love you."

Sarah's lips trembled as she returned the silent endearment.

The bailiff for the day, a burly, ginger-haired male police officer, stepped forward and spoke. "Eyes front for sentencing, and be quiet, please."

Jon turned back around and found McIntyre staring at him, grim-faced. She appeared unimpressed that he was trying to communicate with his wife right before the pronouncement.

Oh well, what more can you do to me? I guess I'm about to find out.

"Defendant, please rise," she said.

His knees shaking, Jon stood alongside a slim young woman, his attorney, Cathy McGregor, who was just out of law school and doing her best to appear professional. She'd tied her light brown hair in a severe ponytail and wore an old-fashioned gray suit that seemed borrowed from a maiden aunt. They exchanged glances, and the corners of Cathy's mouth flickered as she attempted to give him an encouraging smile but failed dismally.

A gentle sobbing started up behind him. It sounded like Sarah, and Jon wasn't surprised, but he couldn't turn to her. Horror froze him, and his heart pounded so fast it was difficult to breathe.

"Ms. McGregor, do you have anything further to add before I pronounce this sentence?" the judge asked.

"No, Your Honor."

"Thank you." Judge McIntyre adjusted her glasses and started reading. "The State of Texas versus Jonathan Raymond Kingsley—found guilty of the murders of Daniel Keith Bell, Gladys Joyce Phillips, and Ranjeet Singhe. The court sentences you to the death penalty, and—"

A small gasp escaped Jon's lips. It wasn't unexpected, but hearing those dreaded words was still a shock.

A gut-wrenching scream of despair that filled the courtroom interrupted McIntyre's pronouncement. Heads turned toward the source. It was Sarah.

"No, you can't kill my Jon, you can't! He didn't do this! I know he didn't!" Her body became wracked with uncontrollable sobbing. Mutterings and murmurings filled the room.

The judge banged her gavel until she regained control. "Mrs. Kingsley, I understand you're upset, and I sympathize. However, if you can't control yourself and refrain from further outbursts, I will instruct the bailiff to remove you from this courtroom. Do you understand?"

Jon watched in misery as his mother-in-law, Rose, an attractive fair-haired woman in her mid-thirties, tried to console his wife. She enveloped Sarah in her arms, pulling her close against her shoulder as she tried to absorb the sound of her daughter's noisy sobbing.

Next to them, and equally devastated, was an immaculately dressed black couple. They were Jon's foster parents, Gus and Winnie Whitmore. Smeared mascara circled Winnie's eyes because of a constant dabbing with her handkerchief, and Gus had unchecked tears rolling down his cheeks.

It was heartbreaking that circumstances beyond his control caused his loved ones this emotional pain. Jon wished he could hug them all but was helpless.

McIntyre continued with the sentencing. "I remand you into the custody of the Harris County Sheriff, who will deliver you to the Texas Department of Criminal Justice. That concludes this hearing. I require everyone to stay seated until the defendant has left the building."

It became too much. As the total weight of it all hit, blood rushed to Jon's head, causing his knees to buckle, and he collapsed into his chair. It felt like he was going to pass out.

The sheriff stepped forward, helped Jon to stand, handcuffed him, and then placed an authoritative hand on his shoulder, pushing him to walk. All Jon could comprehend at this point was the painful thudding of his heart and the sound of Sarah's stifled sobs.

The life he knew was now over, and he could do nothing about it.

Chapter 2

Out of Work

Six months earlier, Jon stood before the manager of G.T. Transport with his cap in hand and eyes pleading. "You sure you've got nothing for me, Garry?"

Garry Thompson was an overweight man with thinning gray hair. His cheeks were bright red, and his forehead dripped with sweat, thanks to the lack of air conditioning in his tiny, cluttered office. Dark, damp patches dominated his gray T-shirt emblazoned with the G.T. Transport logo.

"I'm sorry, Jon. It's the same thing I told you last week. There's not enough work. Otherwise, I'd have you packing shelves for me right now."

"One job's all I need to get enough money to cover this week's rent. You know I've got a wife and kid to support. It's at the point I'll need to tell Sarah."

"You mean Sarah doesn't know? Lord have mercy! I wouldn't want to be you. But as I told you, that new transport company is killing my business."

Garry walked to his office window and pointed at a billboard across the road. In giant letters were the words *Speeditrans—We deliver*, on an image of a green truck. In front of the truck stood a smiling man wearing the Speeditrans uniform handing a small parcel to a well-endowed, attractive young woman.

"They had the cheek to put that sign right outside my business. How can I compete with that? We're only a small, independent transport company, and they're a franchise with locations all over Texas.

"The church next door has offered to buy this building, and my wife wants me to accept. I hate the idea of early retirement, but I have no choice unless I can pick up new clients."

"Well, that will be a sad day, Garry."

"It is what it is. Did you take my advice and ask Speeditrans for a job?"

"Yes, I've tried. But they aren't hiring packers right now—only experienced drivers. I'd need a commercial truck driving license to apply, and I can't afford the training. I'd find a job just like that if I had one." Jon clicked his fingers for emphasis.

"I'm truly sorry. I promise I'll call you if extra work comes in."

"My little girl's hit the terrible twos. Sarah hasn't been coping, and I didn't want to worry her. How can I tell her we'll probably have to move back home with her momma? I'm a lousy husband."

"Kid, stop giving yourself a hard time. You're only eighteen. Most boys your age would have run away if they got a girl pregnant, but not you. I'm sure a good worker like you will find another job real soon."

"Really?" Jon pulled a face. "I surely appreciate the compliment, but I'm a teenage daddy with a juvie record who never finished tenth grade. No one is lining up to hire me, and money's getting tight." He let out a loud sigh and shrugged. "I guess I could always rob me a bank."

Garry's laughter filled the office. "I hear you. If I keep losing business, I'll drive your getaway car." He then rested a sympathetic hand on Jon's shoulder. "But seriously, next time you're at an interview, you get them to call me, and I'll give you a great reference. It's the least I can do."

"Thanks. I know this isn't your fault, and I've taken up enough of your time. Have a good day."

"You, too. Please pass on my regards to Sarah and give that young'un of yours a big hug from Uncle Garry."

"Will do."

As Jon walked outside, the sunlight temporarily blinded him. He put on his cap and adjusted the brim to shade his eyes. At least it was a pleasant day.

He bought the daily paper from a local newspaper stand and bundled it under his arm. Then, he took a brisk walk across the park to his favorite café.

Within five minutes, he arrived. On the window, Anna's in curly, pink letters, outlined in yellow and decorated with sunflowers, sat above an image of a frothy cappuccino. When Jon worked for Garry, the café was his daily lunch spot, but he hadn't visited since his redundancy.

I need a friendly face right now.

Inside, the decor was 50s-style with red leather booths and chairs with white tables on a black and white checked tiled floor. Anna, the owner, greeted him with a huge grin. She was in her thirties, tall and curvy, with long brown curls tied back with a red bow. She wore a red full-skirt dress, a white apron, bobby socks trimmed with lace, and red sneakers. "Hi, darlin'! Where've you been? I haven't seen you for over a week. Is everything okay?"

Jon shook his head, his face glum. "No, not really. My boss laid me off. I missed you, so I thought I'd drop in for lunch while I check out the job section." He pulled the newspaper from under his arm and held it up for her inspection.

"Oh, I'm very sorry to hear that." She gestured toward an empty booth in the corner. "Your booth's awaiting. The usual?"

"Thanks, Anna."

The only other customer in the café was a gangly, pimple-faced youth with oily, shoulder-length, dirty blond hair and pale blue eyes. He wore a black hoody paired with black jeans and sneakers. Jon smiled as he passed, but the youth glared back, averted his gaze, and stared out the window.

It seems I'm not the only one having a bad day.

Once seated at his booth, Jon reached into his pocket for his wallet. A quick inspection of the contents revealed his money situation was grim—not enough for lunch. He jumped out of his seat, ran to the counter to cancel his order, and saw that Anna had finished making his strawberry milkshake.

She looked up at him, her eyes wide with surprise. "What can I do for you, darlin'?"

"I'm real sorry, Anna, but I've just realized I'm short on cash. On my way home, Sarah usually wants something from the store, so I have to keep some money aside. Truth be told, I'm down to my last ten dollars, so I'm wondering if it's possible to put that milkshake on my tab. I promise to pay you when I get my next job."

"Oh, you poor sweetie. Times are tough for you right now, aren't they?"

Jon hung his head in embarrassment. "Yes, ma'am, they are. Do you need help around here? I could wash dishes, fix things, sweep the floors, or whatever you want."

"Oh, darlin', I'd love to give you work, but I only make enough money to keep myself going. I can't afford to pay anyone else."

"That's okay. I was only hoping."

Anna chewed her lip. "I'd hate you to go hungry. A growing boy like you needs more than just a milkshake."

She flicked her eyes toward the gangly youth nearby, still staring out the window, and then leaned across the counter. "Look, I don't have any money to pay you, but I need some heavy boxes rearranged in my storeroom. In return, you get a free feed. How does that sound?"

"It's better than any other offer I've had today. Want me to move those boxes for you now?"

"No, that'll be tomorrow's job after I get my delivery. For today, your meal's on me. Consider it a reward for your customer loyalty."

"Oh, Anna, you're the kindest, most generous—"

"Oh, shush, darlin'! You'll make a girl blush. Now go read your paper and check those want ads. I'm sure there's a job awaiting you in there."

Feeling more optimistic than he had done since Garry let him go, Jon returned to his booth, opened the paper, and began scanning. He started circling the unskilled labor jobs and couldn't help but sigh. Only casual work was on offer. Having to support a wife and child meant he needed something more permanent.

Daydreaming, he recalled that fateful day Sarah told him she was pregnant. Images of her tear-stained face filled his mind.

CHAPTER 3

UNCONVENTIONAL LIFE

"**I**'m late!" Sarah stared at Jon, her face stricken. "I'm never late!"

"But we were so careful. Are you sure?"

"Something must have gone wrong. I told you, I'm never late. Oh, sweet Jesus, Momma's gonna kill me." Her body became wracked with sobs.

Jon enveloped her in his arms. "*Sweet Pea*, I love you. No matter what, I'll stick by you." He gently placed his hand on her stomach. "If there's a baby in your belly, it's a gift from God. We'll love it and cherish it, and we'll make the best parents ever."

Sarah wiped the tears from her eyes and gave him a weak smile. "Do you really mean that?"

"Of course! We talked about having a family one day. It may be sooner than we expected, but we can do this. Trust me."

Despite sounding confident, Jon felt far from it. His foster parents, the Whitmores, preached no sex before marriage. He hated the fact that he would disappoint them.

Before the Whitmores took him in, Jon had never experienced everyday family life. His mother, Katherine, or Kat to her friends, had been a sex worker at *Massage Magic*, a brothel in disguise. She'd been in high demand with her long blond hair, blue eyes, ruby-red lips, and flawless porcelain skin.

With her line of work and hectic schedule, Kat had never factored motherhood into her plans. Pregnancy, therefore, came as a great surprise. Her doctor told her that the brand of antibiotics she took for a persistent kidney infection reduced the pill's effectiveness and, although a rare occurrence, this, along with a condom failure, was the most likely cause. Kat wouldn't consider an abortion because of her Catholic background, so she went ahead.

When her son was born, his dark hair and skin made it apparent that his father was black. However, Kat regularly serviced one-timers and bucks parties, making it impossible to pinpoint the father. She, therefore, accepted that Jon's paternal parentage would remain a mystery.

Kat had intended to put Jon up for adoption, but her dormant maternal urge kicked into overdrive when he opened his big brown eyes for the first time. An overwhelming love instantly filled her heart. So she changed her mind and kept him.

Jon spent his first five years at Kat's apartment or Massage Magic. The brothel owner, Gina, allowed the boy to stay on site because his mother was very popular with the clientele.

The child's presence also seemed good for morale. His sunny nature and ever-present smile made everyone happy to be around him. All the girls adored him and treated him like a beloved pet. Therefore, Jon was never short of a babysitter whenever Kat was working.

His Massage Magic *aunties* enjoyed reading him picture books or the latest romance novel on hand. When Jon wasn't cuddling up to one cosmetically augmented bosom or another, he was playing with his toys or watching kiddy shows.

Despite its unusualness, it was a happy life, and then Rodrigo Garcia came along. He was a short middle-aged Latino who wore colorful bandannas over his shaven head. Gold rings adorned every finger, and a fat gold chain was always around his neck, sporting a custom-made gold medallion engraved with the letter R encrusted with small diamonds.

Rodrigo was a man who usually got what he wanted. The second he saw Kat, he wanted her and started showering her with expensive gifts and buying large blocks of her time. During every visit, he also spoiled Jon with toys and candy.

One day, he turned up with an engagement ring and proposed. Kat saw a way out of her profession and thought her son needed a father figure, so she accepted Rodrigo's proposal despite not finding him attractive.

A few days later, the couple was married by an Elvis impersonator in Las Vegas, with Jon as their little ring bearer. Upon their return to Texas, the mother and son moved into Rodrigo's mansion. That's where the fairytale ended.

Kat soon discovered her new husband was a drug lord, and all his riches came from his cocaine deals. He introduced her to the world of never-ending cocaine. As a kept woman, she quickly became bored having passionless sex with one man and developed a severe addiction.

Two years later, Kat accidentally overdosed. Rodrigo was out when his lieutenant, Emilio, who found her unconscious on the living room floor, called to ask what to do. The drug lord, furious that he even needed to issue an instruction, ordered Emilio, under pain of death, to get Kat to the hospital immediately. The lieutenant bundled her limp form into his car and drove at reckless speed to a nearby hospital emergency room. Unfortunately, the medical response team pronounced Kat dead on arrival. Fearing Rodrigo's wrath for failing to ensure Kat's well-being, Emilio fled the scene and the state, never to be seen again.

It took over an hour for Rodrigo to learn that his wife had passed. Jon was seven years old and attending a local elementary school. The drug lord pulled the boy out of the classroom and took him to the nearest ice cream parlor. There, he broke the awful news as gently as a thug could over a bowl of cookies and cream.

After a mutual sharing of tears, the drug lord held the boy close and said, "Today, you need to become a man. I will look after you, my son, and teach you the family business."

A month later, Jon's initiation began. He delivered pre-paid cocaine to Rodrigo's customers in public areas such as train stations, parks, cafés, and restaurants. It was too easy. No one ever suspected a little boy with a kiddy backpack could be involved with such a nefarious activity. One of the Garcia gang members was always within eyeshot and at a safe distance, ensuring it all went according to plan.

On some level, Jon knew what he was doing was wrong, but the drug lord, in his weird way, gave the boy love and made him feel safe, needed, and valued. During this time, he continued to attend school and learned to accept that his life differed from the other kids in his class.

Jon lived this unconventional life for five years. But that all changed when Rodrigo invited another local drug lord, Louie López, to dine at his favorite Mexican restaurant. The purpose of the dinner was to propose forming a cartel to expand their drug empires. It was a private gathering, and all gang members from both parties were present, including Jon.

Unbeknownst to Rodrigo, an undercover fed called Sanchez had infiltrated his drug ring six months earlier. He knew all about the plan and wore a wire for the occasion, knowing that the dinner presented the perfect opportunity to arrest all members of both gangs. It would be the ultimate coup.

A federal unit parked in a white delivery van sat outside the restaurant, recording all cartel conversations. When Sanchez knew they had gathered enough evidence, he excused himself from the table. He ensured the catering staff remained in the kitchen for their safety and then sent the all-clear signal to the team waiting outside through his wire.

The feds planned to catch both gangs by surprise in a contained environment to avoid civilian casualties. When they burst in, Louie and his five gang members were facing away from the entrance, so they had no chance to turn around. They, therefore, threw up their hands and surrendered immediately.

However, Rodrigo and his new lieutenant, Manuel, surprised them all. Instead of also giving in, they overturned the table before them. Louie and two gang members grunted in pain as the table bounced off their knees and smashed onto their feet. Rodrigo and Manuel crouched behind the overturned table and pulled out their guns.

The other two members of the Garcia gang, Carlos and José, followed suit, injuring the three remaining López gang members across from them. All this happened in mere seconds.

Rodrigo grabbed Jon's arm and pulled hard, causing the boy's chair to crash onto its side and take Jon with it. Rodrigo kicked the chair away and pushed Jon's head to the floor. "Stay down!" he growled.

Carlos, the hothead of the group, fired the first shot. And then it was on. The sound of gunfire filled the air as bullets flew everywhere. All six members of the López gang scrambled to get out of the crossfire.

Jon put his hands over his ears and curled himself into a fetal position. He watched Rodrigo transform from a loving fatherly figure into a crazed gunman with murderous intent in his eyes.

Carlos received a bullet through the head when he popped it above the table in the ensuing mayhem. José then panicked and tried to make a run for it. A fed shot him in the shoulder before he got very far, and he fell, screaming and crying in pain.

Manuel and Rodrigo held their position well. They had just taken out one fed, and another was in their sights when Sanchez stepped in, deciding to blow his cover before they could shoot anyone else. He came in from behind and aimed his gun at them.

"Police! Don't move!" Sanchez held up his badge, revealing he was with the feds. "Drop your weapons!"

For Rodrigo, surrender was not an option. He pushed Jon behind him, then turned to point his gun at Sanchez. "Rot in hell, you bastard!"

Sanchez had no choice but to defend himself. So he pulled the trigger and shot Rodrigo, hitting him in the chest.

The drug lord looked down at the bloody, wet patch spreading across his shirt with a gasp of surprise. He fell back into a crying Jon's lap. Somehow, he found the strength to reach up and gently wipe the tears from the boy's face. "Don't cry, my son. Be brave. I love you." His arm then dropped, and his eyes glazed over as he died.

Now realizing they had him surrounded, Manuel dropped his gun, threw up his hands in surrender, placed them behind his neck, and put his head on the floor. Sanchez moved in and arrested him.

By some miracle, Louie and all his gang members had escaped the bullet storm relatively unscathed, apart from a few bruised knees and crushed toes.

When the feds could move in and make their arrests, they found Jon behind the table, his shirt covered in blood. He rocked back and forth in shock while clinging onto Rodrigo's lifeless form.

Despite his young age and the horrors he had just witnessed, the feds showed him little sympathy. Once they knew he was unwounded, they pulled him to his feet, threw him in handcuffs, and escorted him from the restaurant.

They detained him in remand for a week until he appeared in juvenile court. Sanchez tried to speak up for Jon, as he knew his circumstances. However, when the boy admitted to performing regular cocaine deliveries, the judge determined that a harsh life lesson was required. He sentenced Jon to a year in juvenile detention.

That time passed slowly, and six months into the sentence, boredom led Jon to a service at the onsite chapel. He had never attended church before and found himself captivated by the sermons. It was there that he met Pastor Tim.

The pastor, recognizing a child in need, reached out to him. Before long, he became a confidant and friend as the boy poured out his grief about his feelings of loss. He realized Jon needed a kind, patient Christian family to set him on the right path when he rejoined society. This understanding led him to talk to his congregation to see if he could find the boy a stable and loving home.

Gus and Winnie Whitmore, a middle-aged childless couple, stepped up. When they first met, the connection was instant. A few visits later, they made fostering plans, which resulted in the young man moving into their home at the end of his sentence.

Once settled in, they enrolled him at a local high school. At thirteen, Jon had grown into a tall, handsome young man with a dazzling smile. On his very first day in the classroom, he met Sarah. She had long blond hair, full red lips, and big, cornflower blue eyes, just like his beloved mother, whom he missed dearly.

The young couple exchanged furtive glances all day until their eyes met, at which point Sarah coyly tossed her golden locks and gave him a shy smile. It was love at first sight.

Three years later, this love led them to the birth of their baby girl.

CHAPTER 4

COST OF INDEPENDENCE

"Here you go, darlin'." Anna placed a milkshake and a burger with fries before Jon.

"Thank you so much. You have a heart the size of Texas."

"We aims to please. Now stop your yapping and enjoy your food."

Jon needed little encouragement, having not eaten all day, so he quickly demolished the meal. When finished, he pushed the plate away, fished into his pocket for his phone, and rang Sarah.

On the sixth ring, she answered. "Hi, *Sugar Pie!*"

"Hi there, Sweet Pea. Just on my way home. Do you need anything from the store?"

Before she could reply, their little girl's voice called out in the background. "Daaadaaaa! Daaaadaaaa!"

"Quiet, please, sweetie. Mommy's trying to talk to Dada. Now, play with your dolly. There's a good girl." Sarah huffed loudly with frustration. "She's been driving me demented all day. A few months ago, I couldn't wait for her to learn to walk and speak. Now I wish she was still crawling and would just shut up for five whole minutes."

She let out an enormous sigh. "And those toys! If I roll my ankle on another darn doll, I'll scream! Sometimes, I think leaving Momma's was a big mistake. It was much easier when we were living with her. At least she gave me a break."

Jon chuckled. Maybe telling Sarah his news wouldn't be so bad after all. "You make me laugh, my gorgeous girl. We'll talk about it when I get home. Now, do you need anything?"

"Milk. We always need milk. And some headache pills—preferably Advil. I desperately need some of those."

"Sounds like it. I'll see you in about half an hour."

"Great! Then this little monster's all yours."

"Hush now! Don't be talking about my precious Queenie that way. I can't wait to see her and you real soon. Love you."

"I love you, too. Now hurry home. Bye." Sarah hung up.

Jon stood and went to say goodbye to Anna. However, she was settling the bill with the other young man, so he returned to his booth to pick up his dirty dishes. As he headed back, the youth walked out the door.

"Catch ya later, Lucas," Anna called after him. She then turned back to see Jon collecting the youth's plate. The waitress walked over and stood before him, hands on hips. "What are you doing there, darlin'?"

"Just picking up these dishes. Let me wash these for you."

Anna shook her head, took the crockery and cutlery from his hands, and placed them on the counter. "Don't worry your young head about it. I have this marvelous machine called a dishwasher. And you can also forget those boxes of mine. I want you to spend tomorrow looking for a job."

"But Anna, we had a deal, and I pay my dues."

"And I lied. I don't have anything that needs moving. My delivery guy puts the boxes wherever I want them, and if I need things rearranged in my storeroom, he does it for me. It's all part of the service."

"So why did you say you needed my help?"

"Because I could see you needed mine, and I know how prideful, independent kids like you can sometimes be. I just wanted you to enjoy your meal with a clear conscience."

Jon shook his head in disbelief and then walked over and hugged her.

Anna turned red and pushed him off. "Away with you now. I'm almost old enough to be your momma. Want to make me happy? Then find yourself another job." She strode to the door and opened it, then waved her hand. "Now begone, young man."

"Thank you, Anna."

Jon left the café and walked down the road, feeling good about life again. Everything was going to be okay. It would upset Sarah to learn he'd lost his job and kept it from her, but it would be the excuse she needed to move back in with Momma. Deep down, he knew his young wife wanted this but was too stubborn to admit it.

The irony was that he never wanted to leave Momma's home. But unfortunately, she and Sarah clashed over the baby at every turn.

Momma, known as Rose, was a single parent who became a teenage mother at seventeen. Daryl, her high school sweetheart, was the father. Even though she'd never been with anyone else, Daryl's parents refused to believe their son was responsible. They denied him permission to take a paternity test. Instead, they sent him to a prestigious boarding school in Dallas to escape his responsibilities. Sadly, she never heard from him again.

Fortunately, her parents were very supportive and helped raise Sarah until a car accident took them five years later. The young mother and daughter inherited a mortgage-free home and received a hefty life insurance sum, leaving them comfortable financially.

When Rose first met Jon, getting on board took her a minute. She didn't consider herself racist but never pictured her daughter bringing home a boy of color. However, winning her over didn't take long because he was a polite and God-fearing young man. He soon became a regular feature in their home at many a dinner.

The day Sarah revealed she was pregnant, Rose's heart sank. It appeared history was repeating itself. However, to her surprise, the teens told her they wanted to get married before the baby was born. Although there were concerns, she gave her blessing so her daughter could have the happy ending Rose never enjoyed. The Whitmores also agreed, believing it was the Christian thing to do.

By Texan law, the young couple only needed parental consent if they waited until they were sixteen. The wedding, therefore, took place on Sarah's sixteenth birthday, two weeks before the baby was due. The teens exchanged vows at their church before Pastor Tim. Less than a week later, their Queenie was born.

The Whitmores agreed that the young family would live with Rose because her house was big enough for all of them. The plan was for the teens to take time off school to adjust to parenthood and for Jon to get a job to cover expenses.

However, no one foresaw the clash between Rose and Sarah about raising the baby. From the beginning, the loving grandmother kept overstepping. She constantly took on the mother's role, and the ensuing fights were monumental.

Jon hated seeing Sarah unhappy and decided they needed a place of their own as soon as possible. He had already secured employment at G.T. Transport and planned to save every dollar he could. A year later, a fellow packer offered a sublet for a one-bedroom flat that was only a short walk from work. When this opportunity arose, the teens jumped at it.

It took little time for the young couple to discover the cost of independence. Jon's minimum wage didn't go far with the need to cover rent, utilities, food, fuel for the family car, and catering to the needs of a small child. All the money Jon saved while living at Momma's went on setting up their new home. Now, the young family lived paycheck to paycheck.

Lack of money wasn't the only issue. Over the past year, it had been a rollercoaster ride that Jon called the *Sweet Pea Express* because Sarah's emotions were all over the place. His young wife discovered motherhood was hard work but was reluctant to admit that life was much easier when she had Rose's help.

Yes, moving back in with Momma was the best idea. With no money coming in, it seemed the obvious choice.

Now, all he had to do was convince Sarah.

CHAPTER 5

WRONG WAY HOME

J on headed for the convenience store, lost in thought. Upon turning the corner, he collided with two men huddled together amid an intense conversation.

One man was Lucas, the gangly youth Jon remembered from the café. The other was in his early thirties. He had short black hair shaved at the sides and a shamrock tattoo with a skull in the center on the left side of his neck. Like Lucas, he wore black clothing.

"Watch where yer going, *boyo!*" the older man said with a strong Irish accent. His beady, piercing green eyes glared at Jon.

"Sorry, sir, I was daydreaming."

"Well, fookin' daydream somewhere else."

Jon was naturally a gentle and sensitive soul. He learned young that a big smile, charm, and politeness made life much easier, and this wisdom had always served him well.

He considered producing his trademark disarming grin but thought better of it. Instead, he gave a solemn nod. "I will do that, sir. You have a good day." With downcast eyes, he sidestepped the angry Irishman.

Jon's local convenience store, *Singhe's Supplies*, loomed up less than a hundred yards down the road. A faded sign and graffiti decorated the frontage, and posters for specials covered the windows. A red neon *open* sign flickered on the door's glass panel.

As he entered, a bell chimed, announcing his arrival.

A short, thin Sri Lankan man behind the counter smiled and gave him a polite nod.

"Hi, Ranjeet. How are you?"

"Very good, thank you. What can I be doing for you today, sir?"

"I need some milk ... oh, and Advil for the missus. Do you have any?"

"That I do, sir. I keep a supply behind the counter for special customers like you. Just ask for them when you pay for the milk, okay?"

Jon gave Ranjeet a nod, then headed to the fridge, where he found a well-dressed woman in her fifties. She stood with the door open, examining the contents, trying to decide what she needed. He patiently waited as she made a selection, then grabbed himself a carton of milk.

As he returned to the counter, a tanned, muscular man in his twenties who was trying on sunglasses stepped back to inspect himself in the mirror. He accidentally bumped into Jon as he was passing by.

"Sorry, mate," he said in an Australian accent. He was wearing a U.S. Flag T-shirt—obviously a tourist.

"No problem. It was my fault."

The well-dressed woman was ahead of him when Jon arrived at the counter. She was counting out nickels and dimes to pay for the small bottle of spring water she had selected earlier.

Ranjeet and Jon exchanged amused eye-rolling glances. They could both see plenty of notes in the woman's gaping purse, yet she insisted on offloading her loose change.

As he stood there, Jon noticed an array of flower bouquets sitting in a bucket of water on the ground next to the counter. It was an extravagance he couldn't afford right now, but it might mean he would cop less of an earful for taking over a week to tell his young wife he'd lost his job.

Just as he searched through his wallet and pockets to see if he could find any more change to buy Sarah a bunch, a sudden crash caused him to jump. He turned to see that someone had slammed the door to the shop open so hard that the neon sign had fallen off. Two armed men, fully dressed in black and wearing balaclavas, had burst into the store.

"Nobody fookin' move!" the bigger man yelled in a recognizable Irish accent as he brandished his gun. He gestured to the other man to lock the door.

Jon froze as he hated guns. He knew instantly who these men were, and they would likely recognize him—not good.

"This is a robbery," the Irishman said. "Money and jewelry. Hand it over right now!" He then waved his gun in Ranjeet's face. "Empty all the money from the till into a bag and make it quick."

The other man approached the woman. She stood there with enormous eyes, unable to believe what was happening. "Didn't you hear, lady? Money and jewelry, we want it!" He pointed at the two-carat emerald ring on her left hand. "Nice rock you have there. Take it off and give it to me!"

Eyes still wide, the woman slowly shook her head. "No. I'm afraid I can't."

Jon noticed the woman's cultured voice. She seemed a person more accustomed to giving orders than receiving them.

"It's a family heirloom." The woman placed a protective right hand over the ring on her left. "You can take all my money, but not my ring."

The man started stepping from foot to foot in agitation. "Lady, I have a gun in your face. Don't be dumber than a box of rocks over a stupid fuckin' ring."

"How dare you speak to me like that!" In one quick, angry movement, the woman ripped off his balaclava and dropped it to the floor, instantly revealing the robber's identity. As Jon expected, it was Lucas.

Pale blue eyes stared at the woman in shock. "You fuckin' crazy bitch! Are you fuckin' kidding me!" he said as he ducked down to pick up the balaclava.

Hearing the commotion, the Irishman turned from watching Ranjeet empty the till. Sighing in exasperation, he calmly withdrew a silencer from his coat pocket and screwed it onto the barrel of his gun. He approached the woman and said, "Ah, ma dear, I regret to inform ye, but that was a fookin' dumb move." He pointed the gun at her head and pulled the trigger, causing blood, brains, and bone to spray over Jon's face.

The woman collapsed to the floor, and Jon cringed in fright, traumatized as memories of Rodrigo dying in his lap flooded his mind.

During the cold-blooded shooting, Ranjeet reached down and pulled out a baseball bat but didn't have the chance to swing it. Without blinking, the Irishman turned and shot him right between the eyes.

Ranjeet's head snapped back from the bullet's force into his skull, and he then collapsed, disappearing behind the counter.

The Australian tourist put his hands up and backed away as the gun turned to him. "Mate ... please ... we'll do whatever you want. There's no need to—"

A bullet through the side of his neck, immediately shattering his carotid artery, stopped him mid-sentence, and he made a strangled, gurgling sound as he fell back onto the floor, blood spurting from his wound. It was a horrendous sight.

The Irishman had shot three people with the composure of someone swatting flies. He waited a few seconds to ensure the young man wouldn't ever be getting up again, then pointed his gun at Jon. "Say goodbye, boyo."

Eyes wide with fear, Jon's legs buckled, and he sank to his knees. He was quite prepared to beg for his life. "Please ... please ... I have a young family. Please don't kill me—"

Jon's desperate plea was unexpectedly interrupted by Lucas bursting into tears, causing the Irishman to turn and glare at his young accomplice.

"What the fook? Can't ye see I'm busy here?"

Lucas was beside himself. "What have you done? The police will never stop hunting us. You know that, don't you? And with all that forensic stuff they have these days, we're fuckin' gone, man—totally fucked!"

"Oh, for fook's sake, boyo! Don't go losing it on me now. Ye know this is all yer fault. But as usual, I have to clean up yer mess."

"My mess? I didn't shoot anyone. But it doesn't matter. We'll both get the death penalty for sure." Lucas began pacing back and forth as he imagined the worst. "Armed robbery is one thing. Murder is another."

The Irishman sighed again, but the younger man's words appeared to have affected him. Suddenly, with no warning, he fired a shot at the counter and another at the floor near Lucas's foot, causing him to jump back in fright.

"What the hell, man! You nearly shot my fuckin' foot off!"

The Irishman rolled his eyes. "Stop yer fookin' wailing! I'm working on an idea here." He then walked over to Jon and pointed the gun at his head. "Get up, boyo."

Unable to believe he was still alive, with shaky knees, Jon instantly obeyed.

"I remember ye, boyo, and I know ye already know what I look like, so there's no point hiding ma face." Off came the balaclava. "For that reason alone, I should kill ye. But it's yer lucky day. Ma mate here has given me a good reason to spare yer life."

Lucas looked confused. "I have?"

"Just shut up and keep yer gun pointed at him." The Irishman put his gun in his pocket and grabbed a dishtowel from a nearby stand. He then grabbed the bottle of spring water from the counter and opened it with his gloved hand. He tipped water all over the dishtowel, saturating it, and used it to wipe Jon's surprised face, just as a mother would clean her child.

The Irishman continued until he removed every drop of blood, every bit of brain matter, and bone fragment. He then pulled out his gun, vigorously wiped it, and put it on the counter. When finished, he wrapped the used dishtowel around the empty water bottle and put it in his coat pocket.

He then stood back and inspected his work. "That's better." He turned to Lucas. "Now, give me yer gun."

"Why? Run out of bullets, and you want to shoot me, too?"

"No, I haven't run out of fookin' bullets, ye gobshite. I have one left. So, if yer wanting to get the fook out of here and not worry about anyone coming after us, stop asking me stupid fookin' questions and give me yer gun. Do ye want me to fix this or not?"

Lucas nodded, and the Irishman extended his hand, flicking his fingers toward his palm impatiently in a beckoning gesture. Warily, the younger man handed it over.

The Irishman then pointed the gun at Jon. "Now, boyo, open yer wallet. Show me what's in there."

Jon stared at his wallet in his hand. He obediently flipped it open and held it up for inspection. Inside were his driver's license, a family photo, and a few dollar bills.

The Irishman leaned in, squinting at the image in the wallet's display window. "Nice looking missus and cute kid. Take out the photo and license, and hand them over."

Jon frowned with confusion as he pulled them from his wallet and did as instructed.

The Irishman inspected the address on the driver's license. "I see ye live nearby. Thanks for the info, boyo." He slipped the photo and the driver's license into his top front pocket. Once both were inside, he gave a sinister smile. "I have a photo of yer family, and I know where they live now. So, I can track them down."

Horrified, Jon wondered where he was going with that.

"So, here's what I need ye to do." The Irishmen gestured toward the woman on the floor. "I want ye to shoot the bitch."

"I ... I ... what?"

The Irishman grabbed his gun from the counter and presented it to Jon, who stared at it, feeling confused.

"Are ye retarded, boyo? Take ma gun and shoot the fookin' bitch!" He gave the woman a slight kick with the tip of his shoe for emphasis.

Eyes wide, Jon shook his head. He put his hands up and backed away in horror.

"Take the gun, boyo, and don't be getting any ideas. Ma gun has one bullet left, but this one"—he strode over and pushed the muzzle of Lucas's gun hard into Jon's forehead—"has six."

Sick with fear, Jon took the Irishman's gun. "Please don't make me do this."

"If ye don't do it, I'll not only shoot ye, but I'll take that bullet and shoot it right between those beautiful blue eyes of yer pretty wife's head." Keeping the gun trained on Jon, the Irishman quickly bent down and, with his free hand, pulled an evil-looking knife from a sheath attached to his boot. Engraved into the knife's red wooden handle was a skull on a shamrock, perfectly matching the tattoo on his neck. "And before I shoot yer wife, I'll make her watch me slit yer kid's throat with ma old mate *Reaper* here." He waved the knife blade around menacingly close to Jon's face. "Am I clear enough, boyo?"

There was no choice. Jon pointed the gun at the woman, closed his eyes, and pulled the trigger. He flinched as the weapon made a suppressed crack sound that was instantly followed by a sickening thud as the bullet hit her body. Vomit rose in his mouth.

"Nice shot, boyo. Right through the heart. If the bitch wasn't quite dead yet, she certainly is now." The Irishman pulled Jon to him until their faces were only inches apart. "Take a long look, boyo. This face will haunt yer nightmares. I'll murder yer wife and child if I get even a whiff of anyone coming after me for this. And don't think ye'll be safe if I get arrested. I have friends. Ye can run and hide, but ma people will find ye. It's what they do. Got it?"

"I won't talk. I promise," Jon said, and he meant it. The lack of empathy in the Irishman's eyes made it clear he would carry out his threat. Rodrigo had also made him very familiar with the unwritten criminal code of conduct about keeping one's mouth shut.

"Good boy. Now, keep holding that gun and get back on yer knees. Close yer eyes and start praying. I want ye to wait here until the police arrive."

"Police?"

"Yes. If ye stay here until then with yer eyes closed, holding that gun and praying, then yer family gets to live."

Jon submissively dropped to his knees, bowed his head, closed his eyes, and started reciting the Lord's Prayer.

The Irishman bent and put his mouth close to Jon's ear. "Don't be moving now," he said in a low voice. "Not one muscle. I'll be watching."

Jon stayed still as he heard them leave, keeping his eyes closed, too scared to move. He lost track of time until the shop door smashed open, and the awful words that frightened him six years ago again resounded in his ears.

"Police! Don't move!"

He opened his eyes to see two police officers—one male and the other female—standing above him, guns in hand, pointed at his head.

More guns ... so many guns.

"Drop your weapon!" The male officer leaned in, bringing his gun closer to Jon's face. "Now! Don't make me ask you again."

Jon stared at the gun in his hand. He had been clinging to it as the Irishman had commanded him to, and suddenly, he understood the reason. Immediately, he released his fingers. The weapon slipped out of his hand, tumbled to the floor, and bounced away from him, making a brief metallic clacking noise before coming to rest.

As the police officers stepped forward to handcuff Jon and read him his rights, his traumatized brain couldn't take it in. It was too much.

His mind was screaming, *I didn't do this! I'm innocent!*

But the words wouldn't come out.

Chapter 6

Libby

Libby Davis was having a nightmare. Horrific, disturbing images made her thrash about so much that she fell out of bed and hit the floor with a thud, jolting her awake. Bemused and exhausted, she sat on the floor with her bed sheets tangled around her legs.

It was that awful dream again for the third time this week. The visions were so graphic, so real. Why was this happening?

The intercom perched on the lamp table next to her bed came to life, making her jump. "Hon, are you all right? It sounded like you fell over. Do you need me to come up there?"

Libby rolled over on the floor and reached for the talk button. "I'm fine, Mom. I, um ..." She looked around the room to find a good excuse for the noise her mother had just heard. Her eyes alighted on the nearby desk chair.

Perfect.

"My ... ah ... my feet got caught in the sheets when I jumped out of bed. I just tripped a little and knocked over a chair. I'm not hurt. It's all good."

Guilt made her bite her lip as soon as the words were out of her mouth. She hated lying but didn't want to cause her overprotective mother any more anxiety. There had already been plenty to worry about over the past year, so keeping this nightmare issue to herself was imperative.

"You need to be more careful in your condition. When are you coming down? I'll make you some breakfast."

"Thanks, Mom, but I'd like to soak in the bath first. Give me twenty minutes, okay?"

"All right, hon."

With the mother-daughter intercom exchange now done, Libby extracted herself from the bed sheets, stood up, and sighed. She walked down the hallway to the bathroom and, after turning on the taps to the bath, grabbed her toothbrush and coated it with a generous supply of toothpaste. While vigorously brushing her teeth, she stared sleepy-eyed at herself in the mirror.

Reflected was a stunning curvy girl sporting a luxurious mane of long, wavy brown hair highlighted with streaks of gold. Large brown eyes framed by thick black lashes set in doll-like features stared back at her. She frowned at herself as a headache started coming on. These darn nightmares were taking their toll.

She pulled off her nightgown and dropped it to the floor with a resigned shrug. Once naked, Libby's eyes couldn't resist being drawn to the mirror again. Between her breasts was a long, thin scar. She gently ran her fingers up and down the entire length, almost in wonder. It was not pretty, but a small price for her new life, and her doctor said it would fade in time.

After completing her daily physical inspection, she stepped into the fast-filling bath. When the water reached her shoulders, she turned off the taps and submerged her head, leaving only her nose and mouth above the water. Her hair fanned like a halo, swirling and making patterns as indulgent fingers found their way through the locks to massage away her headache. She luxuriated in the liquid warmth encompassing her body.

Twenty minutes flew by, then thirty, then forty, until the intercom in the bathroom sounded. The distortion effect from the water covering Libby's ears made her mother's voice seem to call her from far away. "Hon, you've been in that bath a long time. You said you'd only be twenty minutes. Are you okay?"

Ever since the operation, her mother had wrapped her in cotton wool. It was a bad idea to agree to the bathroom's intercom, given that the one in the bedroom was intrusive enough. Now, there was nowhere in the house to escape *Big Smother*, aka her mother.

With a groan of frustration, Libby sat up in the bath, gathered her locks, and squeezed out the water. Even more annoying, she discovered the intercom was just out of arm's reach.

Typical! They should have tested that during installation.

Swearing, she hoisted herself to a standing position, stepped out of the bath, dripping wet, and grabbed her towel. An impatient press of the talk button followed.

"I'm fine, *Mother*—I was enjoying my bath—emphasis on the *was*. I know you mean well, but could you please stop fussing?"

"'*Mother*' now, is it? Well, excuse me for caring about your safety. You could be unconscious or drowning up there, for all I knew! It's not the first time you've collapsed in a bathroom, so I think I have a right to be concerned." An indignant silence then followed.

That lecturing martyrish tone made Libby feel like a selfish and ungrateful child. Surrender was her best option. "I'm sorry, Mom. You're right. Next time I plan to take an extra long bath, I'll let you know, okay?"

"Thank you. You know I love you to the moon and back?"

"Yes, I know. I love you, too, Mom. Can I dry off and get dressed now, please? I'm getting water everywhere."

"Okay, hon. See you soon."

Not for the first time, Libby regretted the decision to move back home with her mother during her recovery after leaving the hospital. She should have foreseen full-blown smother mode.

After vigorously rubbing moisture from her body, she tossed the wet towel into the laundry chute and realized her nightgown was now a soggy mess because she had stepped all over it, so it shortly followed. Watching them disappear always made Libby smirk. When she was a kid, she believed the chute was a magical cave that you threw dirty things into, and a kind fairy returned them pressed and folded on her bed. Her mother fed her that tale to ensure little Libby didn't pull off her dirty clothes and leave them where they lay. It worked a treat.

Thank you, kind fairy.

Once she had blow-dried her hair, still naked, Libby strolled back down the hallway to her bedroom to get dressed. It gave her a secret thrill as she imagined her prudish mother's face if she caught her. The thought amused Libby every single time, but it was unlikely to happen. Her mother hurt her knee from a fall at tennis some months ago, which was taking a long time to heal and probably needed surgery, so she avoided coming up the stairs like the plague. Apart from fears for Libby's safety, it was one of the main reasons she insisted on installing the intercoms.

After throwing on underwear and a T-shirt, Libby grabbed a pair of jeans she hadn't worn since returning home from the hospital. While pulling them on, she could feel something in the back pocket. She shoved her hand inside and discovered a crumpled business card for Dr. David Phillips.

The hospital doctor had warned that there might be some psychological hurdles to overcome. He organized a referral for Libby to see Dr. Phillips, a clinical psychologist specializing in organ transplant recipients. She had promised to make an appointment, but it slipped her mind. Perhaps the universe was trying to tell her something, so she picked up her phone and punched in the number from the card.

An upbeat and professional voice answered. "*Phillips and Associates Psychology*, Claire speaking. How may I help you?"

"Hi, Claire. I'm wondering if I could see Dr. Phillips today?"

"Do you have a referral?"

"Yes, I believe I do. Dr. Langston told me he'd send you one. It would be for Elizabeth Davis and sent around late November to early December last year."

"One moment, please." On-hold music played until Claire returned a minute later. "Yes, Dr. Langston has emailed through a referral for you, so that's fine. You're in luck. A spot opened up for ten thirty this morning. Does that leave you enough time to get here? Otherwise, there's nothing available for two weeks."

Libby inspected her phone and saw it was nearly ten o'clock. The clinic wasn't far away, so half an hour was plenty of time. "Yes, thanks. That'd be perfect. I'll head out now and see you soon."

After disconnecting the call, she glanced at the silver necklace hanging from her dresser mirror. It sported an ornately edged, eye-catching red crystal heart pendant.

I mustn't forget you.

Libby grabbed it, and after she had pulled the chain over her head and adjusted the clasp to sit behind her neck, she stared into the mirror at her pendant and smiled. She remembered her mother giving it to her the day after her transplant and saying, "When you wear this, it will remind you to be thankful to that special person whose precious gift gave you back your life."

Not that Libby needed any prompting to feel grateful.

Now, what excuse can I give to get out of the house?

Telling her mother about the psychologist would undoubtedly end up in an interrogation session. She could imagine all the questions.

Why do you need to see someone when you can talk to me?

What's wrong with you?

Is it anything to do with me?

It had been six months since the operation, and the doctors had told her she could start driving again months ago, but her mother wouldn't have it. She insisted on playing the chauffeur and driving Libby anywhere she needed to go. It was ridiculous that she'd allowed her mother this much control but had no strength to fight it during recovery. It was sweet at first, but now it was suffocating. A twenty-two-year-old woman should be free to go outside without her mother's permission.

Nightmares aside, Libby was in excellent shape and felt close to normal, thanks to daily workouts in their home gym. It was time to reclaim her independence, and her mother would have to learn to deal with it.

With her phone set to silent, she grabbed her car keys, walked down the stairs, and headed straight for the front door with grim determination.

"I'm heading out for a couple of hours, Mom. Don't worry about breakfast. I'll have something while I'm out."

"Hon, wait!" her mother called after her. "Where are you going? You're not driving, are you? WAIT!"

The runaway daughter jumped in her car and took off. Glancing in the rearview mirror, she saw her mother standing on the front doorstep, looking confused. Libby opened the driver's side window, stuck her arm out of the car, and gave a cheerful wave goodbye. She knew she'd cop an earful on her return, but it was worth it. Freedom at last!

While driving along, the morning sun warming her face through the windscreen, she became flooded by an overwhelming feeling of happiness to be alive. She shuddered in delight. It was a far cry from lying in a hospital bed, hovering at death's door.

Just over a year before, Libby was an energetic, independent young woman enjoying a successful career as a travel agent. Back then, she was renting a house with three other young women and was on top of the world, having finally saved enough money for her dream vacation—a hiking and trekking tour of Africa.

However, a strange illness struck her when she returned home from her trip, leaving her listless and weak. Her family doctor dismissed her lethargy as the flu or prolonged jet lag, so she soldiered on. She took various over-the-counter medications that did nothing to ease her symptoms.

Then, one morning, she collapsed in the bathroom while preparing for work. She remembered her knees suddenly giving way, falling back against the wall, and slowly sliding down until her bottom hit the cold, hard tiles. And there she remained, propped up against the wall like a rag doll, unable to move, feeling dizzy and confused.

Fortunately for Libby, she was coming out of the bathroom when it happened and had just unbolted the door. She was even more fortunate that all her housemates were home. Given the bathroom was a premium territory in the morning, it wasn't long until one of them found her.

As Libby sat there with her eyes closed, barely holding onto consciousness, she vaguely remembered their panicked discussions about whether to call an ambulance.

Libby heard one ask, "Does anyone know if she has health insurance? It'll cost her a fortune if she doesn't."

They argued back and forth until they agreed the best option was to carry her to the nearest car and drive her to the hospital. On arrival, the emergency department staff took one look at Libby's unhealthy pallor and admitted her immediately, concerned she was at risk of a heart attack.

The housemates gave them her mother's contact details, and she was at Libby's side within the hour of being notified.

After many tests, the doctor looking after Libby discovered, as suspected, the problem was her heart. He told her she had a condition known as *idiopathic viral cardiomyopathy*.

"But what does idiopathic mean?" her mother had asked.

The doctor explained that it was a medical term when the exact cause was unknown. He surmised Libby contracted a virus during her African trek, which resulted in severe and irreversible heart damage. The doctor revealed that Libby would only have months to live without a heart transplant. It was horrific news.

The wait for a donor was then on. Six months passed, and as she lay in her hospital bed, growing weaker each day, suffering end-stage heart failure, a compatible heart became available just in time. Her mother couldn't stop crying.

All Libby could think about when first receiving the news was because some poor person had died, she could live. It was a happy and sad time all at once. It was surreal to imagine someone else's heart would soon beat inside her.

Upon recalling that memorable day, she put a hand to her chest to feel the thud of her donor's heart and said a silent prayer of gratitude. Some amazing stranger's generous decision to be an organ donor saved her life.

Still lost in her thoughts, Libby drove past the clinic ten minutes later. A couple of blocks went by until she realized she had missed it. Swearing quietly under her breath, she continued until she could find a place to turn back around.

The oversight proved lucky, as a car spot freed up out front of the clinic just as she arrived. Hoping this was a sign that her therapy session would go well, Libby grabbed the park and headed inside.

CHAPTER 7

DISTURBING DREAMS

"Hello, may I help you?" A cheerful young woman with freckles and short, curly red hair, dressed in a white uniform, greeted Libby as soon as she entered the clinic. She immediately recognized her voice and glanced at the name badge to confirm it.

"Hi Claire, it's me, Elizabeth Davis. We spoke on the phone half an hour ago. Thanks for squeezing me in at such short notice."

"Think nothing of it. It was good timing on your part. I received the cancellation just before your call, so you were doing us all a favor by filling the spot." Claire slid an electronic tablet with an attached stylus pen across the counter toward her. "Please fill in your patient information, and don't forget to sign at the end."

After completing the questionnaire, Libby sat in the nearest chair and checked her phone messages while waiting. It had been vibrating madly, so as expected, she found that her mother had sent multiple text messages.

Why did you rush out like that?

Are you angry with me? What have I done?

I'm sorry for loving you too much.

Please call me back.

I love you.

Libby bit her lower lip as she read them. She wanted to rejoin the world and make her own decisions again. Sitting her beloved mother down for a heart-to-heart adult conversation about boundaries was well past due.

Heart to heart! How appropriate!

Not for the first time, she wondered about her donor. She had a dear wish to meet the donor's family and have the opportunity to thank them for their generosity, so she wrote them a letter of gratitude from her hospital bed.

Dear wonderful, generous donor family,

I'm so sorry that you lost someone you loved. You must miss them every day.

I'm writing to thank you for the gift of life you've given me. I received your loved one's heart.

During a very upsetting time for you, you had the goodness of spirit to put someone else's needs above your own by donating the organs of your loved one to those in need.

I want you to know I will cherish this beautiful heart and promise to fill it with kindness, generosity, and love.

It would be fantastic if we could meet face-to-face so I can give you my thanks (and big hugs) in person.

Please get in touch with our transplant coordinator if you would like this to happen. No pressure, as I realize this must be a sad time for you.

Whatever you decide, you will have my eternal gratitude.

Lots of love and hugs,

Libby Davis

When finished, Libby gave it to the transplant coordinator to pass on to the donor's family. While waiting for a reply, she imagined who they might be and what she would say. Libby expected tears, perhaps laughter, plenty of hugging, and maybe they'd want to place a hand on her chest to feel the heart of their loved one beating within her. And, of course, she would let them.

She had built the thought up so much that it seemed a foregone conclusion that they would want to meet her. Libby expected to wait a few weeks for them to reply. Therefore, she was surprised when a well-typed response letter decorated with hearts arrived shortly after.

Dear Libby,

Thank you for your very kind letter. I cried when I read it—happy tears.

The heart you received was from my husband. He was a loving Christian family man, taken too soon. It's a blessing that someone as sweet as you received his heart.

Please understand that this has been a tough time for the family. We're not ready to meet with you at this stage. If that changes in the future, we will reach out as you suggested.

All I ask of you is to become the best version of yourself and go for all your dreams because life can be so short, and you don't want to waste a precious second.

Lots of love and hugs right back to you.

Your donor family

Although Libby felt disappointed, she was glad they took the time to write back. At least she learned that her new heart came from a good, kind person. There was always the chance the donor family could change their mind about meeting her later.

She placed the letter in a silver frame embossed with tiny hearts and hung it on her bedroom wall to honor their memory. This small tribute reminded her daily about how wonderful and generous people can be.

"Ms. Davies, Dr. Phillips is ready to see you now," Claire said, breaking through her reverie. "His room is number four at the end of the corridor on the left."

"Thank you, Claire."

The door was slightly ajar when Libby arrived at Dr. Phillips's office. She could see the doctor sitting at his desk, waiting for her. He looked up and beckoned her inside.

"Nice to meet you, Elizabeth." He gestured toward a comfortable-looking leather chair across from him.

Once Libby had sat down, the doctor leaned in, clutching a tablet and a stylus pen. He was a tall, gray-haired, imposing man with horn-rimmed glasses perched on the end of his nose. He quickly scanned her medical information on his tablet. "Hmm, I read here that you had a heart transplant about six months ago. So, what brings you here today?"

"Nightmares, recurring nightmares," Libby responded promptly.

"I see." Dr. Phillips gestured expansively. "Please elaborate."

"It's pretty horrific—guns and violence. The thing is, I don't understand why I'm having these dreams. I'm a real pacifist, so ..." Her words trailed off, and she shrugged helplessly.

"Elizabeth, this is a safe place with no judgment. There's nothing you can say that I haven't heard before. Please continue. I want to hear all about your dreams."

Libby nodded. "Okay, so here it is ..." She closed her eyes, took a deep breath, and then her words came out in a rush. "I was in this convenience store when two robbers wearing balaclavas burst in. Suddenly, their masks are off, and the bigger one shoots three people. He frames me for it, and the police take me away. The end."

Her brown eyes opened wide. "And I've lost count of how many times I've had this dream."

"That's very interesting." Dr. Phillips scribbled some notes on his tablet. "However, I have the impression you're holding something back."

"No, I'd rather not. It's too awful."

Dr. Phillips regarded her over the top of his glasses with one raised eyebrow. It was clear he wouldn't take 'no' for an answer.

"Oh, all right! I admit I skipped a bit. The guy who shot those poor people forced me to take his gun, and ..." Libby closed her eyes as the horror of the vivid memory invaded her mind.

"And?"

"He made me shoot one victim. It was this well-dressed older lady." Guilt overcame her, and she averted her eyes. It still felt so real and so wrong. "But she was already dead, and I didn't do it. It was *him*."

"'Him?' I thought we were talking about you."

"Oh yes, I guess I should have mentioned that. I thought it was me at first. But as I'm reaching out to take the gun, I can see the hands. They're not mine."

"Whose hands do you think they are?"

"That's just it. I don't know. The skin is much darker, and the hands are bigger than mine. They're man's hands." Libby held her hands before her face and stared at them as she recalled her nightmare.

"Have you watched any violent movies lately? The subconscious sometimes locks images away and brings them out in your dreams."

"No. I'm a rom-com movie girl. Scary movies are not my thing, and certainly nothing as graphic as this horrible dream." She shuddered. "I want them to stop and wish I understood why they're happening."

The doctor cocked his head to one side, seeming to assess whether to reveal his thoughts.

Libby noticed his hesitation and frowned. "Why are you looking at me like that? Just hit me with it. Am I going crazy?"

Dr. Phillips pressed his fingers together. "Okay, I have a theory about this. I plan to write a paper on it one day. However, these things are tough to prove, and I'm concerned you may find it disturbing."

Libby rolled her eyes. "I've recently had my heart ripped out and replaced with another. There's nothing much more disturbing than that. So go ahead. You have my permission."

"Okay ... well, there is this school of thought about *cellular memory*."

"Cellular memory?"

"Yes. Most academics in the organ transplant community consider it a pseudoscience, as we haven't gathered enough evidence to support the theory."

"But what does it mean?"

"Cellular memory explores the possibility that memories don't just live in the brain and—"

Libby put her hands to her mouth. "Oh, I don't like where this is heading."

Dr. Phillips leaned back in his chair. "I'm sorry. It's very unprofessional of me. Forget it."

"Are you kidding? Don't you dare stop! I'll shut up, I promise. Please continue."

"Well, okay then. As you know, I'm a specialist in treating organ transplant recipients. As a result, I've been privy to some interesting stories."

"Such as?"

"Some people find that their tastes are changing and enjoy things they didn't like before their operation. It could be food, drink, music, or sports. Some have even shown new talents. *Déjà vu* is also common."

"'Déjà vu?'"

"There is a sense of familiarity about certain situations, places, and, sometimes, even people. Like they've been there and done that. And, of course, sometimes they have strange dreams."

"Dreams like mine?"

Dr. Phillips adjusted his glasses. "I've encountered nothing as graphic as yours. I have, however, counseled patients who've dreamed they're in someone else's body and having experiences that are not their own."

Libby hugged herself protectively. "Creepy."

"Yes. Agreed. By any chance, did you find out who your donor was?"

"No, unfortunately, not really. All I know is what the wife told me in a letter. According to her, he was a loving, Christian man devoted to his family."

Dr. Phillips shrugged. "Look, it's just a theory. Don't worry about it. These dreams will disappear eventually, and, in time, you'll forget you even had them."

"I hope so."

"Have you shared these dreams with your family or friends?"

"No, and I definitely wouldn't tell my mother. She's been worrying and smothering me enough already since the operation. I don't need to give her another cause for concern."

The doctor nodded. "I could prescribe some tablets to help you sleep better, but I believe that would mask the problem. There's also a risk that they might interfere with your immunosuppressant medications. I'm therefore going to suggest another form of therapy."

Dr. Phillips quickly did something on his tablet, and Libby's phone vibrated. "I've just sent you a text about a support group for heart and lung transplant recipients. Sharing and listening to others will help you heal. Nightmares are common after your body has been through such an experience. You're not alone."

"Thank you. It would help to meet other people like me. Sometimes, it's hard to realize that I'm not the only person with a heart transplant."

"I'm here for you, Elizabeth, if you ever need me. Honestly, though, you seem to be a very well-adjusted young lady. I'm confident that a sharing group like this would be the best therapy."

"Thank you, doctor."

Libby left the office feeling lighter after finally sharing her secret with someone. When she returned to her car, she read the information on her phone. The next meeting was on Saturday morning, and she couldn't wait.

It was time to make some new friends and sort out these nightmares. But first things first. She had to work out what to tell her mother.

CHAPTER 8

JAKE

J ake Masters stared at the gun in his hand and struggled to breathe. "Please don't make me do this—"

Suddenly, a loud knocking caused him to wake with a start. Disorientated, he sat up on the couch.

Keys rattled as someone unlocked his front door. Before he could react, his twin sister, Goosy, an attractive, leggy young woman with a multicolored bob, clipped short on one side, burst in. Her left hand held two takeaway coffees in a cardboard cup holder tray, balancing a brown paper bag on top, and keys were in her right.

She deposited the tray on the coffee table beside Jake, grabbed the brown paper bag, and threw it at his head. He deftly caught it with a defensive hand flick before it hit him in the face. From the smell of it, it was a freshly baked croissant.

"Up and at 'em, little bro!" Goosy strode to the nearest window and pulled open the curtains. "You're burning daylight."

Jake, clad in only checked boxer shorts and a black T-shirt, flinched as the sudden bright light streaming through the window assaulted his sleepy eyes. "Morning, Goosy." He ran his hand through his hair and stifled a smile at the accurate imitation of their dearly departed mother. "Thanks for the *nice* wake-up greeting. Have you ever heard of a phone?"

Goosy was two minutes older and never let him forget it. Her real name was Lucy, but Jake started calling her Goosy when she was five. She liked the name, so it stuck, and she became Goosy to everyone ever since. "Check your messages. I've tried calling you three times already. Thought I'd better come over to check you weren't dead."

An inspection of his phone confirmed three missed calls, but the bell icon had a line through it. "Sorry. I forgot to take it off silent."

"So you should be." Goosy pulled the two coffees out of their tray and handed him one. She then stood there, hand on hip, slowly sipping her drink, regarding him, her brow furrowed with concern. "You look like crap."

"Well, thank you kindly, ma'am." Jake's voice dripped with sarcasm.

Goosy noted the pillow and crumpled quilt next to him. "I see you've been sleeping on the couch again." She pointed toward the bedroom door across the hallway. "You realize there's a perfectly good king-size bed in there?"

"I fell asleep watching TV. So sue me."

"Yeah, right! I'll bet you haven't slept in that bed once since you came home."

Jake grinned. "I won't be taking that bet."

Goosy pointed an accusing finger at him. "I knew it!" There was a pizza box sitting on the coffee table. She casually bent down, flipped open the lid, and her nose wrinkled in disgust as she found two remaining stale pieces of pizza. "I see you've been eating well. I'm sure your doctor would *love* to know that you've been looking after yourself. Maybe I should have brought you a salad instead of a croissant."

"You're not my mother."

His sister rolled her eyes. "Could you imagine me being anyone's mother? That poor kid. Jokes aside, are you really going to work today?"

"Sure am. The captain asked me to come in to see her. I can't wait to tell her that my doctor has given me the all-clear. If I get my way, I'll start back today."

Goosy threw herself down on an armchair and continued drinking her coffee. "Suit yourself, but I don't think you're ready. I mean it. You look like crap. Those stupid nightmares again?"

"Yep."

"You know I could access some excellent drugs to fix that."

Jake stuck his fingers in his ears. "I don't want to hear about it. You need to remember what I do for a living."

"You know my opinion about that. I think you should have sued the bastards and taken early retirement."

"Not a chance! You know how much I love my job. Anyway, this was all on me. I was the idiot who turned up without a vest. I'm lucky the captain didn't ask me to hand in my badge."

"She wouldn't dare! You saved a child's life, for God's sake. You're a darned hero who got nothing for his trouble but a chest full of scars and a new set of lungs. They couldn't be that cruel."

Jake frowned and put his hand protectively up against his chest. He never enjoyed being reminded that multiple scars lurked beneath his T-shirt, and his short-term memory loss meant he couldn't recall how he got them.

The last thing he remembered was purchasing strong medication from the pharmacy for a virulent strain of coronavirus that refused to go away. Five days later, he awoke in a hospital bed on a ventilator, with tubes and wires everywhere.

Jake received the grim news that when he attempted to negotiate during a domestic hostage situation, the perpetrator shot him. He was on his phone updating fellow detective and friend Barney about when he would return to work when the call came in.

The area was nearby, so Jake, despite feeling extremely unwell, headed there to help. The police respondents surrounding the house told him a man had shot his wife dead and was using his crying young daughter as a human shield as he made demands.

Jake took over as the highest-ranking officer on the scene and tried to talk the man down. Unarmed, he walked over, hands in the air, offering to exchange himself as a hostage replacement for the man's child. The man accepted, but during the exchange, more police cars arrived, sirens blaring, and spooked him.

He pointed the gun at his child, threatening to pull the trigger, forcing Jake to tackle him. The man panicked and shot Jake three times in the chest at close range before being taken out by another officer.

Fortunately, all three bullets hit the right side of Jake's chest and missed his heart. He was also lucky the weapon that delivered them was a low-caliber semi-automatic. Regardless, his injuries were life-threatening as the bullets shredded his right lung, and blood poured from his wounds.

As the onsite ambulance rushed him to the hospital, Jake babbled incessantly and flirted with the female paramedic looking after him. As she did her best to staunch the blood flow, he kept saying he was fine and even tried to get her number. At least this was Barney's version of events, who arrived shortly after the shooting and insisted on accompanying his friend in the ambulance. Jake remembered none of this, but it sounded like something he would do.

The surgeons rushed him to the operating theater when they arrived. Upon opening him up, they discovered his right lung was beyond repair, so they removed it.

Jake's timing of contracting a nasty coronavirus variant couldn't have been worse, as the virus had ravaged his remaining lung. Things were looking grim.

Miraculously, a compatible set of lungs became available. Goosy was Jake's medical proxy, so the surgeons gave her a choice. They told her they could try to save Jake's left lung and perform a single lung transplant. However, the risk was high that the virus-damaged lung would never work as well as it once did, and if it failed altogether, it would cause significant health issues down the track. Or they could replace both.

The surgeons advised if successful, a double lung transplant would provide a better long-term outcome for Jake.

Goosy made the final decision based on the medical prognosis and chose the latter. So Jake bypassed the waitlist and received both lungs.

The moment of reflection and vulnerability did not escape his sister's attention. Her face softened. "I'm sorry. The whole situation makes me emotional." She shrugged. "That time of the month and all."

Jake gave her a lopsided grin. "Really? Again? Wasn't that your excuse last week?"

Goosy laughed and threw a cushion at his head, which he deflected easily.

"Would you like me to drive you to work?"

"Thanks, but I'm fine with driving myself."

"Are you sure you're ready for this?" His sister's face showed genuine concern.

"Trust me. I'm more than ready. My captain will probably put me on light desk duties until I settle back in, so I don't expect to be doing anything too physical."

"Good to know, little bro. So I guess I should"—Goosy gestured toward the front door—"go."

"Yeah, do me a favor and leave me alone so I can put on some clothes. You'll make me late."

Blowing a kiss, his sister smiled, spun on her heels, and walked out the door without a backward glance.

Peace at last!

Jake sat before his old desk an hour later, feeling like he'd never left. He lost count of everyone who came over to shake his hand. Two female officers hugged him, contravening office protocol, but no one cared.

He had barely settled in when his captain, Sandra Bennett, walked past his desk. She was middle-aged with short, wavy blond hair and wore a tailored navy blue skirt suit. "Don't get too comfortable, Masters. I need to see you in my office. Now, please."

Jake's eyes widened in surprise. It wasn't the welcome back he had expected. He thought the captain had asked him to come in to discuss returning to work, but now he wasn't so sure. Instead, it seemed he was about to cop it for something, but what?

He figured it couldn't be about his failure to wear a vest during the hostage situation because the captain had issued that reprimand months ago when he was still in his hospital bed recovering. Besides, Jake had already paid a high price for that oversight. Maybe she saw the hugs, and he imagined a lecture about inappropriate office behavior.

Upon entering Captain Bennett's office, Jake groaned as he realized it was an ambush.

Oh, hell, no!

Dr. Helen Murphy, the department psychologist, was also there. He warily took the chair beside her.

The captain produced a tight smile that didn't quite reach her eyes. "It's great to see you, Masters. And we're all thrilled you appear to be recovering so well. However, I've got a bone to pick with you. We had an agreement you'd see Helen here at least once a week, and—"

"Yes, I know, but—"

Bennett patiently raised her hand to silence him. "Please don't interrupt me when I'm talking." She paused for effect with stern eyes fixed upon him.

When sure Jake would remain silent, the captain continued. "I hear you haven't even turned up for one session. Is there a reason for that?" She performed a rolling hands gesture when she saw him hesitate, unsure if he could now speak. "You have the floor."

Jake grinned sheepishly and shrugged. "I guess I ... er ... I guess I didn't see a need. I don't remember what happened, so what's there to discuss?"

"Masters, you've been through life-threatening surgery and nearly died. You're fortunate to be breathing. If we didn't break countless protocols and overlook waiting lists to put a new set of lungs into you, you quite literally wouldn't be."

"Yes, I realize that, and I'm very grateful, but I'm doing fine."

Bennett stared hard at him, one eyebrow skeptically raised.

An uncomfortable silence followed until Jake felt compelled to continue speaking. "Oh, all right! I admit I've had a few bad dreams, but I think it's something I've conjured up to deal with the fact that I can't remember the shooting. That's about it."

"Nightmares are often the mind's way of coping with traumatic events," Helen said.

Jake gave his captain a triumphant look. "There you go. So it's all good. My brain's sorting stuff out all by itself. There's no need for therapy."

The psychologist shook her head. "I didn't say that. I know you may not remember the shooting and think you don't need my help. However, I recommend you talk to someone about your dreams and how you feel about your organ transplant."

"But why? I told you before that I'm fine. I admit the physical recovery was difficult, but that's all."

Bennett folded her arms in frustration. "Because it's protocol, that's why, and we must follow the correct procedures when one of our people goes through a traumatic event."

"And if I disagree, then what happens?"

"Simple. If you don't let Helen or someone else properly assess your mental state, protocol demands that we send you back home until you're ready to comply. It is, of course, ultimately your choice."

"So now you're blackmailing me! Well, that's just *awesome*!"

Helen shook her head. "No, Jake, we're not blackmailing you. It's just procedure, and I'm sorry you're feeling pushed into a corner. We're just trying to help you, not hurt you."

Jake folded his arms, mirroring the captain. He didn't like feeling coerced into submission.

"Until you feel ready to speak to me, I have something else I'd urge you to consider." Helen reached into her bag, pulled out a card, and offered it to Jake. "This is for a heart and lung transplant support group. It's only about fifteen to twenty minutes north of here. I know the psychologist who runs it."

"Great! It still sounds like a head-shrinking session," Jake said as the psychologist put the card on the desk and pushed it toward him. He ignored it.

"Enough, Masters!" The captain's patience appeared spent. "I've been cutting you some slack because of what you've been through, but I have my limits. I suggest you shut up and listen to Dr. Murphy."

Jake glared at them, did a zipping of his lips together gesture, and then resumed folding his arms.

Helen tapped the business card on the desk with a manicured fingernail. "This group will help you to open up, and you'll get the chance to listen to other people's stories."

"Is that it?" Jake asked. "It's all touchy-feely, and I just turn up and listen?"

"No, not that simple. It's a *sharing* group. They want you to tell them about your transplant experience, any problems you've had, and how you feel. Once you've done that to my colleague's satisfaction, we can consider signing off on your therapy."

"Right now, I'm *feeling* very annoyed. And it's nothing to do with being shot. One visit? Is that it?"

The psychologist stared at him with a pained expression. "Possibly. Share well, and we'll see."

Bennett smiled at Helen. "Sounds reasonable." She then turned to Jake. "It's this, or you consider retiring from the police force altogether. What'll it be, Masters?"

Jake's shoulders dropped in defeat. "It seems that I don't have much of a choice. When's the next session?"

"They meet on the first and third Saturday of every month, so there's one this coming Saturday morning at ten o'clock." Helen pushed the business card on the desk closer.

With a deep sigh, Jake picked it up and slipped it into his shirt pocket. "Okay, I'll give it a go. So is that it? Captain? Doctor? May I be excused?"

"Yes, that will be all." Bennett flicked her hand dismissively. "You can go home for now. We'll reassess the situation in a week or two."

"Bless your hearts."

If inclined, one could easily interpret Jake's departing comment as *fuck you*. He pushed his chair back from the table, stood, and strode out of the office.

Saturday couldn't come fast enough for him.

It's time to put this issue to bed once and for all.

CHAPTER 9

SHARE WITH CARE

Jake sat in his car across the road from the church hall, regarding it warily. It looked harmless enough. Now, he just needed to reveal his innermost thoughts to strangers. What a waste of his time! However, he'd agreed to do it, so there was no choice but to ruin his Saturday morning in group therapy.

Various people of all shapes and sizes walked into the hall. One young man was so thin and pale that Jake figured he had come straight from the hospital. Otherwise, it seemed a typical selection of people you would find at the nearest shopping mall.

And then *she* arrived—curves in all the right places and long, wavy brown hair with golden highlights that caught the morning sunlight, creating an angelic halo effect around her head. She wore a red, fully buttoned-up top decorated with a long necklace and a heart-shaped pendant. Her jeans appeared sprayed on, and he couldn't help but admire her full, rounded butt. She was the most stunning young woman he'd ever seen. Maybe this meeting wouldn't be too bad after all.

Jake watched her go inside, then jumped out of his car, strode across the road, and into the building. He was barely through the door when a friendly, overweight woman in her forties greeted him. She had shoulder-length straight black hair, a tad too much makeup, and wore a multicolored floral dress that looked one size too small.

"Welcome to our little group. My name's Trish." The woman ushered him in and pointed to a table at the back. "Please grab a drink and a cookie and join the sharing circle. The session will start in a few minutes."

"Thank you, Trish. The name's Jake, and I look forward to it."

She gave him a warm smile and then turned to the next person who entered the room.

When Jake arrived at the drinks table, the attractive young woman was already there, pouring herself a glass of water.

"Reasonable turnout." Jake grabbed a cup and placed it under the tap of the coffee machine.

"Is it? I wouldn't know."

"Ah, so you're a first-timer like me?"

She nodded and took a sip of her water.

"Heart or lungs?"

"Excuse me?"

"It's lungs for me," Jake banged a fist against his chest. "I've been breaking in this set for a few months now. I'm not sure if I'll keep them." He gave a short, self-appreciative laugh.

However, the young woman's pained expression suggested that his attempts at light humor were falling flat. She placed a protective hand on her left breast and walked away without responding.

Way to go, Jake! What a stellar first impression.

A tinkling sound interrupted his thoughts.

Trish was walking around the room while ringing a small hand-held silver bell. "Okay, everyone, the meeting's about to begin." She gestured toward the circle of chairs where a few people had already taken seats. Perched on one chair was a big teddy bear with a red heart embroidered on its chest. "Please take a free seat anywhere in the sharing circle. Just leave the chair with the bear. That's mine."

Jake noticed that the young woman deliberately chose a spare seat between two people, ensuring he couldn't sit beside her.

Great! Okay, lady, I can play hard to get as well!

He selected the chair that was furthest from her.

Once everyone had joined the circle, Trish walked over to the teddy bear, picked it up, and tenderly placed it on her lap after she took its chair. Once sure she had the group's attention, she began.

"Welcome, everyone. Allow me to introduce myself to those who don't already know me. My name is Patricia Goldstein, but you can all call me Trish. I'm a fully qualified psychologist. My younger brother had a heart and lung transplant five years ago, but his body rejected the donor organs. He died shortly after the operation."

She paused and waited for the usual reaction. As expected, there were sympathetic expressions all around. "To honor the memory of my brother, I started the Larry Goldstein Heart and Lung Support Group for organ transplant recipients of a heart, lungs, or both, and for the people who support them."

A middle-aged man in the circle applauded. The others politely followed suit.

"Thank you all for coming along, and to those familiar faces, welcome back. I see we have four new people this morning. For their benefit, I'd like to go around the circle and get you all to introduce yourself by your first name. If you're an organ recipient, please also state what kind of transplant you had and how long ago. For support people, please tell us which person you support and what your relationship is with them."

Trish turned to the slim, pale, effeminate, twenty-something man on her left. His platinum blond hair was mainly buzz cut, apart from a long strip at the front, which now flopped over one of his eyes. "Let's start with you, Damien."

The young man pushed the hair from his eye and waved at the group. "As Trish said, my name is Damien. As most of you know, I'm here to support my boyfriend, Chris." He reached for Chris's hand.

Jake smirked inside as he realized, from his earlier observation on arrival, that he thought Damien was an organ transplant recipient. His slight frame, pale skin, and deep dark circles under his eyes suggested he needed a decent feed and a good night's sleep.

Chris, who appeared to be in his early thirties, had short black hair, a muscular build, and broad shoulders. His attempt at a polite smile toward the group appeared more of a grimace as he quickly extracted his hand, much to Damien's dismay. "Hi, I'm Chris. I had a heart and lungs transplanted a year ago."

Next to him was a girl dressed emo-style who sported tattooed arms, a ring through her nose, and blue dreadlocks with black roots. She nodded at the group and, in a monotonous, emotionless voice, said, "Skye—heart—eight months."

With her share over, Skye turned to the young man next to her. He was also emo and heavily tattooed. He took Skye's lead and introduced himself briefly, "Mick—Skye's boyfriend—support person."

Next to Mick was the attractive young woman. Her huge brown eyes circled the group as she gave them all a warm smile. "Hi, everyone. It's nice to meet you all. My name's Libby, and I had a heart transplant six months ago."

Jake couldn't have been less interested from thereon. As three more women and two men briefly introduced themselves, he became lost in thoughts about the mysterious Libby. She only looked to be in her early twenties, and nothing was adorning her ring finger, which he hoped meant she was single. His thoughts drifted to wondering what it would be like to be in a serious relationship with someone like her and—

What the hell are you thinking, Jake? He mentally berated himself as he cut off the unfamiliar romantic notions flooding his head. *This is not like you at all!*

Until the day of the shooting, Jake led the life of a playboy. His line of work meant unusually long and irregular hours, making social planning difficult. It was, therefore, not surprising that this lifestyle didn't suit most women.

Early in his career, he decided casual relationships were his best option. A few friends with benefits, he could call at a moment's notice, satisfied any carnal desires, with no emotional attachments being part of the deal. It was all very upfront, so the ladies knew where they stood. Everyone was on board and had a good time.

However, not having a partner to love and care for him hit home during the transplant recovery process. Both his parents had already passed away. First was his mother, who had pancreatic cancer and died only a month after his nineteenth birthday, just over eight years ago. His father pined over the loss of his wife so much that he committed suicide by overdosing on sleeping pills six months later.

Sure, his twin sister was there, but she took the loss of their parents very hard. Her grief over her mother's death turned to anger when their father took his own life. Goosy had always been a daddy's girl and couldn't understand how her father could leave her like this.

As a result, she shut down emotionally, determined that no one would hurt her like that again. The sweet and cuddly sister, who threw herself at him and clung on while smothering him with kisses when they were kids, had disappeared entirely. A wise-cracking, tough little smartass took her place.

These days, Goosy's version of caring was rough, with zero physical affection. Jake craved a hug while he fought to regain strength after the operation. However, all his sister could do during that time was continually punch him in the arm and berate him. She was furious that he had almost left her alone in the world.

Goosy's anger was understandable. Not wearing a vest when putting himself in mortal danger was reckless. Barney nicknamed him *Maverick* years ago, as this behavior was not unusual. But his luck ran out this time, and he paid a life-changing price.

Of course, the ladies who casually frequented his bed were nowhere to be seen during his recovery. They were suddenly way too busy to make time for him. It made him realize just how empty his life had become.

Jake became so lost in thought that he almost didn't notice the person next to him tapping on his shoulder. He turned in surprise to face a slightly overweight, middle-aged man with a bad comb-over and ruddy complexion. "What?"

The man nodded toward the group. "It's your turn to introduce yourself."

Suddenly realizing all eyes were on him, he gave an embarrassed grin. "Sorry. My name's Jake. I had a double lung transplant six months ago."

One more woman introduced herself, and it was then back to Trish. The bear still perched on her lap like a small child. She smiled and, using the teddy's arm, waved it at everyone, causing a couple of people to giggle.

"For those who don't know, this is my furry friend, Cherie."

Jake dropped his head and rolled his eyes inwardly. *This day keeps getting better and better!*

"Cherie is our group mascot and our resident share bear. She has a special place in my heart because I gave her to my brother when he was in the hospital." A moment of pain flickered through Trish's eyes. "We'll pass her to you when you're ready to share. Whoever's holding Cherie controls the conversation, and the rest of us must listen without speaking or interrupting them. The only person who can break this rule is me. I might ask questions to assist you with your sharing.

"I also realize that some of you might find it tough to share, so we won't judge you if you want to hug Cherie. She loves cuddles and received many from me after my brother died. So, who'd like to be the first to share today?"

Everyone in the circle looked at each other, willing someone else to volunteer. Finally, Damien slowly raised his hand.

"I knew I could rely on you, Damien," Trish said with a smile as she passed him the bear.

The young man clutched Cherie to his chest and dropped his chin on her furry head. "I want to talk about how sometimes, since his operation, I feel Chris is pushing me away—"

"Oh, here we go again!" Chris put his head in his hands and groaned.

"The bear!" Damien admonished. "I have the bear. You're supposed to listen to me. That's the rule."

Chris looked up at him and rolled his eyes in frustration.

Damien pointed at him accusingly. "See how he treats me! I get this all the time. He always shuts me out like this whenever I try to tell him how I feel. And I'm sure you all saw what happened when we introduced ourselves. I tried to hold his hand, and he rejected me." He dramatically tossed the hair off his eye and turned to his partner. "That hurt, Chris, and you embarrassed me when I was just trying to show everyone how much I love you and want to be here for you."

Damien's over-the-top behavior was very comical. Not wanting to appear an insensitive jerk, Jake had to bite his lip to suppress the urge to laugh.

Chris suddenly sat up straight and snatched Cherie. "Enough. It's my turn to speak now." He looked at Trish for permission. She shrugged and waved her hand for him to continue.

"Do you know why I don't want to hear about *your* feelings? It's because *I'm* the one who almost died! *I'm* the one who had the operation! I've had to deal with someone else's heart and lungs in my chest. Yet somehow, you have made this all about *you*! And I'm sick of it."

Damien looked stricken. A tear rolled down his cheek. "Oh, baby, I'm so sorry! I didn't know I was making you feel this way. What a selfish bitch I've been! I've just been so worried about you. I'm truly sorry."

Chris's face softened. He dropped the bear and pulled Damien to him for a hug. "Sorry, too. I know I've been distant while dealing with my transplant, which has been hard on you. I promise to let you in more. Okay?"

Damien nodded, and his cheeks flushed pink, finally giving color to his pale face. He bent down, retrieved Cherie from the floor, and passed her back, smiling apologetically.

"Well, that's what I call a good share," Trish said. "It was full of emotion and honesty. These boys have shown that there's no holding back here. Now, we need to hear from one of our new people." She looked around the circle, and her eyes settled on Skye. "How about you, Skye?"

Trish offered Cherie, but the young emo flopped back in her chair with folded arms, shook her head, dropped her chin to her chest, and closed her eyes.

"Ah, okay. I see Skye is not ready to share today." She turned to Libby with a hopeful look.

"Thanks, Trish, but I'd like to listen to some other people a bit more first."

Jake looked around at the reluctant group. Most people rated public speaking their number one fear, and he always wondered why. It just seemed to come naturally to him. Probably because being the twin of a sister with high-intensity energy, like Goosy, who was the ultimate charmer and possessed the singing voice of an angel, forced him to step up and compete to get his parents' attention when he was younger. His communication skills made him a good interrogator and negotiator, so his career advanced quickly in the police force despite being only twenty-seven years old.

Helen told him he needed to share to get Trish to sign him off as fit for duty. He, therefore, would give them a sharing experience they'd never forget. Jake put his arms out for Cherie when Trish looked his way.

"Hit me, Trish. I'm ready to *bare* all." He appreciated the scattered laughter as some people got his play on words.

"Oh, wonderful. I was hoping we'd hear from you today." Trish gave the bear to the woman beside her, who passed it on.

Once Cherie was in his lap, Jake mimicked Trish's teddy bear wave with Cherie's arm. The entire group laughed this time.

Sharing's going to be fun.

"As I told you guys before, the name's Jake. I'm a detective with the police force. I'm here because my boss won't let me return to work until I share my experience. So, here's me, sharing, and I hope Trish will sign me off afterward." He turned to Trish. "Okay, Trish?"

Looking unsure, she shrugged and gestured for him to continue.

"Anyway, as I mentioned earlier, I had a double lung transplant. I needed one because I got shot in the line of duty."

A murmur of shock ran around the group.

"Don't worry. I don't remember a thing. One minute, I was driving to work, and the next, I woke up in the hospital with someone else's lungs inside me. Sure, recovery was tough, but I'm good now." Jake turned to Trish. "All I need, doc, is for you to sign me off so I can return to what I do best." He held Cherie out, offering her back. "There you go. How was that?"

Trish put up her hand, rejecting Cherie. "Yes, Helen told me to expect you. I'm very interested in hearing what you have to say. However, I believe you're holding back."

"In what way?"

"She mentioned something was troubling you, but I can't say what without breaching confidentiality. If you understand what I mean, would you care to elaborate?"

Jake thought for a second, then realized what Trish was asking him. "Are you referring to the nightmares?"

Trish smiled and nodded.

"Okay, well, there's nothing much worth mentioning. I've just been having this recurrent dream. I'm sure it has something to do with the shooting. It's all good, I promise you."

Once again, Jake held out the bear, trying to make Trish take it back, but she ignored him.

"I'm sure the group would love to hear more about these dreams. We find it's always good to share them. They often hold the key to our innermost thoughts and feelings."

He sighed in frustration. Trish wasn't making this easy for him. "It's nothing really, I'm sure."

She stared at him with a fixed, benign expression on her face. It was apparent she wouldn't budge on this and wanted more.

With a sigh of resignation, Jake knew he couldn't escape sharing his nightmare. "Okay, if you must know, I dreamed about these two guys in balaclavas, holding guns, who tried to rob this convenience store."

There was a loud gasp. It was Libby, and everyone turned to look at her. She blushed, dropped her head, and gestured toward him to go on.

"Okay, well, the older one shoots three people. Then he gives me his gun and threatens me to make me shoot this dead woman on the ground, and—"

Suddenly, Libby jumped out of her chair and ran from the room. Everyone looked surprised as they watched her leave.

"Hmm, I think I'd better hand back the bear before I clear the room with my horror stories," Jake said, hoping to lighten the mood. It worked because some group members tittered as he held Cherie out to Trish again.

This time, the psychologist accepted the bear, then stood up and placed it in her seat. "Please, chat amongst yourselves, everyone. I need to go after Libby and check she's okay."

As Trish left the room, Jake frowned.

Well, that was a train wreck! I can't seem to put a foot right with that girl!

It was a shame. Although Jake felt he had made a lousy first impression on Libby, something was magnetically compelling about her beyond her stunning good looks.

He couldn't help but wonder what it was.

CHAPTER 10

NOT JOKING

L ibby sat inside the church hall toilet cubicle, head down with elbows resting on knees, as her heart raced wildly. She couldn't believe it. Jake's dreams were the same as hers. How was this possible?

Deep down, she knew the answer. The handsome young detective must have had the same donor. If her psychologist's theories were correct, it would make perfect sense.

As soon as she laid eyes on Jake, Libby could sense something drawing her to him apart from his obvious good looks. However, when he first came near her, her heart started beating so fast it was almost painful. It may have appeared dismissive, but she had to get away to collect herself.

It was unfortunate because she had to admit he was her type—tall and muscular, with light brown hair, a clean-shaven square jawline, deep blue eyes, and a playful, crooked smile. He was also cheeky yet charming, making him seem even more attractive.

Before she became sick, had they met at a party, given half a chance, she would have probably made out with him. Not likely now. She made a *great* first impression by snubbing him at the drinks table and running out of the room in the middle of his sharing.

The sound of someone gently tapping on the cubicle door broke into her thoughts.

"Libby, are you okay?" Trish called through the door.

"Yes, Trish. Please, don't worry about me."

"It's just that you rushed out so suddenly."

"Sorry, but I felt unwell and didn't want to throw up on anyone." She opened the cubicle door, gave Trish a weak smile, and walked to the basin. "It seems it was a false alarm. I'm okay now. It's all just a bit embarrassing."

"Nothing to be embarrassed about, my dear." Trish waited for Libby to finish washing her hands and offered the crook of her arm. "Let me walk you back in," she said.

Returning to the meeting room, they noticed the group had moved to the drinks table to chat. A couple of people saw them enter and greeted Libby with sympathetic smiles.

Trish clapped her hands to get the attention of the rest of the group. "It looks like we've broken into the social part of the meeting earlier than I'd intended, but that's okay. So carry on, unless someone else wants to share today?" No one raised their hand, so she nodded and joined the discussion.

Libby spotted Jake standing at the back of the group. His concerned eyes met hers, and she realized they needed to talk. Today might be her only chance, so she smiled and strode over.

"Hi there. I must apologize for running out in the middle of your share."

He waved her off. "No, I'm the one who's sorry. It was my story that upset you. I should've kept my big mouth shut. I hope you're okay."

"Yes, I'm fine, thanks. Nothing to worry about." Her heart was now beating normally around Jake, which was a relief. She shifted from foot to foot. "I wanted to ask if you'd be interested in chatting about what you said during your share. Would you like to ditch this meeting and go for a coffee somewhere?"

Jake's face lit up. "Sure. I'd love to"—he held up a finger—"but just give me one minute, as I need to do something first."

She watched as he walked over to Trish, pulled a folded paper from his back pocket, and offered it to her. The psychologist shook her head, took his arm, and led him to the room's corner for a private chat.

There was an exchange between the two that Libby couldn't hear above the group chatter. She saw Jake speaking and gesturing energetically, appearing unhappy with what he was hearing. Trish calmly faced his annoyance with a resolute expression, her arms folded.

When the conversation finished, Trish held out her hand. Looking disappointed and defeated, Jake reluctantly shook it. He then shoved the paper back into his pocket and returned to Libby.

"Is everything okay?" she asked.

"No, not really. I feel like someone sold me a bill of goods. Anyway, I'll tell you later. I'm ready to blow this joint. I've had enough share bears for one day to last me a lifetime."

She nodded, and the two of them went outside.

"So, where'd you like to go?" Jake asked.

Libby pulled her phone from her bag and spoke to it. "Hey, Google, show me the nearest café." A map with pin drops and café names came up in response to her question. "There's a café on the other side of the park. Up for a short walk?"

"Sounds good to me." Jake gestured for Libby to lead the way.

As they slowly strolled side by side down the street and across the park, she gave him a curious sideward glance. "So, what happened with Trish that upset you so much?"

"Oh, yeah, that. Trish thinks I'm suppressing my emotions about the shooting, and they're coming out in those disturbing dreams. She said she would recommend to my captain that I have another month off work while I sort out my *issues*."

"A bit more time off to relax surely isn't that bad."

"I get most people would think that, but I *want* to return to work. I'm over being stuck at home. The worst bit is that Trish said I need regular private therapy sessions with the office shrink. I came to the group session to avoid those, but it sounds like they will happen anyway." He frowned. "Darn it! I wish I'd never mentioned those stupid dreams. Like I said earlier—stitched up!"

Libby shrugged. "Sounds like they care about you. I wouldn't take it too hard. Anyway, I may know why you're having those dreams."

Jake's eyebrows shot up with surprise. "Really? Color me intrigued."

She gave an enigmatic smile. "I have some theories to share with you over a drink. Stay tuned."

A short stroll later, they arrived at the café. Libby stared at the image of the frothy cappuccino and flowery writing on the window. It seemed super familiar, causing her to wonder if she'd been there before. But that was unlikely, as this wasn't a part of town she frequented. They walked inside.

A well-preserved woman in her fifties waved at them and walked over. She wore a red, short-sleeved top paired with black pants, and the name *Anna* was on her badge. Like the café, she also seemed familiar, but not to the same degree—something seemed different. But Libby could have sworn she had seen those kind eyes before.

"Howdy, guys!" Anna gestured toward a nearby table for two. "Go take a seat, and I'll be right over."

"Do you mind if we have the corner booth?" Jake asked. "I'd prefer it, and it seems to be free."

"Go for it."

Libby also felt inexplicably drawn to the corner booth. *How strange.* She shook the thought from her head and followed Jake.

They had barely sat down when Anna came over to serve them. "Howdy, folks. The specials of the day are on the board." She pointed to the chalkboard on the wall. "Do you need more time, or are you ready to order?"

Jake looked her up and down quizzically. "Have we met somewhere before?"

"Darlin', I pride myself on never forgetting a face. I rarely see good-looking men like you around these parts. If we'd met, I would for sure remember you."

Libby cut in. "You'll never believe this, but I was about to ask you the same thing."

Anna blushed and seemed flustered. "Well, you're a pretty young lady and equally unforgettable. But no, I haven't met you either." She put her hands on her hips. "Folks, this is very flattering, and I don't want to seem rude, but I've other customers to serve. So, may I take your orders, please?"

Jake nodded. "Sorry. I'll have a cappuccino, thanks. No, wait. Scratch that. Make mine a strawberry milkshake. And whatever the young lady wants."

Coincidentally, Libby also craved a strawberry milkshake, which was unusual, as she preferred chocolate. "Ditto, please."

They made polite small talk until Anna came back with their milkshakes. As she walked away, they both leaned in to sip them.

Their eyes met as Libby watched Jake suck hard on his straw, emptying the brain-chilling liquid from the glass in one go.

Impressive.

"It's strange, but I could have sworn I met that woman before," she said between dainty sips. "And all this"—she waved her hand at their surroundings—"seems familiar, too. Were you feeling the same, by any chance?"

Jake sat back, licked his lips, and shrugged. "It's just some strange coincidence, I'm sure. There's always a rational explanation. Changing the subject, I have to say, you asking me out was a surprise. It didn't seem like I'd made a great first impression."

"Funnily enough, I thought the same."

He smirked. "Thanks for agreeing that I didn't make a good first impression."

"No, I meant—" Libby cut herself off as she realized he was making a joke. "Oh, okay. Hilarious. Perhaps we should start over."

"Great idea." He leaned across the table, his hand extended. "My name's Jake. Pleased to meet you."

Libby smiled, happy to play his game. "Nice to meet you, Jake. I'm Libby," she said, raising her hand to meet his. However, the second they touched, she felt an incredible connection flow like energy to her soul. Was he feeling this, too? She noticed Jake's eyes were wide, probably mirroring hers, and he seemed equally entranced.

Time stood still. Their handshake seemed to go on forever until, with an awkward laugh, they released simultaneously.

Self-consciously, Libby twiddled with the heart pendant on her necklace. Her donor was never far from her mind, and, in particular, not now. The reason she and Jake felt so connected seemed all too clear. All she needed was verification that this wasn't just in her head. It was time to launch right into it. "So, you said you had a double lung transplant six months ago?"

"Yes, that's right."

"Well, that's what I need to talk about."

"You mean you haven't invited me here for my considerable charm? I'm shattered."

As much as she enjoyed the banter, there were better times for flirting. "I need you to tell me exactly when and where you had your transplant. Trust me, it's important."

"So much for formalities. It was at Memorial Hermann Hospital last November, if you really must know."

"Last November ... er ... was it on the 18th?"

"Okay, yeah, it was on the 18th. How did you know that?"

Libby closed her eyes. "I knew it!"

"Knew what exactly?"

"I had my transplant at the same place on the same day." She leaned across the table and looked deep into Jake's eyes. "I believe *your* lungs and *my* heart have come from the *same* donor."

"Really? I'll admit it's a coincidence. But—"

Libby flicked her hand, dismissing his objections. "I need to talk to you about your dreams."

"More like nightmares, really, and annoyingly persistent. I wish I knew why I keep having them."

"I think I know." She paused for dramatic effect. "I believe they're memories from our donor."

Jake frowned. "*Alleged* same donor. And what makes you say that?"

"Because I'm having the same horrible dreams, so it seems pretty obvious that—"

"Hang on a minute. Are you serious? The *same* dreams? How's that possible?"

"My psychologist told me about this theory called cellular memory, which means storing memories in organs other than the brain. So, I think we're experiencing our donor's memories through our dreams."

A range of emotions crossed Jake's face as he processed what she said. He then shook his head. "Oh, come on. Do you expect me to buy into this nonsense?"

"Well, how else do you explain it?"

"Oh, I don't know. You could be some loony girl who frequents these support programs trying to pick up strange men. You listen to their shares and tell them crazy stories to convince them that there's this way-out connection."

From Jake's skeptical expression, Libby could see he didn't believe her.

"Okay, I'll prove it to you. Ask me about anything from the dream that only you and I could know."

"Hmm, this could prove interesting." His eyes raised to the ceiling as he tried to recall something. "Okay, I've got it. What's special about the guy who does the shooting? It's something about the way he speaks."

"Oh, you mean the Irish accent?" She enjoyed his look of surprise.

"Okay, that was a lucky guess. Maybe I mentioned that during my share."

"You didn't."

"Nope. I'm not sure now. Let's try something else."

Again, Jake paused as he thought of something to test her. He then clicked his fingers. "Okay, I have a tricky one for you that will seal the deal. So, what nickname did the Irishman have for his knife?"

"That's easy. It was Reaper."

Jake dropped his head into his hands. "This is crazy."

"Yeah, I know, right? So, do you believe me now?"

He leaned across the table, hands under his chin. His eyes locked on hers, and she could see he was struggling to accept what she was telling him. Seconds later, a slow smile spread across his face. "Dammit, I've got it. I'm such a moron! I've just worked it out. Goosy put you up to this, didn't she?"

"Pardon? Who?"

"Don't play coy with me, young lady. You must be a friend of my sister, Goosy, and this is one of her jokes. My sister knows all about my dreams in every detail. I also told her I'd be at this meeting today. Oh, come on, show me your phone. It wouldn't surprise me if she's listening in on this conversation and is laughing her ass off." Jake leaned in and spoke to Libby's bag perched on the side of their table. "If you're still listening, Goosy, you got me, but good."

Libby pulled her phone from her bag, unlocked it, and handed it over for inspection to show that no one was listening. "Check my contacts. You'll see Goosy isn't in there."

Jake wasted no time taking up her offer. His inspection went on for over a minute. Libby worried he had found some compromising photos she'd forgotten to delete. As a bit of a wild child before the heart condition took over her life, her photo gallery had plenty of pouty selfies showing cleavage for the benefit of boys not worthy of her time.

She held her breath until he finally handed it back.

"All right. I may have come up empty, but this proves nothing. Goosy would have told you I'm a cop, so for all I know, you could have deleted part of your call history and her number from your contacts, and offering your phone was part of an elaborate ruse to convince me."

Seriously?

"I swear I don't know your sister. Call her if you must, and you'll see I'm telling the truth."

"I'll do just that." Jake pulled out his phone. "Hey, Google, call Goosy."

The call was on speaker, and the answering service kicked in after four rings. "Hey there! It sucks that you've missed me. You know what to do. Leave a message after the beeeeep!"

"Goosy! I know you've been messing with me. Call me back as soon as you get this message." Jake punched the hang-up icon with his finger to disconnect the call and threw the phone on the table. He stared at Libby. "You got lucky."

Oh, for the love of God!

"Jake, I'm not joking here. You need to listen. I think these dreams will keep haunting us until we find out who our donor was."

"Okay, let's play. Assuming I even consider going along with your fairy story, what do you want me to do about it?"

Is this man deliberately being obtuse?

"Well, aren't you supposed to be a police detective? Shouldn't you be able to access this information somehow? I can't explain it, but I feel this is important."

Jake's skeptical expression showed he remained unconvinced.

"Just give me your phone, and I'll put my number in it," she said. "Or give me your number, and I'll prank call you so you can save it."

"No way, lady." Jake placed a protective hand over it. "You're not going anywhere near my phone, and I'm not giving you my number. Sorry."

Libby gritted her teeth, trying not to lose her temper. She snatched a pen from her handbag, pulled a pink paper napkin from the dispenser, wrote down her contact details, then folded and placed it on Jake's phone. "Here's my name, number, and email address. Please talk to your sister. You'll see I'm telling you the truth."

"Oh, I'll be talking to my sister all right. You can count on that. Now, I need to take off and be literally anywhere else but here. I've had enough crazy for one day. I'm happy to walk you back to your car, but that's it. Are you coming?"

Libby stared at her half-finished milkshake with downcast eyes, holding back tears, and shook her head. "No, thanks. I'm going to sit right here and finish my drink."

"Okay, well, thanks for the chat. It's been entertaining, at the very least." Jake picked up his phone and the napkin from the table. He also snatched up the check Anna had left with their milkshakes.

"But I invited you out, so I should be the one who—"

He ignored her and headed to the counter. Libby watched him banter in full charm mode with Anna as he tapped his phone against the Google Pay device she held toward him. He then shoved the phone and napkin into his jacket pocket and turned back to Libby. "See ya."

Libby chewed her lower lip and fought back the tears she could feel welling up inside her. Not trusting that her voice wouldn't crack, she gave him a nod of farewell.

Jake presented the most charming, cheeky grin, a polite wave goodbye, and then walked out the door.

How can someone so gorgeous be so stupid?

Why was their connection not clear to him?

Jake's police background was making him overthink this. When he learns this wasn't a joke from his sister, perhaps his curiosity will compel him to investigate, and then he will call her. At least, she hoped so.

Now, all she could do was wait.

CHAPTER 11

LAST GASP?

Jake glanced over his shoulder at Libby sitting in the window of Anna's café as he walked away. She looked dejected as she watched him leave, and he felt guilty.

What a gentleman you are! Not even waiting for the lady to finish her milkshake.

He had to admit it had been a very entertaining morning. First, he witnessed a gay couple having a soap opera-style spat. Next, he cuddled an enormous share bear while he spilled his guts to complete and utter strangers, and then there was the lovely Libby. What kind of girl would let Goosy talk her into playing a practical joke on a man with a double lung transplant? She would have to be a bit on the crazy side.

However, he noticed that his breathing became difficult as they talked about the dreams and their supposed donor. What was up with that? It had to be psychological. What other explanation could there be? This girl almost messed with his head until he realized it was a stupid joke!

A beep from his phone alerted him to a text. He stopped walking and pulled it from his pocket to read the message. It was from Goosy. She had sent an edited photo of Jake with a shrunken head on a normal-sized body. He smirked, now sure his sister was behind the Libby joke.

Nice one, Goosy. Oh, you're gonna cop it when I catch up with you!

His phone returned to his pocket, and he continued walking, trying to think of a witty response. Only a few steps later, he found his breathing become labored.

No!

The doctors had warned him his lungs might fail, but that was in the early days and shouldn't be happening now. It was like breathing through a tiny straw while submerged underwater—horrible!

As his head spun and his knees buckled, Jake lurched toward a nearby tree, reached for support, and sank to the ground.

This is it! I'm going to die!

He fought to breathe, and red spots floated before his eyes. He didn't notice the sudden gust of wind until something papery and pink fluttered toward him and plastered itself against his leg. It looked familiar, and Jake reached out to grab it despite his breathing distress. To his surprise, the second his fingers enclosed it, he found his lungs started working again.

As he sucked in long, grateful breaths, he turned it over to see Libby's name, number, and email address scrawled in large letters. He frowned. It was the pink napkin she had given him at the café. It must have fallen out of his pocket when he retrieved his phone. Annoyed, he screwed it into a tight ball and threw it away from himself.

To his horror, straight away, his lungs started failing him again.

Nooooo!

His head spun from the second assault of oxygen deprivation. He grabbed his chest, choking for air, until another gust of wind caused the pink paper ball to bounce and skip back into his lap. He snatched it in frustration, ready to toss it away when his lungs began working again.

Jake propped the napkin ball on the tips of his thumb and forefinger, staring at it as if it were magical.

What's going on? This is nuts!

He then carefully placed it beside him on the ground and waited. Nothing happened, and he felt fine.

Yep! Definitely losing my mind.

He decided he wouldn't let this stupid napkin make him its bitch. Jake grabbed it, stood up, drop-kicked the pink paper ball, and watched it arc until it landed, bounced along, and settled twenty feet away. He then stood waiting—still nothing.

He walked over, picked it up, and looked at it.

Who is this crazy Libby girl? She should move to Hollywood with those acting skills. She looks way too healthy for a person who's had a heart transplant, with that gorgeous honey-colored skin of hers and that long, shiny brown hair with those golden flecks, that kick-ass body, and—

He needed to cut those thoughts off, as he didn't like where they were heading. A bin was nearby. With his mouth set in a determined line, he launched the ball of paper basketball-style, then gave a Mexican celebratory wave when it dropped dead center in the bin.

Decision made—time to forget this girl and focus on returning to work. I will fight those darned shrinks and get my old life back!

Jake rolled on his heels and turned, planning to head off to his car. And then it happened. He felt the wind knocked out of him like a punch to the stomach.

What the hell? Not again!

He fell to his knees, gasping, feeling worse than before. Now, he couldn't breathe at all.

Nooooo! Jake's eyes turned toward the bin. *Could it be?*

With only seconds before losing consciousness, he pulled himself to his feet. Making an awful, desperate gurgling noise that sounded foreign to his ears, he lurched toward the bin and threw himself into it headfirst. Jake tossed rubbish everywhere as he sought the balled napkin. All was turning dark when he wrapped his fingers around it. As soon as the paper ball was in his hand, his constricted lungs released, allowing him to suck in the air he needed.

"Fuuuuuuck!" As soon as the profanity was out of his mouth, Jake looked around. Guilt riddled him as he half expected the ghost of his dead mother to come and slap the back of his head. Until his mother became bedridden at the end stages of her cancer, she'd drag the family to church every Sunday. She was very religious and frowned upon any form of swearing—particularly the f-bomb.

After their mother died, the family spiraled, as their father couldn't cope with the death of his wife. He was agnostic, so attending church was no longer a Sunday requirement. When he killed himself, the twins ditched religion altogether, deciding God had let them down. Despite this, they agreed never to utter the forbidden word out of respect for their mother's passing. Sometimes, however, a horrible situation makes it seem impossible not to do so.

Jake glared at the napkin ball. Something supernatural was messing with him, informing him of Libby's importance.

As he stood there, catching his breath again, his phone rang. He pulled it from his pocket to look. It was Goosy.

"Hi, sis. I tried calling you earlier."

"Like, duh! Why do you think I'm phoning you back? As usual, you must have called when I was in the shower—every single time, dude ... like *every* time. I'm sure you have hidden cameras in my place, so you can do it to bug me.

"I haven't been up long, to be honest. The gig at our new venue last night ran super late." A loud yawn followed. "Best night ever! The crowd loved us, and management has booked us up for the next month. Can you imagine—your big sis is finally becoming a rock star! A few more regular gigs like this and no more bartending for me!

"By the way, did you see the pic I sent? Pretty funny, right?"

Typical Goosy—chatting nonstop at high speed.

"Yeah, that was some nice editing. And congrats on the gig, but I need to ask you something important since you obviously haven't bothered to listen to my message."

"So, what have I missed? You sound weird. Is something wrong?"

"You tell me. Now listen. We've played some pretty good practical jokes on each other over the years—"

"Yeah, like when you pinned toilet paper to the back of my first prom dress when we were thirteen and let me walk around like that all night, and no one had the decency to let me know. That was just *hilarious!*"

"And you took all the ants from our ant farm and filled my bed with them the same night. I didn't realize until the next morning when I woke up covered in ant bites. So yeah, fun times."

"Even funnier to discover your allergy to formic acid and see your face puff up like a balloon."

Jake smirked as he remembered that empathy was not one of his sister's strong suits. "Yeah. The joke you pulled today was funnier than anything you have ever done to me. Nice one, sis. You had me going there. All I want to know is, how did you talk Libby into it?"

"Who? What are you talking about?" Goosy sounded confused.

"You know, the Libby joke you played on me today. Admit that you're the puppet master. It's the only rational explanation. I need you to be honest with me."

"Little bro, have you been drinking? I know you've been through a lot. So why would I torture you with some stupid practical joke right now? Dang it, I almost lost you! I'm not that big of a jerk."

So, this wasn't Goosy after all. What the hell is going on?

Jake frowned as the uncomfortable realization hit that Libby may have told him the truth.

"I'm sorry, sis. Something strange happened today, and I thought you were responsible. I'm not mad or anything. Seriously, it's all good."

"Well, if someone's messing with you, they mess with me, little bro. You know that, don't you? So, who's this Libby person? Say the word, and I'll take care of her for you. What else are big sisters for?"

"You're a crack-up! Look, I'm going now. Don't worry about me. I can take care of myself."

"You're my little bro, and you know I'll always be there for you. Call any time if you need me, okay?"

"Thanks. Will do. Bye." With that, he hung up.

Jake stared hard at the balled napkin, wondering what to do next, and an idea occurred to him.

Time to try something new.

He unfurled it, punched Libby's contact details into his phone, and saved them.

And now, for experiment number three.

He wrapped the napkin around a rock, placed it on the ground, and cautiously backed away. He then sat on a nearby park bench with his eyes locked on it for five minutes. Jake wasn't taking any chances. This time, nothing happened.

What a relief!

The curse of the pink napkin appeared to be behind him. It was now time to take things a little further.

Jake brought his phone to his mouth. "Hey, Google, call Libby."

Taylor Swift's *'Shake it off!'* happened to his right. He turned in surprise to find Libby walking toward him, fishing in her handbag for her phone, until she spotted him sitting there.

He grinned, pressed the call-end button, and gave her a silly wave. "Don't bother trying to answer that. It's just me. Hello again."

"What are you still doing here? I thought you'd be long gone."

"Yeah, about that—it's a story for another day. Instead, I'd rather tell you some good news." He patted the seat beside him and gestured for Libby to sit down. She complied, and he turned to face her. "Let's just say I plan to investigate our respective donors to see if they're the same person. However, could I ask you to do one thing first? Of course, you can say no, but it would help."

"Anything. What do you need?"

"Your scar from the transplant—could you show me just the top of it? I need to know I'm not going crazy, and what you're telling me is true."

With a nod, Libby stood up, stepped back, unbuttoned her red blouse, and pulled it open, revealing a black, lacy bra and the long scar between her breasts. There was nothing more beautiful yet sad all at the same time.

Jake hadn't expected this, thinking she would protest. Deep in her eyes, he saw her pain. This was no joke. Somewhere in the recesses of his mind, he always knew it. His practical, *prove-it-to-me*, and *there-must-be-a-rational-explanation-for-this* nature had tried to blind him. But now he could see, and a lump rose in his throat. It was mortifying to have put her through this indignity.

He stood and, with gentle hands, reached out to close her blouse. "Sorry. I've been a real idiot and a jerk. I believe you."

A single tear rolled down her cheek. "You do?"

He nodded. Sensing Libby's need, he opened his arms, and she fell into them. He rested his head on top of hers as they held each other.

Libby buried her face in his chest, and the floodgates opened. "I felt so alone," she said between sobs. "I thought no one would understand what I was going through."

Jake took a deep breath. Although it made him uncomfortable when a woman cried, having this girl in his arms felt right. It was like Libby's energy was becoming one with his, and something within told him he could trust her. It was emotional, and he didn't want to let her go. "Me, too," he said, his voice sounding choked.

Oh my God! Keep it together, Jake!

Seconds felt like minutes until finally, by silent, mutual consent, they parted and regarded each other in slight embarrassment as they tried to regain control. Jake couldn't remember coming this close to losing it in years, not since his parents died. This girl was amazing. To think he wanted to toss her away until his lungs persuaded him otherwise.

He offered her his hand. She took it, and they walked back to her car. Their connection was tangible. They didn't even have to say a word. Why hadn't he noticed this before?

Jake knew what he needed to do. He had to employ all his detective skills to investigate the heck out of this situation, and then maybe they could both get a good night's sleep.

CHAPTER 12

FLOWER POWER

Later that afternoon, Jake stood before Teri Johnson, the charge nurse of intensive care at Memorial Hermann, eyeballing her in frustration. "Since you refuse to tell me what I need to know, I want to speak to Doctor Bourke."

Teri shook her head. "The doctor is in surgery right now, but even if he weren't, he would just say the same thing. Donor information is confidential, even to the police, so don't waste your time."

"I could organize a warrant."

"On what grounds?" Teri planted her hands on her hips. "You were very fortunate to receive such a fine set of lungs. Some might say you should be grateful and leave it at that."

As they spoke, Jake became distracted by a short, blond woman in her fifties, all dressed in pink, bustling around as she arranged flowers in a large vase at the nurses' station behind Teri. The woman was staring at Jake and seemed glad he noticed her. She winked and presented him with a cheeky grin. He smiled in return, realizing it was Alice, the volunteer flower lady who often popped into his room for a chat during his recovery in the hospital six months ago. Despite Alice being twice his age and a married woman of twenty years' standing, they enjoyed an over-the-top flirtatious relationship.

The charge nurse followed Jake's gaze and turned to face the flower lady with a glare of disapproval. "Are you right there? I thought you had already arranged those flowers today."

"Sorry, Teri. It's just that it's Jake, and I wanted to say hello." Alice turned her attention to Jake. "So wonderful to see you. Handsome as ever. You look great!"

"You, too! Have you done something with your hair? You're even more ravishing than I remember. Your husband had better treat you right, or I might have to steal you away for myself."

Alice batted her eyelashes, patted her golden curls, and gave a girlish giggle.

Teri rolled her eyes and stepped between them, facing Jake. "Are we done here, *detective*?"

Jake's shoulders slumped in defeat. "I guess so. Thanks for looking after me while I was here, anyway."

"You're welcome. And I'm glad you're looking so well. It's always nice to receive visits from past patients and see how they're doing. I'm sorry I can't help you, but, being a detective, you would understand that we need to maintain confidentiality."

"I do. Thanks anyway."

With that, he turned on his heels and strode away down the hospital corridor, contemplating his next move, until a voice called him.

"Jake, please wait for me!"

Jake turned to see Alice chasing him down, her high heels clacking on the floor as she approached. No longer in the mood for flirty banter, he considered lying that he couldn't stop as he had to get to another appointment, but then his conscience kicked in, telling him the kind-hearted flower lady deserved better. So, resignedly, he waited for her to catch up.

Alice arrived at his side, slightly breathless. "You move fast with those long legs of yours!" She then looked left and right and lowered her voice to a whisper. "I overheard your conversation with Teri and—"

Jake frowned. "Alice, that was supposed to be private."

"Okay, I'm sorry, but I have some information that might help you."

"Help me? With what?"

"With your donor, of course."

"Are you serious?"

"Sure am. Maybe we could—"

Jake put a silencing finger to her lips and guided her to the nearby visitor room, where he and Goosy had spent many hours chatting during his recovery. It was a relief to find it empty. He pulled out a chair at a nearby table and gestured for Alice to sit, which she did.

He plopped himself in the chair opposite and leaned toward her across the table. "Okay, tell me what you know about my donor."

Alice's worried eyes looked toward the door. "I thought you might take me out for a drink or something. I'm not sure if this is the best place. As an unpaid volunteer, no one asked me to sign a confidentiality agreement. That said, I love visiting with the patients and would hate to lose the privilege because of sharing classified information."

Jake followed her gaze and noticed the door didn't have a lock—probably because of safety reasons. His eyes then dropped to the chair next to him.

I'll sort this out.

Without hesitation, he stood up, dragged the chair to the door, and propped it under the handle so no one outside could open it without some difficulty. He then promptly returned to his chair. "Okay. I've bought us some privacy for now. So, spill!"

Delighting in his focused attention, Alice went into full-blown gossip mode. "You might not realize this, but as a volunteer, the medical staff often treat me like wallpaper and forgets I'm around. So, sometimes, they will talk about private patient matters that someone in my position shouldn't hear. Like today, for instance."

Jake nodded and started rolling his hands impatiently. "Speed it up, Alice. Do you know the name of my donor?"

Alice folded her arms and raised a disapproving eyebrow, pursing her lips into a petulant pout. He could see she didn't like his tone or being interrupted.

Jake felt like she was channeling his dearly departed mother. The best option was to own it. "Sorry. It was rude of me to cut you off like that. I appreciate your wanting to help. Please go on."

"Thank you." Alice gave him a curt nod. "Okay, well, I know *what* the person was, but not exactly *who* they were."

"What do you mean?"

"Okay, well, here it is. From what I heard, your lungs came from"—The flower lady's eyes locked with his, and she leaned in for dramatic effect—"a *D.R.D.*"

Jake's eyes widened as the full implication of this information sank in.

It had been two years since Texas had legislated that death row inmates could donate their organs. The subject of the *death row donor*, known as a D.R.D., became additional information to learn as part of ongoing police training.

It hadn't been easy to get this legislation through. There was also a problem with the Texan execution method—lethal injection—which damaged the organs, rendering them unviable. An alternative approach was, therefore, required.

Harvesting under anesthesia seemed logical, as removing any vital organ would cause death. However, medical advisors stated that this method contravened the Hippocratic Oath and required a humane brain death of the D.R.D. first.

The discussion panel floated and rejected many more ideas until someone joked they should treat a death row donor like a cow for slaughter by putting a bolt through the brain. An animated discussion ensued amongst the medical advisors, who stated that it could be the answer if someone could design a high-precision device more suitable for humans.

Several mechanical engineers applied for the task and delivered many prototypes for consideration. Jake remembered reading that the engineer who created the winning prototype loved the iconic '80s film *The Terminator*, and he named his invention the *Boltinator* in homage to his favorite movie.

To facilitate the Boltinator execution method, later known as B.E.M. for short, a preliminary medical team needed to restrain, anesthetize, and put the death row donor on a ventilator. They would then leave the room. Next, the executioner would wheel in the Boltinator.

The executioner would place a helmet on the donor's head, designed with a hole on both sides to line up the rods of the Boltinator. Once set in place, one button push would deliver two high-temperature, razor-sharp, hollow bolts that would meet and close off in the middle of the brain stem in milliseconds, causing instantaneous brain death.

During the projectile process, the bolts would gather and contain in their core all bone and brain matter in their path. The electric current heating them would cauterize the wound, and then the Boltinator's high-powered suction unit would remove everything collected in the hollows of the bolts.

The advantage of the Boltinator execution method was that it was precise, quick, and clean. Jake remembered hearing that, after the bolt extraction, if you lined up your eye with one of the helmet holes, you could see straight through the donor's head. It sounded gruesome despite the lack of blood.

Once a medical practitioner confirmed brain death, a surgical team would enter the room to harvest the donor's organs and pack them for transportation.

In the early days, death row donors were huge in the news, and many debated the ethics of the practice. A few bleeding hearts protested against it. However, once the government passed legislation, most people lost interest and moved on to other subjects of discussion.

Jake remembered hearing that when the organ donation option became available, many prisoners on death row dropped their appeals and volunteered for execution. Having endured countless years being locked away, devoid of loving human contact, many welcomed the idea of a meaningful death—particularly those who had found God. The more devout of the latter believed organ donation to be an opportunity to make amends for their wrongdoings and hoped this self-sacrifice would be enough to receive salvation.

Jake frowned as he tried to push the hole-in-the-head imagery from his mind.

It's a quick, humane death, but still—

Alice reached over and patted his hand. "Oh, I'm sorry. Maybe I shouldn't have told you. If I were in your shoes, I wouldn't be happy to find out I had a killer's organs inside *my* body."

He shook his head as the meaning behind his recurring dreams became all too clear. "Don't be so sure about that."

"Sorry?"

"Nothing." Jake pulled her in for a bear hug and then planted a big kiss on her cheek. "Look, Alice, I've got to go now, but thanks. You've been an enormous help."

Once released, she was bright red and breathless. "You're most welcome. Just one thing. You haven't told me why you wanted to know."

"Sorry, but that's confidential."

Alice put her hands on her hips, Teri style. "No way! Are you kidding me?"

Jake shook his head. "It must be that way, for now, I'm afraid. One day, I'll reveal all, but first, I have some investigating to do ..."

CHAPTER 13

REVELATIONS

The following morning, Jake sat perched on the edge of his couch, wearing baggy sweatpants and an old, faded T-shirt. In his right hand was a piece of cold leftover pizza. He took a bite of the latter and slowly chewed as he contemplated the closed laptop on the coffee table. He was stalling, and he knew it.

It wasn't his fault. He planned to investigate Alice's death row donor claims the second he got home, but Goosy had sent a text message demanding to catch up with her *little bro* and to hear all about the *shrink fest*. She also wanted to know everything about the *Libby person*.

A Goosy interrogation session was unappealing. Jake's twin connection with his sister made it nearly impossible to lie to her. Her ability to see straight through him was unnerving. She was territorial and overbearing toward any women he was seeing, which never mattered to him until now.

Why now?

Jake knew the answer but wasn't ready to admit it to himself.

So, he suggested they see a movie. They met just before it started, and he took off straight afterward, claiming to be tired. Goosy wasn't thrilled but let him go. Interrogation averted.

Once his front door swung shut behind him, Jake knew he would never get to sleep if he fired up his laptop and ventured down a potential rabbit hole of information. Instead, he ordered a late-night pizza and, as usual, fell asleep in front of the television.

Yet again, the convenience store robbery haunted his dreams, and they were even more graphic than usual. As soon as Jake awoke, he knew he had to end these nightmares. The first step was to confirm his donor was a D.R.D.

Time to do this! No more procrastinating.

With a resigned sigh, he shoved the rest of the pizza slice in his mouth and flipped the laptop lid open.

As soon as it powered up, he opened his browser, typed *executions U.S.A.* into Google, clicked the web address link, and looked up the information for the previous year. Seventeen names popped up. A quick scan showed that only one execution occurred on the 18th of November in the entire United States of a man called Jonathan Kingsley. All he needed to do now was to see if the information matched up.

State, Texas, check. Method, B.E.M., check. D.R.D., check. Bingo!

If Alice's information was correct, this man was his donor. He just had to Google Jonathan Kingsley to see if the history panned out.

Hmm, not so easy.

There were quite a few people called Jonathan Kingsley on the internet. To refine the search, he typed *Jonathan Kingsley murderer.* Instantly, a link courtesy of *Murderpedia popped up in the number one spot.* Jake was familiar with the crowdsourced database website, having used it in other police investigations.

Feeling slightly sick inside, he clicked the link to Jonathan's story, and the haunted brown eyes of a handsome young black man staring at him from the web page greeted him, instantly searing his soul with pain. It was a mug shot, most likely taken around the time the police arrested him.

Geez, he was only a kid back then!

Jake scanned the basic information summary to confirm he had the right person.

Let's see—convenience store shooting, three victims and executed on the 18th of November. Yep, it looks like our guy.

His eyes then dropped to read the details of the crime.

> An anonymous female witness alerted the police to a shooting at Singhe's Supplies convenience store via the 911 emergency response team.

Upon arriving at the scene, the police discovered three victims with fatal gunshot wounds. They were Ranjeet Singhe, the store owner; Gladys Phillips, a local woman; and Daniel Bell, an Australian tourist. Police found Kingsley with a gun in his hand, kneeling and praying next to the body of Ms. Phillips.

When brought in for questioning, Kingsley proclaimed innocence, stating the murders were the actions of two mysterious men in balaclavas, who instructed him to kneel at the body of Ms. Phillips until the police arrived.

Forensic ballistics confirmed the gun found in Kingsley's possession was the murder weapon, and gunshot residue on his right hand revealed he had fired it. When presented with the latter evidence, Kingsley claimed one man forced him to shoot Ms. Phillips. Police dismissed this story as a wild fabrication.

Investigations revealed that G.T. Transport retrenched Kingsley the week before the murders. His former boss, Garry Thompson, testified on the witness stand that Kingsley had visited him earlier that day of the shootings, begging for work and said he felt he needed to rob a bank. Thompson stated he believed it was a joke, but the prosecution thought it spoke to Kingsley's state of mind.

After sentencing and incarceration, Kingsley spent nearly twenty years fighting the death penalty and proclaiming his innocence until he dropped his appeals and volunteered to become a death row donor (D.R.D.).

PRIOR CRIMINAL HISTORY

Under Texas law, the rules of evidence prevent prior criminal acts from being presented to a jury during the guilt-innocence phase of the trial. However, once a jury finds a defendant guilty, they receive information about the defendant's prior criminal conduct during the second phase of the trial to help determine the defendant's punishment.

The court learned that Kingsley's mother was a sex worker who overdosed two years after marrying notorious Mexican drug lord Rodrigo Garcia. Kingsley was seven at that time.

Garcia groomed Kingsley to be a drug dealer. This association ended during a police shootout in which Garcia, a gang member, and a federal policeman lost their lives. Afterward, Kingsley, then twelve, spent a year in juvenile detention.

This past criminal history caused the jury to consider Kingsley a damaged and dangerous young man who was beyond repair and unsuitable for rehabilitation. They, therefore, sentenced him to death.

There were copies of court transcripts from Kingsley's sentencing, his appeals, and photos just before his execution. He still looked so young, apart from some streaks of premature graying at the temples. Not surprising after what he had endured.

Jake dropped his head, unable to look at his donor's sad face any longer. Deep down in his soul, he knew that this poor man was innocent and had spent more than half his life on death row waiting to die for a crime he didn't commit. A lump rose in his throat, and he felt a pang of guilt.

When Jake was a young Christian, he was against the death penalty, believing everyone deserved a chance for redemption. However, after a few years as a police officer dealing with the scum of the earth, he hardened up and changed his view. But now, the realization hit him—he had it right the first time and wondered how many innocent people Texas had executed by mistake.

With a few more Google searches, photos of all three victims and details about them came up. Memories from his dreams flooded his mind, shattering any remaining concern that he and Libby were experiencing a shared delusion.

Jake wanted to call and tell her but felt it best to deliver this information in person. He picked up his phone, which was sitting next to his laptop.

"Hey, Google, call Libby."

A few seconds later, Libby answered. "Hi, Jake. Great to hear from you. How's the investigation going? Do you have any news on our donor?"

"Really? That's fantastic. Well, don't hold back. Tell me everything."

"I will, but I'd rather do it face to face."

"Oh, come on! You can't keep me in suspense!" Libby sounded disappointed.

"I'm sorry, but I'm uncomfortable talking about this over the phone. How about I take you to dinner tonight if you're free, and I'll tell you then? I'm even happy to drop by and pick you up."

"Okay, great. I live in Northside Village. I'll text you the address."

"That's perfect. It's only about ten minutes from my place. How about we aim for dinner at eight, and I'll pick you up around seven-thirty?"

"Sounds like a plan. See you then."

As soon as Jake hung up, he sent the web page image to his printer. When the job finished, he snatched the paper from the print tray, folded it, and placed it next to his phone to remind him to take it to Libby's later.

Now, there was nothing more to do than relax until it was time to pick up Libby. Jake looked forward to seeing her again but wondered how she would handle the news about their donor. He hoped it wouldn't be too much of a shock for her. He felt responsible for making her cry the day they met, and he wasn't in a hurry to make that happen again.

Jake shrugged off the uncomfortable thought, reached for another cold pizza slice, flung himself back on the couch, and finished eating.

CHAPTER 14

A DATE WITH FATE

L ibby's bedroom looked like a bomb had hit it, as clothes were everywhere. She pulled on a black, figure-hugging dress, stood before the mirror, and sighed. It was a favorite because it was simple and elegant, showing off her ample cleavage. But, unfortunately, it now also displayed her scar.

She tilted her head to one side. It was frustrating. It seemed all her favorite dresses now paraded the scar like a badge of honor. She didn't feel ready to endure all the sympathetic looks people would undoubtedly give her.

Oh, well—a great excuse to buy new clothes—

The noise from a car pulling up outside broke into her thoughts. She ran to her window and saw an old black Mustang parked in their driveway. Seconds later, she watched Jake jump out of it and head for their front door. Libby grabbed her phone to look at the time—right on seven-thirty.

Crap! Why did he have to be so punctual?

The next thing she knew, the doorbell sounded. A mental count of ten followed, and right on cue, her mom's voice rang out from the intercom.

"Hon, just letting you know your date's arrived."

Date? Why did she have to say that? It's so embarrassing!

Libby bent down and pressed the talk button. "Okay, Mom. Could you make him a drink or something, please? I need a few more minutes."

"Okay, hon, I'll take care of him until you're ready. See you soon."

"Thanks, Mom." She then turned back to the task at hand.

What to wear, what to wear?

Libby noticed Jake's casual dress of jeans and a T-shirt, so it seemed pointless to glam up.

Stop overthinking this!

Decisively, she threw off the dress, dragged on her trusty jeans, and was about to don her favorite red blouse when she realized this was the same top she had worn for the group therapy session.

That would never do!

She quickly discarded it in favor of a black V-neck, which she put on. However, she soon realized it was yet another cleavage top.

How annoying!

Changing yet again would take too long. Instead, Libby rushed to the cupboard and pulled out a bright, multi-colored scarf to tie around her neck. It hid her scar beautifully.

That'll work!

On went her favorite boots and her heart necklace. Then, full of anticipation, she headed downstairs to meet Jake. She found him sitting on the couch in the living room, waiting for her. He was in the middle of reading something on his phone.

"Hi, Jake."

He looked up and presented her with a broad grin, and she felt a sudden rush of happiness to see him again.

God, he's handsome!

She tried to stay composed and sat on the couch next to him. "Sorry to keep you waiting. Where's Mom? She was supposed to be looking after you."

"She *is* looking after me. Coffee is coming. My instructions were to wait here and make myself at home. I have to say that your mother is a stunning woman and so young! Until she told me who she was, I thought she must be your sister."

Libby's smile froze on her face.

Great! And the Most Beautiful Mother award goes to ...

It wasn't the first compliment she'd heard about her mom. It was a prime reason she didn't bring boys home when she first started dating.

"Thanks. It might have been better to meet at the restaurant. Unfortunately, you'll have to run the Mom gauntlet before we leave. I apologize for all the personal questions she'll probably ask you."

"You're making her sound awful when she seems like a real sweetheart."

"Appearances can be deceiving. My mother is a very caring woman, but since the operation, she has treated me like a porcelain doll that'll break if she doesn't control every aspect of my life."

"That sounds excellent. I wish I still had a mom who cared that much—or a dad, for that matter. They both died years ago."

Libby instinctively put a comforting hand on top of his. "I'm so sorry to hear you lost your parents so young."

He shrugged. "Parents are supposed to go before the kids. I only wish mine hung around for longer."

"I remember you mentioned you had a sister. Are you close?"

"Yes, very. Goosy's not exactly the nurturing type. But she loves me when she's not giving me a hard time."

"It must be nice having a sibling."

"Ah, so you're an only child, then?"

"Yes, I admit it. I'm spoiled rotten and the center of my mother's universe."

"And your father?"

"He was a soldier who went missing in action, presumed dead in Afghanistan when I was a small child. I vaguely remember sitting on his knee as he read me bedtime stories. But that's about it. I fantasized for years that he was still alive and would come home one day, but he never did."

"Oh man, and here I am going on like I'm the only person in the world who knows what it's like to lose a parent."

Libby cocked her head to one side. "It is what it is. Anyway, enough of our sad tales of woe about the past. Let's talk about the present. What did you find out about our donor?"

"I don't think you'll like what I'm about to tell you, but, anyway, here goes—do you remember hearing about the D.R.D. program? It was on the news a couple of years ago."

"Sorry, no. The what?"

"Okay, well, in a nutshell, the D.R.D. program allowed people on death row to donate their organs after being put to death, and—"

Libby reached out and gripped Jake's arm hard. "So, you're saying my heart and your lungs came from an executed person?" Her eyes widened with shock. "Oh, my lord! That's horrible! I had no clue that was even a possibility. So, how did you find all this out?"

"From a private source. Afterward, it was simply a matter of doing an internet search and finding a death row inmate executed around the same day we received our organs. It was a little too easy, truth be told."

Libby felt her heart beating wildly. "Sorry, but this will take a bit for me to process. I guess I'll have to learn to deal with it. So, do you have a name? A photo?"

Jake nodded, pulled the page he had printed earlier out of his pocket, and handed it to her.

She unfolded it, then frowned. "This is terrible! I can barely read it, and the photo's just a blob. Haven't you anything better than this?"

He grabbed the page back and looked at it. "Sorry. I just printed it off and folded it without checking. My printer can be flaky sometimes. It looks like it needs a realignment. Hang on. I'll bring the web page up on my phone." Jake did a quick internet search and presented it to her.

Libby reached for the phone to inspect the image. This was it! She was finally going to see the face of her donor for the very first time.

She enlarged the photo with an expansive thumb and index finger sweep. To her surprise, someone familiar was staring at her with big brown eyes.

What the?

"Hang on a minute." Libby stood and hurried to her mother's nearby bedroom. Within seconds, she returned with a father-daughter photo in an ornate silver frame taken on her second birthday.

"Am I going crazy?"—her eyes fixed on Jake as she presented him with the framed photo and the image on his phone side by side—"or does our organ donor, Jonathan Kingsley, look exactly like my father?"

At that precise moment, an enormous crash caused them both to jump. Libby's mother had entered the room and dropped a tray of tea, coffee, and biscuits. She was now standing there with her big, cornflower-blue eyes transfixed in shock.

It was Sarah.

CHAPTER 15

GIFT OF LOVE

S ix months earlier, Sarah glared at Jon through the small window of the prison communication booth.

Cathy McGregor was sitting beside her, telephone handset to her ear. The young, slim attorney who represented Jon nearly twenty years ago was now a slightly overweight married woman in her early forties with three kids. Believing in Jon's innocence, she had supported him pro bono since then, launching appeal after appeal to keep him alive. Texas would have probably executed Jon years ago if it weren't for her.

"No! I won't allow it!" Sarah threw her handset on the bench before her, in disgust, unwilling to listen anymore.

A nearby guard admonished her. "Ma'am, if you don't respect the equipment, I'll have to ask you to leave."

"Sorry about that, sir. It won't happen again." Cathy's concerned eyes turned to Sarah. "Will it?"

Sarah folded her arms. "I'm not making any promises."

The attorney sighed deeply, picked up the discarded handset, and offered it back. "Jon's trying to talk to you. It would be best if you listened to him. It's important."

Sarah locked eyes with her husband. He looked distraught as he pointed at the handset and gestured for her to take it, but she shook her head, folded her arms, and turned to Cathy. "Whose idea was this? I swear if this was you, I'll ... I'll ..."

"No, it wasn't me. Jon made this decision all by himself. We wouldn't be having this conversation if it weren't for the blood type."

"Blood type?"

Cathy spoke into her handset to Jon. "Tell your wife what you told me about the blood type." She then pressed the other handset to Sarah's ear, forcing her to accept it, which she finally did, snatching it from her hand.

Angry eyes turned to Jon. "Oh, all right! Speak if you must, but it'll change nothing."

"I'm so sorry. I know this is a lot, but I need you to listen. You know our Queenie has O-negative blood and—"

"Of course, I know that! I'm her mother!"

"Well, the doctor would have told you that even though Queenie can be a universal donor to everyone else, she can only receive organs from other O blood type people. Therefore, the waiting list is much longer for her, and you know our Queenie can't afford to wait."

Sarah shook her head in confusion. "So, what does that have to do with *you*?"

"Here's something you probably won't know about me because I only recently learned this myself—apparently, I'm also O-negative."

Jon waited for this information to sink in and then continued. "Because they knew I was the right blood type, they ran other tests to be sure I was compatible, and the results showed I was a perfect match. I'm sorry, Sweet Pea, but I see this decision to become a death row donor as the only way to save our girl."

"Don't *'Sweet Pea'* me, Jon! Now is *not* the time. How could you go ahead with this without consulting me?" Sarah pressed the handset mouthpiece against her breast and turned to Cathy. "Sweet Jesus, why didn't you tell me he was planning this? What kind of attorney are you?"

"I'm sorry, but attorney-client privilege prevents me from doing so. If my client has instructions for me, particularly regarding becoming a death row donor, then there are rigorous protocols that I must follow."

Sarah felt her emotions overwhelming her, so she took a deep, controlled breath. She couldn't bear to lose Jon, but her beautiful daughter's heart was failing, and with each passing day, it seemed less and less likely they would find a suitable donor in time. That said, they couldn't seriously consider this as the solution.

No! No! It was too much.

She shook her head vehemently and vocalized her thoughts. "No! We can't! It's not right! I couldn't live with this!" She put the handset on the bench and desperately grabbed Cathy's hands. "We have to stop him. We can't let him do this. I love my daughter and want to save her, but Jon's an innocent man. He can't die this way."

"Sorry, but I represent your husband and not you, and he's called me in as his facilitator to represent him in the D.R.D. process. I have to abide by his wishes." She gestured toward Jon. "Now, please listen so he can help you understand. Our visiting time is nearly over, and he has something important to tell you."

Sarah reluctantly put the handset to her ear once again. She felt determined that nothing would make her change her mind.

"Are you okay?" Jon's eyes were full of concern. "I'm so sorry I sprang my decision on you like this. Maybe I should've written you a letter to explain it better."

"Explain how you want to be the ultimate hero and sacrifice your life for our child. Yep, that would have made a great letter. You realize I might end up losing you both, right?"

"You can't think like that. Without a donor's heart, our Queenie will surely die."

"Don't you think I understand that?!" Tears of frustration rolled down Sarah's face. "She's on the donor list, and we'll find one. It doesn't have to be *you*! Sweet Jesus, Jon! I wish I'd never told you about her condition."

"Well, I thank God that you did. I've prayed every day for Queenie to find a heart. But she's been waiting for nearly six months, and her time's running out. I want my beautiful girl to live. This way, I'll be with her forever. I'll never escape this living hell, but my heart can. Can't you see that? I want this, and I'm ready to go."

"*Hell?* I thought you had a fairly good life here. I thought they were treating you well."

He dropped his head. "Forget it. Don't worry about it."

"Jonathan Raymond Kingsley! You look me in the eye right now! What do you mean by 'hell?'"

"Sorry, I should've told you sooner, but I was trying to protect you. All this was hard enough on you, and I didn't want you to worry about this, too. Please find it in your heart to forgive me for lying to you all these years. I meant well. I truly did."

Sarah put her hand up to the glass. "Jon, you're scaring me. What is it? What have you been lying about?"

"It's a living hell in here. I spend most of the day locked in my cell. It's a tiny cell with only a single bed, a fixed stool with a small table, and a toilet with a sink. They shove my meals through a hole in the door. I only get out when they take me for a shower or to the exercise facility, and that's only for an hour each day. Even then, I don't get to talk to anyone because the guards segregate me from the other prisoners.

"When I'm in my cell, I hear other inmates yelling as they try to talk to each other, which is nearly impossible. Then some scream and cry as they go slowly insane from the isolation."

Jon's eyes filled with tears, and he knuckled them away. "The only thing that's kept me from losing my mind in this place is you, my darling—you and all your beautiful letters and weekly visits with stories about Queenie."

Sarah felt confused. "But what about your job in the library, where you said you got to read books all day and chat with other prisoners? And that cooking class where you learned to make scones that would rival mine? And then there's that basketball team you played in every week. You made this place sound like a health resort."

"Well, the reading part is true. I've consumed thousands of books, but only within the confines of my cell. My little radio is all I have to keep me in touch with the world. But the rest of it ..." Jon looked stricken. "I'm so sorry, but I've been lying to you all this time. I've told you about what I wished it was like here. But, in reality ..."

Shrugging helplessly, Jon unconsciously pulled hairs out from the right side of his head behind his ear. As he temporarily turned his face away, a large bald patch became visible, showing that he'd been plucking hairs for quite some time.

It was a familiar condition. Pulling hair out was a habit Jon developed during stressful times. However, Sarah hadn't seen him do this since she told him she was pregnant with Libby and then again during the trial.

Sarah thought he was on top of things and wasn't doing it anymore. But, then again, they were always so lost in each other's eyes during visiting time, and he was careful never to turn his head away like this. He would back away from the glass, forming a love heart with his fingers and blowing kisses when saying goodbye. Now she understood why.

"Oh, Jon, you should've told me. Instead of prattling on about my stupid life, I would've fought for you against these inhumane conditions. I can't believe you've been living like this and keeping quiet about it all these years ... just to protect me."

Grief-stricken, she placed her hand on the glass, and Jon did the same. They hadn't touched each other once during those long years since they unfairly took him from her. It was the closest they ever got. Sarah lost count of how often she wished she had a sledgehammer to smash through the grimy plexiglass between them. She shook her head, choking back tears as the true horror of her husband's sufferings became apparent to her. "Oh, my poor, poor Sugar Pie."

Jon hung his head. "There's more, but I'll let Cathy tell you."

"More?" Sarah's questioning eyes flicked to Cathy.

The attorney shifted uncomfortably in her chair and pressed her hands down as she readjusted her gray pinstriped skirt. "Yes, I'm afraid there's more I need to tell you." She glanced at Jon to ensure she had his permission to go on.

He nodded his assent.

"Well, as you're aware, I've exhausted every avenue trying to prove Jon's innocence, and we all know it would only be a matter of time before Texas will want to move forward again with setting an execution date.

"The thing is, Sarah, there are only so many appeals the state will allow. Very few death row inmates make it beyond twenty years. The chances are high that they'll overturn our next appeal, and Jon gets executed anyway, so—"

"So, I want my death to be meaningful," Jon said, interrupting her. "We know they will execute me eventually. But if I choose to go voluntarily, our beautiful daughter gets the heart she needs, and I can leave this world on my terms."

Sarah felt overwhelmed with anguish. "But it's so unfair. You're innocent. You don't deserve this."

"I have prayed on it a lot, and God spoke to me. I believe His plan for me all along was to die so our daughter could live. All this"—Jon gestured around the tiny communication room—"all our suffering was, for one reason—to save our Queenie. If I weren't in here, I wouldn't have been able to give her my heart. So, I wouldn't change a thing. And after it's over, He will take me to Heaven to wait for you until it's your time. I know it."

"But Jon, what if our daughter wants to know her donor? What am I supposed to say to her?"

"I can answer that," Cathy interjected. "Donor families have the right to confidentiality. The hospital staff will tell her that, anyway. They're even more tight-lipped about death row donors. Libby won't be able to find out where her heart came from unless you decide to tell her."

"I want this, my darling." Tears formed in Jon's eyes. "There's no need for Queenie to know that it's my heart beating inside her. All I want is for her to live and enjoy her life. The policy states that we can donate our organs to relatives who need them, and if I choose, I can allow the state to donate whatever is left. Of course, I want to help others. It would give my death even more purpose."

Sarah could see that her husband had decided. She could do nothing to stop him short of telling Libby, which would be like opening Pandora's Box. Given her daughter's fragile state, shocking news like this could be dangerous.

"I disagree with this, Jon, and I'll never give you my blessing because I love you too much. It's unfair of you to make me choose between you and Libby. So, I won't do it."

"I love you, too. But the thing is, it's not your choice. I'd never do that to you. As much as I'd like you to support my decision, I don't need your blessing. Cathy and I have been working on this for some time now. The wheels are already in motion, and they've set the date. I just wanted to help you understand my decision, give you a chance to prepare yourself, and say goodbye."

"Wha-what? They've set a date! When?"

"One week from today."

Sarah heard no more. Instead, she felt herself swaying. Then, finally, her limbs became loose, and the handset tumbled out of her hand as she fainted in shock.

CHAPTER 16

UNCOMFORTABLE TRUTH

Sarah fell to her knees and started picking up the broken crockery from the floor to put onto the tray. "Oh, my goodness," she said with a nervous laugh. "Excuse my butterfingers. What a terrible mess!"

Libby dumped Jake's phone and the photograph on the coffee table. She walked over and bent down to her shaking mother, trying to still her frantically busy hands. "Mom? Please stand up and talk to me."

Sarah pulled her hands away and put them to her face. "No ... no ... you weren't supposed to find out. I told him you'd work it out somehow. You're a clever girl ... such a clever girl. But 'No,' he said. 'Be strong, Sweet Pea. Smile and be happy about your daughter's new heart.' Be happy? Like I would ever be happy again!" She was becoming hysterical.

Oh God, she's losing it.

"It's okay, Mom. Let me help you up. I'll make you a nice fresh cup of tea." Libby gestured toward Jake. "Help me—help me with her, please."

Jake, who'd been quietly watching this little drama unfold, immediately jumped up from the couch, assisted Sarah to stand and supported her to a nearby dining chair.

Libby dropped to her knees before her mother and held her hands. "Mom, look at me."

Sarah tried to turn her head away, her eyes tightly shut, and tears rolled down her beautiful face. "I can't! I can't!"

"Mom, you need to look at me. Mom! Mom! MOTHER!"

Sarah's eyes flicked open as if Libby had slapped her. "I hate it when you call me Mother."

It was a deflection, and Libby knew it. She looked up at Jake. "Pass me the photo and your phone, please."

Jake retrieved them from the coffee table and deposited them into her outstretched hands.

Although Libby was only two years old when she lost her father, her grief was profound. So, Sarah printed two copies of her favorite father/daughter photo to soothe her little girl and put them in identical silver frames, one for each bedside table.

"He's watching over you, hon, and still loves you," Sarah said as she presented the photograph. "Talk to him whenever you like, and he'll hear you. I promise."

Libby spent much time with that photo, staring into her father's loving eyes and having countless imaginary conversations.

Comparing the images once again confirmed her fears. Those eyes staring at her from both photographs—the resemblance was unmistakable. Her father and Jonathan Kingsley were either identical twins or ...

It was too horrible to contemplate. Feeling sick inside, as if trapped in a nightmare, Libby held the phone before Sarah's face. "Mom, why does this man, Jonathan Kingsley, look like my father?"

Her mother stared at the image on Jake's phone. Tears formed in her eyes, and she turned away. "No! Y-you'll h-hate me. You'll n-never forgive me."

Libby could feel her heart beating wildly, and she placed a protective hand on her chest. "You need to tell me the truth right now, Mom. If you force me to find out myself, and it turns out to be what I'm thinking, I swear to God, I'll walk out of this house, and you'll never see me again. Do you hear me? Never!"

She stood and was about to walk away when her mother grabbed her hand.

"I'm so sorry. Please let me explain."

Jake rested a supportive hand on Libby's shoulder. "Your mom's in shock. Be gentle with her."

"Gentle with *her?* If what I suspect is true, I want to throttle her right now. Okay, *Mother*, go ahead. Explain."

Sarah dropped her head in defeat and nodded. "It's true. Jonathan Kingsley was your father."

Libby's eyes widened in shock. She'd asked for the truth, and there it was. "But you told me my father went missing in Afghanistan. You told me he was a hero, and we were to pray every day that they would find him and bring him home again. I was right there on my knees beside you when we prayed—for years! I can't believe you *lied* to me. What kind of mother does that?" Tears began falling down Libby's face. "I need to hear you say it. Do I have my father's heart inside of me?"

Sarah blinked rapidly, then dropped her head in her hands, unable to maintain eye contact with her daughter. When she spoke, her voice was barely audible. "Yes … yes—sweet Jesus, forgive me—it's your father's heart."

Bile rose in Libby's throat, but she pushed it back down. She wanted to be wrong and for this to be some crazy coincidence. She prayed for any other explanation than this.

Sarah's eyes were pleading. "We were trying to protect you. Do you understand? It wasn't my choice. I was against it, but your father insisted, and he went ahead with the death row donor process without my blessing."

"Without your *blessing?* What about all those years that I've been without a father? He was alive in jail all this time. I could have visited him and gotten to know him. What the hell, Mom!"

"You were only two years old when they took your father away. Neither of us wanted you growing up worrying about him rotting in jail and facing execution."

"So, you thought lying to me by telling me he was missing in action was better?"

Tears were now flowing freely down Sarah's face. "He was such a good, kind man, and I wanted you to think of him as a hero, so I came up with a story to give us hope he may return home one day. I kept praying for a miracle that someone would come forward and prove him innocent. But no one ever did."

"Explain one thing. Why isn't my surname Kingsley?"

"Your father had terrible press back then, and the victims' families were so angry. He was worried about a backlash against us and was fearful for our safety. He insisted I change our family name, so we took my father's surname. We thought it was a safe option because he was never part of my life. Your father wanted it, and your grandparents agreed it was in your best interests."

Libby had never felt angrier in her entire life. Her voice was low and cold. "Did any of you consider what *I* would have wanted? You, of all people, knew how much I missed my father. How do you expect me to forgive you for this?" She pulled her hands away from her mother's and turned away.

"Please don't hate me." Sarah started wailing, and she fell to the floor. "You're my world. You have always been and always will be the most important person in my life. I only agreed to keep this from you because I love you so much."

As Libby turned back and stared at the shattered woman crawling on the floor toward her, many things became apparent. It now made sense why she often caught Sarah quietly crying more times than she could count for a month after the transplant.

Libby remembered thinking her mother's behavior was strange and how she never seemed truly happy for her. She had put it down to anxiety and concerns about organ rejection. Sarah's smothering behavior and the endless lectures about protecting her new heart, Libby now realized, was not only grief for losing her husband but a need to preserve Jon's precious gift to his daughter.

"So, how often did you see him?"

"Hon, I went to see him every visiting day, every single one. They only let him have one personal visit each week, and I never missed a session. I would go when you were at school or leave you with Granny Rose or Meemaw and Pop and pretend to go shopping.

"And in that last week leading up to his execution, they let me see him every day. It's a courtesy they afford D.R.D. volunteers. But I have to say that was the most horrible week of my life, Libby. All I wanted to do was curl up in a ball and cry myself sick, but I had to keep it together for his sake and yours, as I was also visiting you in the hospital during that time.

"Just know that I loved your father just as much as I love you. He was my only love. Why do you think I never remarried or even had a boyfriend?"

"And here I was, always pushing you to get out and meet someone. I get you protecting me when I was a little kid, but I'm an adult now. When you knew he was planning to be a death row donor and give me his heart, why didn't you say something then? We could have stopped him."

Sarah sadly shook her head. "He'd put the wheels in motion without my knowledge. By the time he told me his plan, they'd set the execution date. It would have been pointless and cruel when you couldn't do anything about it.

"I also feared you might reject his heart if you knew where it came from. As much as I hated it, at least this way, his death had meaning. You'd live, and we both keep a piece of him forever. I didn't want you to find out, and I prayed every day that you never would. I'm so sorry."

Libby's knees buckled, and she joined her mother on the ground. Sarah pulled her into her arms, and they both lost control of their emotions. Mutual tears fell in torrents as they held onto each other.

Jake stood by, looking acutely uncomfortable and helpless, but Libby didn't care. This revelation was too much, and she needed to process it.

After they'd cried it out, mother and daughter slowly parted and stared at each other. It was weird. Libby had never felt closer to Sarah, yet so distant. Who was this woman who'd raised her? What a dark secret to hold in for so long. It must have been hell.

After an awkward silence, Jake stepped forward with a helping hand, and soon, both ladies stood.

Although not wanting the answer, Libby still had to ask the question. "So, Mom, what did they accuse Dad of doing?"

Sarah shook her head. "I don't think you'd want to know."

"Yes, I do. It's important."

Jake interjected, "You don't need your mom to tell you. They accused your father of murdering three people during a convenience store robbery and convicted him of the crime. I'll send you the link. It's all there."

Their eyes locked. "All of it?" Libby asked.

"Uh-huh. Yep. Do you understand? *Everything's* there."

She nodded, realizing he was talking about their shared dreams.

"Don't believe it, hon." Sarah ran the back of her hand across her eyes. "What your father went through was traumatic, and he never wanted to talk about it other than to say he didn't do it. But deep down in my soul, I already knew he was innocent. Your father hated guns and would never own one. He didn't have it in him to hurt anyone."

Jake and Libby exchanged knowing glances, and Sarah noticed. She fixed her eyes on Jake. "I'm sorry, but who are you? I thought you were just some guy Libby had met on one of those dating apps, but you turned up at our home with a photo of my Jon. So why do you have this information about my husband? What's it all to you, anyway?"

Before Jake had the chance to speak, Libby quickly jumped in. "Okay, Mom, you got us. Jake and I met at a heart and lung transplant support group yesterday. I didn't want you to worry, so I told you I was catching up with a friend.

"Anyway, Jake had received a double lung transplant. We had this instant connection when we met and discovered we had received our transplants on the same day. I was curious to find out if we had the same donor. Jake—being a detective with the police force—investigated and, well, here we are."

Her mother put her hand to her mouth, and fresh tears formed in her eyes. "So, my Jon is a part of you as well?"

Jake nodded. "It's certainly looking that way."

"Jon said he would help others with his sacrifice, and he was right." Sarah pulled a startled Jake into her arms for a hug and buried her face in his chest. When she pulled away, she looked up at him. "Don't believe the lies you've read about him. They're not true."

"We know he's innocent, Mom, and—" Libby cut herself off.

Shut up, Libby! Just shut up! She's not ready for the entire story.

Sarah frowned in confusion. "How could you?"

Libby thought quickly. "We can *feel* it, Mom. I can't explain it. We just *know*."

This answer seemed to satisfy Sarah, and she nodded sadly. "I understand. Your father's a part of you now. You'd have to feel his goodness. He was such a kind man." She then turned to Jake for confirmation that it was the same for him.

"Yep," was all that he could manage.

Libby breathed deeply, knowing she couldn't leave Sarah and needed to learn more about her father. She turned to Jake. "I'm very sorry about our dinner plans, but I need to spend some time alone with my mother. There's a lot to discuss. I'm sure you understand."

"Yes, of course. I'll leave you both to it, and we can chat again tomorrow if that's okay?"

Libby nodded in agreement.

As Jake turned to leave, Sarah reached out and grabbed his hand. "You need to prove my husband was innocent. You must find out who killed those people because it wasn't my Jon."

"That's the plan."

Libby walked him to the door. With sad eyes, they shared a long hug.

"We both know what the killer looks like," Jake whispered in her ear. "I'll make it my mission to find this guy, and he'll pay for what he's done. I promise you that."

"Thank you," she whispered back.

Libby saw him out and then returned to Sarah. Her mother's eyes were bright with sorrow.

It was going to be a long night.

CHAPTER 17

FREAKY COINCIDENCES

J ake was sitting on the couch drinking coffee when his phone rang. He grabbed it from the side table and saw it was Libby. He smiled and wasted no time in answering. "Well, hi there. I was thinking about calling, but you beat me to it. So, how are you? Is your mom okay?"

"Much better than she was last night. We were up talking until two in the morning. As you would imagine, I had a lot of questions."

"And what about you? The news about your dad must have been an enormous shock."

"That's an understatement. I'm still trying to wrap my head around everything—so surreal. I don't know how Mom could hide this from me for so long."

"Did you tell her about our dreams?"

"No. I don't think Mom could handle it. She's worried enough about me. I decided months ago I should keep that to myself."

"I tried to keep my dreams from Goosy, but my sister always knows whenever something's up with me. She kept bugging me until I told her all about them.

"Anyway, I have some good news. Because my captain won't let me return to work right now, I have plenty of time to investigate. My only problem is that I can't access the police databases. My friend Barney is looking into it. He's putting together some files for me and—"

A knocking interrupted the conversation. Jake went to his front door and looked through the peephole. A bald, slightly overweight black man in his mid-thirties, dressed in a dark blue suit and a white shirt with a blue and black striped tie, stood waiting. It was Barney.

Jake took his phone off speaker mode and put it to his ear. "Sorry, Libby, I've got to go. Barney's here. I'll call you back with an update soon."

After hanging up, he opened the door to his friend and waved him inside. "Thanks for coming over, Barn. What have you got for me?"

Barney pulled a USB flash drive from his pocket and handed it over. "Here's all that info you wanted." He then strode to the couch and plopped himself down. "I copied everything I could find on our database. So, who's this Jonathan Kingsley to you, anyway?"

"I'm pretty sure that he's my donor."

Unconsciously, Barney rubbed his hand across his chest. "You mean?"

Jake nodded. "Yep. I believe it's thanks to this man"—he held up the flash drive—"that I'm standing here breathing and talking to you."

"*Shoot!* There'll be a record of me accessing this data. I could be in some serious trouble here. If this guy is your donor, you're not supposed to know. D.R.D. protocols are in place for a good reason."

"Yep, I'm well aware of the death row donor rules. I'm sorry for not telling you, but all my investigations point to this guy being my donor, and I want to learn as much about him as possible. It's a history lesson for my future children. It'd be cool to say to them, 'Guess what, kids, my lungs came from a guy accused of murder, so don't mess with your old man.'"

"Yeah, *great!* I wouldn't be so happy about it if it were me." Barney grimaced. "What makes you so sure he's your donor? Where did you source your info?"

Jake shook his head. "Sorry, Barn, I can't tell you that. My source is confidential and needs to stay that way for their sake."

"Yeah, yeah, I get it. Well, keep it to yourself that I gave you this. Otherwise, we'll both be up to our necks in it with the captain."

"No problem. I sure appreciate you doing this for me. Feel like staying for a coffee?"

"I'd like to, but I have work to do back at the precinct." Barney reluctantly stood and started heading for the door.

Jake saw Barney out. "Thanks again."

"No worries. Feel better soon, Maverick. I sure miss you. The captain's got me training this rookie detective. I'll be ditching him as soon as you're back."

The second Barney was gone, Jake ran to his laptop, inserted the flash drive into a port, and flipped open the lid. He swore under his breath as it took forever to get out of sleep mode. His laptop was sorely overdue for a reboot and probably a rebuild, but he could never get motivated enough to dedicate the time to it, and certainly not right now.

Finally, the screen lit up, and he navigated to the flash drive. There were four folders entitled 'Appeals,' 'Audio,' 'D.R.D.,' and 'Legal,' respectively.

The legal folder caught his attention first. There, he found a report from one of the attending police officers on the scene, a copy of Jon's original statement, a revised statement, and documents of the Court Transcripts for the trial and sentencing.

Jake had read the Court Transcripts on Murderpedia, so he skipped to the original statement, as the latter was unavailable online. While reading it, the nightmares replayed in his mind.

Everything was consistent with what he remembered, but he noticed Jon claimed he couldn't identify the true culprits of the crime because they wore balaclavas. Jake didn't find this surprising. Jon was likely too frightened to describe them because of the threats to his family.

In his initial statement, there was no mention that the murderer forced him to take his gun to shoot Gladys. That information came later when forensics found gunpowder residue on his hands.

Jake shook his head. It sounded too far-fetched to be believed. Jon's past criminal history and the evidence damned him.

The Appeals folder contained copies of multiple stays of execution. Libby's father had been living on borrowed time.

The Audio folder contained code-numbered MP3 files and many subfolders—probably documents and transcripts from the trial and Jon's interrogations. Jake figured he would get to those in time. For now, he only required the essential information.

He wanted to see inside the D.R.D. folder the most. When he opened it, there were only three documents—the application, the declaration, and the organ recipient list.

The organ recipient list was the most critical file. He pointed the cursor at the document. His index finger tentatively hovered above the left mouse button, knowing one click would open it and reveal all.

All good things come to those who wait.

Instead, Jake right-clicked the document and selected the print option. He had serviced his printer the night before when he had nothing better to do after Libby sidelined their dinner plans to spend time with her mother, and he needed to test that it was now working correctly. Besides, seeing the information in print seemed more fitting. And he knew Libby would want a copy.

This investigation was their baby, and looking at the recipient list to confirm everything they believed they knew without Libby sharing the moment seemed a tad wrong.

While the file was printing, he distracted himself by reading the declaration.

> I, Jonathan Raymond Kingsley, being of sound mind and body, declare that I consent to be executed by the State of Texas via the Boltinator execution method (B.E.M.)* to facilitate becoming a death row donor (D.R.D.).
>
> My heart is to go to my daughter, Elizabeth Rose Kingsley, also known as Elizabeth Rose Davis. I agree to donate all remaining organs and tissues for transplant only.

Jake groaned. *Darn it! Spoiler!* He knew he shouldn't have read it. The declaration just confirmed that Libby had Jon's heart inside of her.

The document was full of legal jargon, ending with a graphic description next to an asterisk concerning the Boltinator execution method in tiny print. Jake winced as it left zero mystery about how the donor would die. Regardless, Jon had signed and dated the declaration.

Imagine facing that voluntarily! Talk about fatherly love and sacrifice.

Jake's eyes flicked to the printer. The organ recipient list sat on the output tray. It looked like it printed okay, and he felt tempted to snatch it up to read it but refrained.

Jake turned to his phone, which was on the charger dock. "Hey, Google, video call Libby."

Within seconds, Libby's confused face appeared on the small screen. "Why the video chat?"

"Because of this." Jake walked over to the printer, grabbed the document from the output tray, and held it up in front of the phone, facing Libby.

"How do you expect me to read that? It's too small. No, wait a minute. I can make out the heading. Oh, my lord! Is that the organ recipient list in your hand?"

"Yes, ma'am, it certainly is."

"So, what does it say?"

Jake nodded, flipped the document around, and quickly scanned the list. Everything was there—all donated organs, the recipients, and their contact details listed alphabetically by organ. As expected, Libby's name and details were next to the heart, and Jake's name was further down the list for the lungs. They had confirmation—Jonathan Kingsley was their donor. There was little doubt, but it was good to see it in writing.

"Yep, it's official. Your dad's our donor—both yours and mine." He immediately regretted his enthusiasm and bluntness as he saw tears forming in Libby's eyes.

"Oh, I'm sorry. That was insensitive. I'm such an idiot!"

Rapidly wiping the tears from her eyes, she shook her head. "That's okay. I'm not surprised, anyway. All that bit of paper does is make it more real. You and I need to find that man who killed those people. We have to clear my father's name."

"We will. I'll not rest until we see that darn Irishman behind bars. I thought it might be worth going to the scene of the crime. Something might jolt our memories to help us."

"Where's that?"

"It's a convenience store called Singhe's Supplies. I'll look it up. Hopefully, it's still in business and not too far away."

Jake punched the business name into Google on his laptop, and a link to the location popped up. His eyebrows shot up in surprise when he clicked on it and zoomed in. "I don't believe it!"

"What's the matter?"

"Just a crazy coincidence! You remember that café we went to after our support meeting?"

"You mean Anna's? Yes. I remember we both found the manager and that place very familiar."

"Yeah, well, Singhe's Supplies is only around the corner."

"You don't mean—"

"Yep. It's pretty likely your dad frequented that café. Hang on. Let me look up something else. According to what I read, your dad worked for a transport company before he got laid off and went to see his old boss on the day of the shootings. Maybe that's somewhere in the area."

Jake punched G.T. Transport into Google. His eyes widened in shock as he scanned the information that popped up. "Oh, seriously! This whole thing is becoming freakier and freakier."

"What is?"

"You know that church hall where we met for the support group?"

"Yes."

"Well, it wasn't always a church hall. It was once a small warehouse. The church next door bought it to convert into a community hall nearly twenty years ago. Try to guess the previous owner."

"I wouldn't have a clue. But I suppose you're going to tell me."

"G.T. Transport. That's the place where your dad used to work before they had to let him go. They shut down the business less than a year after they put your dad in jail."

"Oh, my God! The odds on that would be—"

"Yeah, it's way too big to calculate. I think you and I need to check out that convenience store. Can you be ready in twenty minutes?"

"I certainly can."

"Okay, great! I'll see you soon." Jake disconnected the call and grabbed his jacket.

We're coming for you, you stinking Irishman!

And with that thought, he was out the door.

CHAPTER 18

LIVING NIGHTMARE

As they stood at the entrance of Singhe's Supplies, Jake turned to Libby. "Are you ready for this?"

"As ready as I'll ever be."

"Okay, here goes." Jake strode forward, pushed open the door, and ushered her through. "Ladies, first."

"Thank you."

Everything in the store seemed very familiar, yet somehow different. It only took three steps when suddenly, Jake found breathing challenging.

Oh no! Not this again!

He groaned and put his hand on his chest. "Man, I'm not feeling too good."

"Yeah, I'm not feeling so great myself." Libby's face was ashen.

"Can I help you guys?"

The two turned their heads in surprise, and what they both saw immediately distracted them from their physical discomfort. Behind the counter stood a man like the shopkeeper from their dreams.

What the? But it can't be!

"Ranjeet? Ranjeet Singhe?" Jake asked without thinking.

The man nodded. "Yes. That's me. Who's asking?"

Jake frowned with confusion and then mentally kicked himself. If this were the same man, he would be much older. He remembered from the transcripts that Ranjeet left behind a wife and son. The latter, wearing the same uniform his father wore twenty years ago, made the similarity remarkable and quite unnerving.

Libby had no such insight. The shock seemed to cause rational thought to escape her because she blurted out, "But, Mr. Singhe, I thought you died twenty years ago!"

Jake felt his eyes bugging out of his head.

Oh, hell no!

The shopkeeper glared at her. "Is that a joke, young lady? That was my father. Did the local kids put you up to this? If so, you can kindly leave my store now."

Libby went bright red. "Apologies, Mr. Singhe. My mistake. It's just that you look like your father."

"But how could you have met him? You could have only been a small child when he died. So, I need to repeat, is this a cruel joke?"

Jake knew he had to step in.

Time to shut this down.

"Please excuse my *associate*. She's just a little confused. Allow me to introduce myself. I'm Detective Masters with the Houston Police." Jake produced his badge and flashed it. It proved handy in situations like this, and he was glad his captain didn't make him hand it in along with his gun while recovering from the transplant.

Ranjeet inspected the badge. "Okay, detective, but that doesn't explain why you're in my store. Or why your associate mistook me for my father."

"We"—Jake gestured toward Libby—"are reinvestigating the details of the robbery that took place here in your store twenty years ago when your father lost his life. As for my associate, she ... ah ... saw photos of your father, and your resemblance to him was a bit of a surprise. It was for both of us, I admit. Blame it on a very late night with little sleep. We apologize for upsetting you."

"Once again, I'm very sorry, sir," Libby said. "No disrespect intended."

The shopkeeper, with a curt nod, accepted their apologies. "I'll never forget the day my father died, and we still miss him, even today. It was a horrible time for my mother and me. At fifteen, I had to drop out of school to keep the store going. We heard they executed the man responsible for my father's murder last year. Shouldn't the case be closed?"

"Yes, it was, sir," Jake said, "but we reopened it because additional evidence has presented itself, leading us to believe the state executed the wrong man."

"You mean Kingsley wasn't responsible for my father's death? How could that be? They found the murder weapon in his hand, and he'd fired it. At least, that's what the police told my mother and me."

Jake, realizing he had said too much, exchanged glances with Libby. "Sorry, sir. It's classified information at this point. We've just returned to the crime scene to check your store's layout to ensure certain things align with Kingsley's statement. So, Mr. Singhe, is the layout different from back then?" Jake already knew the answer, but had to play the game.

Ranjeet shook his head. "No. It's the same as my father left it. It was the optimum setup, so my mother and I saw no need to change it."

"Thank you, sir. Do you mind if we take a wander through your store?"

"Please go ahead. If Kingsley didn't kill my father, my mother and I want to know who did."

"We're still investigating, sir, but we will certainly be in touch when we catch the real perpetrator." Jake gave Ranjeet a curt nod and gestured to Libby to accompany him.

When they walked over to the fridge, something unexpected happened. Jake's vision blurred, and he blinked rapidly. When it cleared, the middle-aged, well-dressed woman from his dreams stood in front of the milk section with the door open—so real she seemed tangible. He started hyperventilating and closed his eyes hard for a couple of seconds. When he reopened them, she was gone, and the fridge door was now closed.

Am I going crazy?

Jake swung around to Libby. "Did you see that?"

Libby, whose attention was elsewhere, turned in surprise. "What?"

Jake shook his head. *Yep, I'm losing it.* "Doesn't matter."

"Okay. Well, I don't quite see the point of all this. I missed my morning coffee, so I'm ordering a cup. Want me to get you one as well? My treat."

"No thanks, but you go ahead. I want to look around a little more."

Libby nodded and headed back to the front counter.

While Jake wandered through the store, deliberately retracing Jonathan Kingsley's steps as he remembered them from his dreams, he felt a sense of impending doom. His breathing became increasingly labored. He ignored it, sure his mind was playing tricks on him, and kept going.

Now, where was it that the police found Kingsley?

Jake walked to the center of the store when suddenly everything started spinning. It was disconcerting, so he closed his eyes hard. It worked last time, and he hoped it would work again. Unfortunately, when his eyes reopened, the Irishman stood before him, pushing a gun muzzle into his forehead.

Somewhere in the recesses of his confused mind, Jake realized he was standing in the exact spot where Jonathan Kingsley had stood, terrified all that time ago. Reluctantly, his eyes dropped to the floor before him, and he flinched. The well-dressed woman was lying face up, vacantly staring into space. A bullet hole sat above her left eyebrow, and a pool of blood surrounded her head.

What's going on? Is this really happening?

Jake stared into the beady green eyes of the Irishman—evil incarnate—and unwillingly reached out to take the murder weapon. Its weight rested heavily in his hand.

He wanted more than anything to shoot his tormentor. It would be so easy if he had some control over his body. However, he felt little more than a puppet.

A knife blade waved in his face as the threats he had heard many times before in his nightmares offended his ears. Jake helplessly pointed the gun at the dead woman on the ground and pulled the trigger. Afterward, as the Irishman ordered, he dropped to his knees, shut his eyes, and started reciting the Lord's Prayer, something he hadn't uttered since his mother's funeral.

"Our Father, who art in heaven, hallowed be thy name. Thy kingdom come, thy will be done, on earth as it is in heaven. Give us this day our daily bread, and forgive us our trespasses as we forgive those who trespass against us. And lead us not into temptation, but deliver us from evil ..."

As Jake kneeled, praying on the floor, he could hear someone calling him. The voice seemed to come from the other end of a tunnel, but he couldn't move, and his eyes refused to open. He felt trapped inside his mind until a hard slap across the face suddenly brought him back to reality.

Libby was kneeling in front of him, her eyes wide with concern.

Ranjeet was standing above them, looking agitated. "What's the matter with him?"

"Sorry, sir. I think he needs his medication. Detective, have you taken your insulin today? It's been a long time since breakfast."

Jake stared at her in confusion. "Breakfast?"

"You know—being a *diabetic* and all."

The charade became apparent, and he gave them an embarrassed grin. "Yeah, my *insulin*. Right."

With Libby and Ranjeet's help, Jake staggered to his feet. Once upright, the shopkeeper backed off, but Libby noticed Jake was struggling and continued to support him.

"Sorry for the inconvenience, sir," she said. "I'm just going to take my partner back to the car. We have some insulin there. Thanks for your cooperation."

Jake's legs were like jelly. Being forced to lean on Libby was embarrassing, but her ability to keep him standing was impressive.

You're a strong one, Ms. Davis!

Ranjeet rushed ahead to open the door as the two left. "Are you sure you don't want me to call an ambulance?"

Libby shook her head. "No. Detective Masters will be fine. I've seen this before. All he needs is a shot of insulin. Sorry about the coffee. I'll have to leave it, I'm afraid. I have my hands full here, as you can see."

"Of course. Don't worry about it."

The pair staggered outside, and Jake couldn't help but notice the shopkeeper's expression of relief that they were out of his store as he shut the door behind them.

CHAPTER 19

BREACH OF CONFIDENTIALITY

O nce outside, Jake felt better with every step he took from the store. He rubbed his eyes a few times to ensure the hallucination had passed.

As they headed toward the corner, he was already feeling relatively normal again, but he allowed Libby to continue to support him in case Ranjeet was still watching. Once around the corner, he patted her hand to let her know he no longer needed her to hold him upright.

Libby raised an eyebrow and released him. "So, can you tell me what just happened?"

"I wish I could, but I don't know myself. It was bizarre. I could hardly breathe at first, and then I was stuck inside our nightmare, except I was awake. Everything was so real that I felt the gun in my hand and even the breath of that evil Irishman."

"Hmm, I may not have had those visions, but I must admit my heart was beating painfully fast when I first walked in. Then I saw Ranjeet and became so distracted that my heartbeat became normal. I was fine after that until you went all weird."

"Well, I seem to be okay now. I want to go for a walk to clear my head. Is that all right with you?"

"Sure. Where to?"

"How about the park across the road?"

"Okay."

Minutes later, the two walked past the tree where Jake had collapsed two days earlier. He shuddered.

"What's the matter?"

Jake shook his head and led her to the park bench. After both had sat down, he turned to her and said, "I need to tell you something, but I don't want to worry you."

"Like what?"

"Well, this isn't the first time that something strange has happened to me, apart from our dreams."

"Okay."

"You remember that day we first met?"

"Of course."

"Well, after I left you in the café, something freaky happened with that napkin you gave me with your number on it."

"Freaky?"

"Yeah. Every time I tried to get rid of it, I couldn't breathe. Like, I truly thought I was going to die. But as soon as I punched your number into my phone, my breathing returned to normal. Until today, of course."

"Funny you should say that. At the support meeting in the church hall, I found my heart rate was uncomfortably high, particularly when I met you. I put it down to nerves or something like that. But then it happened again back at the café just after you left. I came good again as soon as I walked outside and started heading toward you."

Suddenly, Libby's eyes widened. "You know what I think?"

"What?"

"It's almost like our organs are ... haunted"—Libby's eyes flicked left and right—"by the ghost of my dad."

"Yeah, well, I didn't want to say, but I've been thinking along the same lines since the park incident. That's crazy, right?"

"Not really. My dad spent nearly twenty years on death row. He had nothing else to do but replay what had happened in his mind. Remember me telling you about cellular memory back in the café? It wouldn't surprise me if this memory about the convenience store murders embedded itself in every cell of his body. So, here's another thought—"

Jake's brows shot up quizzically. "Yeah, what?"

"What if the other organ recipients are experiencing the same nightmares?"

"Well, if you asked me six months ago before all this, I would've recommended they put you in a looney bin. We have psychics who work with the police, but I've always considered clairvoyance hocus-pocus mumbo-jumbo. But now, I suppose, anything is possible."

Suddenly, Jake's mouth broke into a grin as he realized something. "Want to find out?"

"How do you propose we do that?"

Still smiling, Jake reached into his jacket pocket, pulled out a folded piece of paper, and presented it.

"What's that?"

"It's the recipient list of our death row donor. I brought it to show you because I knew you couldn't see it properly on your phone."

Like an impatient child, Libby snatched the list from Jake's hand and read it. "Oh, my God! Dad donated so much to so many. They took the corneas, intestines, kidneys, liver, and pancreas apart from the heart and lungs. There would hardly be anything left of Dad by the time they finished with him."

"No, I guess not." Jake could sense Libby's sadness and placed a comforting hand on hers. "It was very generous of him to help others. I wouldn't be here if he didn't."

A single tear trickled down Libby's cheek. She quickly knuckled it away, nodded, and smiled at him. "And I'm grateful you're here. It would be so hard dealing with this on my own."

Their eyes locked. Jake wanted to kiss her and sensed she felt the same, but he knew this wasn't the right time.

Libby blushed, looked away first, and, appearing slightly flustered, returned her attention to the list. "I noticed they've even got addresses and contact numbers next to all the names. So, are you proposing that we call these people?"

Jake shook his head. "No. That would be way too intrusive. Besides, I've flashed my badge once in this investigation, so I must tread carefully. I hope Ranjeet forgets my name because I could be in serious trouble here if he reports me to the police and my captain hears about it."

"I didn't think of that. How was that conversation going to go, anyway? Something like, 'Hi there, I'm just wondering if you had a transplant last year on the 18th of November. Oh, and by the way, have you had any scary dreams lately?' I remember how well that information went down with *you*."

"Yeah, my thoughts exactly. It might be better to do this as a text message and allow them to respond. The only thing is, we would probably have to do it on your phone. I need a low profile in this investigation for obvious reasons. As a regular citizen, you have a little more leeway."

Libby ran her finger down to the first name on the recipient list. "How about we start with Claudine McDonald, our cornea lady?"

"Okay, let's go."

Libby immediately opened her handbag, pulled out her phone, and typed in Claudine's number. She stared at the blank message screen, then her eyes flicked to Jake. "Do you have any ideas of how to phrase this?"

Jake shrugged. "Just keep it friendly and casual."

Libby screwed up her mouth and thought for a second. "Right, I've got it! The perfect message." She then clicked the microphone on the phone's keyboard and used talk-to-text to create it. "Hi there. You don't know me. I'm reaching out because you had a transplant last year on or around the 18th of November. We had the same donor. To celebrate his life, I would love to meet with you. Please call me back if this idea interests you. Best regards. Libby." She turned to Jake for his approval. "How does that sound?"

"Perfect."

Libby nodded, quickly checked the transcribed text, and then offered Jake her phone. "Want to do the honors? It's ready to go. You only need to hit that send arrow."

Jake nodded and was about to do so when concerns about breaching confidentiality flooded his mind. If this got back to his captain, his career would be over.

Texas legislated to keep D.R.D. information confidential because people receiving these organs go through enough trauma. Most wouldn't handle knowing they have the organs of an executed death row inmate inside them. For that reason, the protocol strictly prohibited this information from being disclosed.

The more Jake thought about that, the more he realized this was a bad idea. He shook his head. "No, I've changed my mind. It could be psychologically damaging, not to mention breaking the law."

He roughly handed the phone back as if he were holding a weapon. However, Libby hadn't quite grasped it when he let it go. The phone bounced from hand to hand as they both tried to catch it. They failed, but Libby stuck her foot out in one last desperate attempt. She winced as it bounced off her instep onto the ground.

"Oh, darn!" she said and bent to pick it up. After a brief examination for damage, her eyebrows suddenly shot up. "Uh-oh!"

"What do you mean, 'uh-oh?' Is it broken? Don't worry. I'll buy you a new one. It was my fault."

Libby shook her head. "Much worse than that. Something must have happened when we dropped it." She held the phone in front of Jake's face. "Look, the message is now showing up as sent. One of us must have accidentally hit the send button when we tried to catch it."

He grabbed it from her hand, scrolled through the messages, and his eyes widened.

No! No, no, no, no! Oh, crap! This can't be happening!

Jake thrust it at Libby. "Quick, unsend it before she reads it."

She snatched back the phone, but before she could do anything, the 'Shake it off' ringtone sounded, causing them both to jump. The incoming call number on the screen caused her eyes to widen. "Oh, my lord! I think it's her."

"The cornea lady?"

A rapid scan of the details on the recipient list confirmed it. "Yes," she said. "What do we do? Should we answer it?"

Jake felt conflicted. On the one hand, this was a disaster waiting to happen, but on the other, his curiosity was well and truly piqued.

"Oh, screw it!" Ignoring the horrified look on Jake's face, Libby took the call. She put it on speaker. "Hello? It's Libby Davis speaking."

A bubbly, high-pitched voice greeted her. "Well, hello there! It's Claudine McDonald here. I got your text, and it was great to hear from you. I've been trying to find out who my donor was for months. How did you get that information? Also, how did you get mine?"

"I ... um ... I ... er ..."

Seeing Libby struggle, Jake felt forced to lean in and speak up. "Hello there, ma'am. Apologies for contacting you out of the blue."

"Who are you?" Claudine sounded confused. "I thought I was talking to Libby."

"Yes, you were, ma'am. But I'm here with her. I'm Detective Masters with the Houston police, and Ms. Davis is ... uh ... assisting me with some investigations regarding your donor. We are calling to find out if you've been experiencing any strange symptoms since your transplant."

"You mean symptoms such as horrible dreams?"

Libby jumped back in. "Yes! Awful dreams."

Jake put his finger to his lips, begging her with his eyes to remain silent. "Ma'am, is there any possibility that we can come and interview you?"

"Oh, lordy, yes!" Claudine sounded excited. "I'd love it! I've been going crazy with these dreams over the last few months, and it would be great to talk to someone about them."

"Thank you, ma'am. We have your address listed here in the suburb of Independence Heights. Are you still there?"

"Yes. Same place for the last fifteen years."

"What time could you see us for the interview? We could come today if that's convenient for you?"

"Yes, that's fine. I'm an artist, so I work from home. You're welcome to come over now if that suits you both."

"Thanks, ma'am. That'd be great. We'll be on our way to see you shortly. Expect us in about twenty minutes."

"I'll put the kettle on. Do you like tea?"

"Tea would be lovely," Libby said, butting in again.

"See you soon, ma'am." Jake then ended the call and handed it back. "So, it seems your hunch was right. We're not the only ones having these bad dreams. Ready for another road trip?"

Libby nodded.

Jake held out the crook of his arm. "Shall we?"

With a smile, she took it. "We shall."
The two laughed and walked back to the car.

CHAPTER 20

IMAGES OF EVIL

Twenty minutes later, Jake and Libby stood outside a quaint red brick cottage with a white picket fence, a beautifully manicured garden, and a cute postbox replicating the house. It looked like something straight out of a children's picture book.

As they approached the front gate, two little dogs ran toward them, barking madly. One was completely black, and the other was black and white.

"Oh, cute!" Libby seemed delighted.

"Humph!" Jake stared at them with disdain. "Rat dogs, the pair of them. I'm not a fan. Give me a real dog any day, like a German Shepherd or at least a Labrador, if you prefer cute and cuddly."

Libby rolled her eyes.

The front door opened as the two stood on the other side of the gate, pondering the best way to get past man's best friend. A petite, curvy woman in her early fifties with long, straight red hair stepped out. She wore stylish glasses with a pinky-purple rim and a flowing, multicolored kaftan.

"Onyx! Indigo! Heel!" The woman extended her hand as she opened the gate for them. "Detective Masters and Libby, I presume? Hi there, I'm Claudine." She gestured toward the door. "Do please come in. Oh, wait a minute. Just let me put the dogs around the back." She whistled, and the two dogs obediently followed as she led them away. Claudine returned via the front door a minute later and beckoned them inside.

As Jake and Libby entered, they noted the eclectic furniture. Despite nothing matching, the selection was aesthetically pleasing.

"Please, take a seat." Claudine pointed toward the floral couch, and the pair sat. She pushed toward them the tray of tea and biscuits perched on the coffee table. "Please help yourself." She then sat down in a green chair opposite them and leaned forward. "I'm quite excited to have you here."

Claudine's eyes flicked toward Libby. "So, your text said we share the same donor. Why would you put such a lie in your message if you are only involved in an investigation? I don't understand."

Before Libby could answer, Jake jumped in. As a detective with undercover experience, lying came quickly to him. "Sorry for the deception, ma'am. We didn't want to raise any personal concerns with the text. It seemed better to go with a gentle approach, so we—"

"I think we should tell her," Libby butted in.

Jake gently elbowed her in the ribs and turned to her with pleading eyes, willing her to shut up, but she ignored him.

Claudine frowned. "Tell me what?"

"That we both received organs from your donor. I got the heart, and he"—Libby nodded toward Jake—"got the lungs."

Jake shook his head and sighed.

Good one, Libby! No chance of remaining professional now!

Claudine's eyes were wide with surprise. "Oh! I didn't expect that! I thought the two of you were here because some of our donor recipients had been experiencing strange symptoms since their transplant. So you're not a detective?"

Jake had to take charge and somehow salvage this situation. "Once again, apologies, ma'am, for confusing you." He produced his badge. "Yes, I'm a detective. We truly are here to investigate any symptoms associated with this donor. You said you were experiencing strange dreams. Would you care to elaborate?"

Claudine nodded. "It's difficult to talk about this with my friends because it's so out there. I was thinking I was losing my mind."

"So, what exactly have you been dreaming?" Jake asked.

"They're more like nightmares about this robbery where three people get killed. It's just awful!"

Libby couldn't help but nod enthusiastically.

Jake gave her a look, willing her to calm down, and then returned his attention to Claudine. "Please go on, Ms. McDonald. Could you give us a few more details?"

"Okay. Well, there's this Irishman and a skinny young man. They've come into this store to rob the place. Things become out of control, and the Irishman shoots three people. And then the worst bit happens." Claudine's nose wrinkled with disgust. "That awful Irishman makes me shoot this poor woman he's already killed."

Claudine stared at the pair with a horrified look in her eyes. It was clear she was replaying the images in her mind. "I know it sounds crazy, and I wish I could get some therapy, but I can't afford it since the government cut off my disability benefits thanks to the success of my cornea transplants. I've also developed an obsession preventing me from returning to my profession."

Jake raised a curious brow. "What kind of obsession?"

"Well, before my sight started failing from corneal dystrophy, I was a professional portrait artist. However, since the transplant, I only want to paint images of the evil men from my dreams. I've been pulling them from my head onto the canvas, trying to stop these nightmares, but it hasn't worked so far."

"You mean you have portraits of these men?"

"Oh, yes. Heaps of them. Would you like me to show you?"

Jake jumped to his feet. "Yes, that would be very helpful. Please lead the way."

Claudine stood up. "They're in my studio out the back. Follow me."

They all walked down a long corridor, which ended in a large annex with floor-to-ceiling windows. Through one window, they could see the two little dogs. The pair jumped up, paws and noses against the glass, tails wagging, clearly wanting to be let inside. Claudine ignored them.

A painting on a nearby easel made them stop in their tracks. Libby nudged Jake hard in the ribs, and he nodded. It was a large headshot portrait of the Irishman who haunted their dreams. They stood transfixed as the beady, green eyes burned into their souls.

"He's an evil-looking S.O.B., isn't he?" Claudine pulled a face. "I don't think people will line up to buy this painting. It's frustrating because this strange compulsion to paint him and his skinny little friend stops me from relaunching my business for paid portrait work."

Claudine walked over to a nearby room and came back with another painting. The gangly youth from their dreams stared out at them from the canvas.

"You're some artist, ma'am," Jake said.

"Oh, thank you!" Claudine looked pleased. "I do my best. Anyway, I've given you all that I've got. How about something in return? I want to know more about my donor."

Libby locked eyes with Jake. It was clear she wanted him to reveal more. He knew if he didn't say something, she probably would.

"Okay, ma'am, well ... I don't know if I really should tell you this, but it seems unfair if I don't. Our donor is a D.R.D."

"A D.R.D.?"

"A D.R.D. is what's known as a death row donor."

"Oh, I remember hearing about that on the news when the legislation came in. Lord have mercy! Are you telling me I have the corneas of a killer?"

Libby could not contain herself. "He's not a killer! Surely your dream showed you that! You've seen the truth through his eyes, after all!"

Claudine turned to Libby in surprise. "How do you know that? I thought the Irishman might have been my donor. So it's someone else?"

"Yes. Your dreams are through the eyes of our donor. And our donor is my father!"

Jake closed his eyes in frustration. He knew bringing Libby along for this investigation was a mistake.

Claudine's mouth dropped open. "Your father? Oh, my lord!" She turned to Jake. "And you? Have you been experiencing these nightmares as well?"

"Yes, ma'am. Okay, we've established we're all experiencing these dreams. As a detective, I felt it was my duty to reopen this case."

"So, what I'm seeing is through my donor's eyes? Well, that makes much more sense, I guess. Silly me. I should've realized." Claudine turned, grabbed Libby's hands, and patted them. "I'm so sorry for your loss, Libby, but this is amazing! Your dad is trying to reach out to us."

"I thought you'd be quite shocked."

Claudine shook her head. "No, not at all. I've always believed in life after death. I used to do tarot card readings years ago before my portrait business took off. So, let's say the spirit realm is very familiar to me. You should let me do a free reading for you sometime."

"Well, our goal here, ma'am, is to prove our donor's innocence," Jake interjected. "I wish I could tell you more about him, but other than revealing that he's a D.R.D., I feel I have breached confidentiality quite enough for today."

Claudine nodded. "I understand." She rubbed her hands together with excitement. "I can't believe these dreams have meaning, and I'm not going crazy. So what can I do to help you?"

Jake indicated the paintings. "Well, ma'am, you're helping us enormously right here. We don't have the artistic skills to bring these visions to life. Not like you've just done."

Claudine blushed. "Well, thank you, kind sir."

"We want to prove our donor's innocence and find the actual killer." Jake pointed at the Irishman. "This man." He then nodded toward the portrait of the gangly youth. "And this is his accomplice. I'd like to photograph your paintings if that's okay. We can then put them through the police database and, hopefully, track them down."

Claudine put her hands to her mouth. "Oh, wow! Can my paintings do that? How amazing!" She stood aside. "Please take as many photos as you like. I have a lot more paintings of them here." Claudine ran to a nearby room and brought back ten more portraits. There were six more of the Irishman and four of the young accomplice.

Jake carefully photographed every single one with his phone, closely followed by Libby, who did the same with hers.

Ten minutes later, after exchanging pleasantries, the pair took their leave.

"Thank you, ma'am, for your cooperation. You don't know how helpful you've been," Jake said.

"It's my pleasure. I hope you catch that evil Irishman and his accomplice. You must lock them up for what they did, particularly that Irishman."

Shortly after, Jake and Libby sat silently in the car, pondering what they had learned. It had been a big day.

Finally, Libby said, "So, what now?"

"I'll send the portraits to Barney to run through our police database."

"Sounds like a plan."

As soon as Jake had dropped Libby home, he called his friend.

"Well, hello there, Mav. Have you opened that little present I gave you this morning?"

Jake realized Barney must have other police officers nearby and couldn't speak freely. "Yeah, I've opened it, thanks. Now I just need another favor."

"Man, you're milking this almost dying thing. Well, I'm at your service. What can I do for you now?"

"I have a few images I'm sending to your phone. I want you to run them through the police database."

"Seriously? You know the station monitors all police checks!"

"I wouldn't ask you to do this if it wasn't important."

Barney made a grumbling noise. "Oh, all right! Send them through, but if the captain finds out and sacks me, I'll come over to sleep on your couch and live off your pension, assuming they don't cut you off for this!"

Jake couldn't help but laugh. "Deal. How soon can you do it?"

"Give me half an hour, and I'll call you back. Oh, I see you've sent the images through already. I guess you weren't planning on me saying no."

"Of course not. I know I can always depend on you."

"More like take me for granted, but yeah, okay. Chat to you in half an hour."

"Thanks, Barney."

Jake headed home, and as he waited for Barney to call back, he reread Kingsley's case details. He found it hard to concentrate as his mind drifted back to Libby.

Maybe when all this was over, they could—

His phone rang, interrupting his thoughts. It was Barney. "Please tell me you have some good news."

"Sorry, but I got nada."

"Nothing at all?"

"The database produced hits of men with similar characteristics, but none matched what you sent me. It's just too hard to narrow down. So how old are these images, anyway?"

"About twenty years old."

"Well, I'd say that no one has arrested your guys in that time frame, so, unfortunately, I think this cold case of yours has to remain cold."

"That's disappointing, but thanks anyway, Barn. You did your best. Catch ya later."

Jake flung his phone down on the couch beside him and sighed with frustration. If ever he wanted to utter the f-bomb, it was now. He knew Libby was probably expecting him to call with some news, but no, he decided. Let her have one more night of hope.

With that thought, he headed off to bed. An early night was just what he needed. He would start afresh tomorrow.

CHAPTER 21

NAME AND SHAME

Jake was dreaming again, but instead of about the convenience store, he was inside Anna's café, where he and Libby had their milkshakes the first day they met.

In front of him was a waitress whose name badge said she was Anna but looked very different. Now, she wore a red and white '50s-style outfit and appeared much younger than he remembered. She pointed, and he started walking toward the corner booth. It was the same one he and Libby had sat in when they were there.

On the way, he turned his head. The gangly youth from his nightmares sat at a window table, glaring at him.

Suddenly, the dream jumped slightly into the future, and Jake wandered around, picking up dirty plates. He noticed the youth walking out the door.

"Catch ya later, Lucas," Anna said, waving goodbye.

Jake awoke and sat bolt upright in bed.

Well, that was different.

He realized that the accomplice frequented Anna's café often enough that she knew him by name. He had a lead!

Thanks, Mr. Kingsley!

His phone rang as he sat there, recovering from his dream and wondering whether to call Libby. Without looking, he picked it up and answered. "Yeah?"

"Well, hello to you, too! What a *delightful* greeting."

Immediately recognizing Libby's voice, Jake blinked rapidly, trying to dispel the sleepiness from his eyes. "Sorry, ma'am."

"Could you please stop calling me that? I'm only twenty-two years old, for God's sake. I'm far too young for anyone to call me '*ma'am.*'"

"Sorry. Force of habit."

"Okay, I understand. I just wanted to call you because I had a strange dream about that café we visited after the meeting. I discovered the accomplice's name, and that waitress also seems to know him."

"Wow! So you had the same dream? Why am I not surprised? Your dad is sending us another message, and I may have worked out why."

"Why do you think?"

"I got my friend to run the images Claudine gave us through the criminal databases, and nothing came up for either. It seems they avoided getting arrested in the last twenty years, so there's little hope of identifying them. But now we have another way to find them. We need to make a trip back to Anna's café."

"You're reading my mind."

"How soon can you be ready?"

"Give me half an hour."

"Okay, I'll pick you up then."

Forty-five minutes later, a familiar café window loomed up.

Walking inside, they were happy to see Anna behind the counter. They suspected Jonathan frequented this café and knew this woman—their dreams confirmed it. One by one, the puzzle pieces were coming together to form a picture.

Anna smiled and waved at them. "Well, howdy. Nice to see you folks again."

"You have an amazing memory," Jake said.

"I remember all my customers, and it was hard to forget you two, especially since you both claimed to have met me before, but I knew you hadn't. I pride myself on never forgetting a face."

"Oh, that's right. You mentioned that when we were last here." Jake casually leaned on the counter. "So, I'm curious. Exactly how far back does this impressive memory for faces go? Could it go back as far as, say, twenty years?"

The waitress raised an eyebrow. "I'm good, but I'm not sure I'm that good. For me to recall them after twenty years, they'd need to be pretty special."

"Just wondering if you remember Jonathan Kingsley?"

"Hmm ... that's strange ... I *have* heard that name before somewhere, but I can't seem to put a face to it."

"Okay. Well, does this photo jog your memory?" Jake produced the image he had of Jon on his phone.

Anna squinted at the photo. "Oh, my lord! That's Jon. I never knew his full name. He was just Jon to me and used to be a regular customer of mine back in the day."

"So, what do you remember about him?"

"Well, even though that was a long time ago, I do recall Jon was a lovely, polite young man with a smile that would light up a room. Unfortunately, he was down on his luck when I last saw him. The poor love had lost his job, so I gave him a free meal."

"Anything else?"

"Let me think. I recall Jon having a wife and child. I remember him showing me a photo of them in his wallet. Jon used to talk about his little girl all the time. He was so excited about everything she did—her first steps, her first words, and that kind of stuff. He was such a proud father. Now, what was the nickname he had for her?"

Anna frowned as she searched her memory, then her eyes lit up, and she snapped her fingers. "Got it! He called her Queenie because they gave her the same name as that English queen on the throne back then. You know. *Elizabeth.*"

"I go by Libby these days." Tears filled Libby's eyes.

"Oh, my goodness! I can't believe it's Jon's little Queenie all grown up! Time goes way too fast. So, how's your father these days?"

"If you can remember Jon," Jake interjected, "can you recall hearing about a robbery at the nearby convenience store back then?"

"Oh my lord, yes. That was Singhe's, which is just around the corner. I don't read the papers or watch much television—never seem to have the time—but I remember the police visiting and telling me about it." Anna gestured toward a security camera mounted above the counter. "All the shops in the area got video surveillance after that. Poor Ranjeet. His son took over the store when he was only a kid. I heard they caught the man who did it."

"No, they didn't!" Libby said. "The killer set my father up."

Anna stared at her in confusion. "Sorry?"

Jake gave a loud cough and stared hard at Libby, directing her with his eyes to stop talking, but she ignored him.

"They arrested my father for the crime. But he didn't do it. He was innocent."

"Wait! I remember now," Anna said. "The police told me that Jonathan Kingsley was the name of the shooter. No wonder that name was so familiar. I just didn't put it together." Her eyes widened in shock and disbelief. "No! That can't be! That's not the Jon I remember."

Libby was suddenly angry. "You're not listening to what I just said! I'm telling you, he didn't shoot anyone. We're here because we're trying to track down the real killer."

Jake shook his head and sighed deeply. Talk about laying all their cards on the table yet again. This investigation was the most unprofessional he had ever conducted. His breakdown at the convenience store was awful enough. Then there was the D.R.D. confidentiality breach with Claudine, and now this. If anyone reported him to his captain, he would be toast. She would never let him back on the force. It was time to take back control of the narrative.

"Sorry, ma'am, for not explaining the situation better. What Libby is trying to say is that we've reopened the investigation into the murders at Singhe's Supplies." Jake flashed his badge. "We believe there were two other men responsible. We suspect one or both may have frequented your café that day." He pulled out his phone and flicked through his photo gallery. He found what he was seeking and offered it to Anna. "This picture is of one of those men. Would you mind looking at it?"

Anna nodded and took the phone. "Certainly. Anything to help Jon."

Jake could see Libby was about to speak, and he knew she would reveal to the waitress that the state had already executed Jon for the crime, but that would only waste more time. He quelled her with a stern look.

The first image displayed was of the Irishman.

Anna screwed up her nose. "I can't say this one's familiar. I'm sure I'd remember *that* face if he ever came into my café."

Jake took back his phone, found an image of Lucas, and held it up to show Anna. "Okay. Well, how about this one?"

Tilting her head to one side, she nodded. "Yes, I know him. That's Lucas. He's one of my regulars. He looks a little different. Maybe younger, but definitely him." Her eyes became huge again. "Oh, my goodness! Are you saying he was the murderer? That would be hard to believe. He's always struck me as skittish."

"No, not the killer, but the accomplice. Would you know his surname?"

"I'm good at first names and faces but not so great at remembering surnames, but hang on a minute. I might have something for you." Anna ducked behind the counter and popped up, holding a battered-looking electronic tablet. "I'm positive Lucas signed up for my loyalty program."

As Anna hit the power button on the tablet and waited for it to start up, she continued chatting. "Lucas was a bit of a momma's boy. He was always short on cash and could never seem to hold down a job, so he lived with his mother until she died—such a lovely lady who thought the sun shone out of him. The two used to have lunch here regularly until she became sick. Lucas told me he inherited her house when she passed."

Anna returned her gaze to the tablet. "Let me search." A few clicks later, she gave a triumphant smile. "Here he is. Lucky for you, I've only got one Lucas in the program—Lucas Doyle." She turned the tablet around and presented the details—name, address, and number.

Jake took a photo with his phone. "Thank you, ma'am. You've been a tremendous help."

"I must admit, I thought Lucas had some drug problems. He seemed to get skinnier and skinnier over the years and always had a strung-out look. I suspected he was on heroin or some such drug. People do all kinds of evil things for money when addicted."

"Yeah, they do, unfortunately. Well, we'll be going now. Thanks again, ma'am."

Once they had returned to the car, Jake commanded his phone to show him the way to Lucas Doyle's address. Google Maps popped up, giving directions.

That's only two blocks from here. How convenient.

"So, what now?" Libby asked.

"Well, since we're in the neighborhood, we could head to Doyle's place, hoping to catch him at home. But perhaps I should leave you here at the café."

"Are you kidding? There's no way you're leaving me behind. I'm coming with you."

Boy, this girl is stubborn!

"Oh, all right. You can come. But this time, you must stay in the car. Okay?"

"No problem. Deal!"

With a nod of agreement, Jake started the engine and headed off.

CHAPTER 22

SPECIAL DELIVERY

Five minutes later, the pair drove past Lucas Doyle's home. The house had a mint green clapboard exterior, its frontage spoiled by the overgrown garden and the pile of used auto parts decorating the middle of the front lawn. In the driveway sat an old white Ford pickup. Jake wished he had easy access to the police database to confirm Lucas was the owner and, therefore, still lived there—only one way to find out.

He parked the car a few houses away to avoid the risk of Lucas taking down his number plate and to keep Libby at a safe distance.

"Okay, stay here!" Jake jumped out of the car.

Libby saluted. "Yes, *sir*, Detective Masters, *sir*!"

"I mean it!"

"Okay, don't have a cow! Understood!"

Satisfied, Jake went to the boot and pulled out a cardboard box. He kept it there to organize his groceries after shopping, but it would serve another purpose today. He planned to catch Lucas off guard and hoped it would work.

Jake strode to the front door, acting more confident than he felt. He mentally steeled himself to prepare for anything and hoped Lucas was unarmed.

Such a typical dumb Maverick move! Oh well, here goes!

He knocked loudly, and while waiting, he noticed someone peek through the blinds of the front window.

"Hello?" Jake called out, holding up the cardboard box. "I have a delivery for a Lucas Doyle."

A familiar male voice responded. "I don't remember ordering anything. Just leave it out front and fuck off. Thanks!"

Charming!

"Yes, sir. Certainly, sir." Jake placed the box far away from the door and pretended to walk away. Instead, he stepped to the side, hid behind a nearby bush, and waited.

The front door cracked open a minute later. A man's head with long, stringy blond hair popped out and looked around to ensure Jake had gone. He then walked out to retrieve the box.

Now was his chance! As soon as the man bent down, Jake sprang from the bush, lurched forward, and ran at him.

The man cried with fright and dropped the empty box. He ran back into the house and tried to slam the door shut. A quick thrust of Jake's foot in the doorjamb thwarted the plan.

The man panicked and tried to run for it, realizing he couldn't keep him out. Jake chased him up the hallway and tackled him. The man fell facedown to the ground. Still trying to get away, his arms flailed everywhere, and he rolled over onto his back but quickly found his shoulders pinned to the floor.

Pale blue, very recognizable eyes, wide with fright, locked with Jake's. Although the man was twenty years older than the one in his dreams, there was no mistaking that this was Lucas Doyle.

"Get the fuck off me, man! What do you want? I told Joey he'd get his money next week. There's no need to get heavy."

Jake pulled the scared man to his feet and threw him into a nearby chair. It seemed Lucas had money issues and thought that this Joey person, probably some loan shark or drug dealer he owed money to, had sent a thug around to rough him up.

Jake planned to reveal he was a police officer but realized he could use this mistaken identity to his advantage.

Time to bluff.

"Joey's not happy, Lucas. He wants his money, or some kneecaps will get broken. Do you feel me?"

Lucas nodded, his eyes wide with fear. "I'll get Joey his money. I promise. A couple more jobs will do it, and I'll have the cash."

"Joey's not a patient man." Jake put a threatening fist up to Lucas's face. He then stood up with his hand to his chin, pretending to contemplate something. "But there might be a way that I can buy you a bit more time."

"Yeah, man, yeah! Anything you want. What can I do for you?"

"We're looking for your Irish friend." Jake pulled up the image of the Irishman on his phone and displayed it to Lucas. "We know you hang around with him."

Lucas frowned as he stared hard at the image. "Man, where did you get that? Is that a painting or one of those arty apps? It must be fuckin' old because Sean looks nothing like that anymore."

Jake fought hard to suppress a smile, as Lucas had unwittingly given him enough essential information to take a calculated risk. He folded his arms and rolled his eyes. "Yeah, I'm aware of that. Sean looked like this when he murdered those people at Singhe's Supplies with you as his accomplice. About twenty years ago now, wasn't it?"

"How could you know that?" Lucas asked, his eyes bugging out. "Sean swore me to secrecy, and I've fuckin' told no one. Why would he tell *you*?"

Jackpot!

In a conspiratorial manner, Jake tapped the side of his nose. "I have my ways. Anyway, Joey knows Sean's good with guns and threatening people. He wants to have a little chat with your Irish friend about it. We might have a job for him."

"Yeah, okay, man, okay. So, what do you want from me?"

"I want you to tell me where we can find him."

Lucas's eyes started darting everywhere, and his brow furrowed with worry. "Oh, man, I wouldn't know. I ... uh ... haven't seen him for a while now, so ... uh ..."

Jake knew he was lying. He learned from years of police training how to spot all the signs. He grabbed Lucas by his collar and pulled his face close to his. "Don't lie to me, Doyle. Do you want me to come back with Joey? You can imagine how that will go."

"No! There's no need to do that. Okay, okay. I used to catch up with Sean for a beer at Molly's—you know, that Irish pub down on Main."

"Yeah, I'm familiar with the place. And when is Sean likely to be there?"

"Well, they have a happy hour every Friday night. During those years we hung out together, he never missed it."

"Okay, Doyle. Thanks for the info. And there's just one other thing"—Jake pulled Lucas in even closer so they were nose to nose—"This discussion is strictly confidential. I better not hear about you telling Sean we're looking for him. If I do, you can expect another visit where I'll break some things, and I'm not talking about household items. Got it?"

Lucas nodded emphatically. "Got it, man. We're cool. Seriously, I won't tell him."

"You'd better not!"

And with that, Jake released Lucas and strode out of the house, feeling very pleased with himself. He quickly jumped in the car with Libby and drove away.

"So, how did it go?" she asked.

"Much better than expected. I got some info on the Irishman."

"Seriously?"

"Yep. The Irishman's name is Sean, and he hangs out at Molly's Irish Pub on Main every Friday night. So I guess that's where I'll be this Friday."

"And me!"

"Oh, no way! You know how dangerous this man is and what he's capable of. You're not coming along, and that's final."

"Oh, really? Well, let's see you try to stop me!"

CHAPTER 23

BEER BAIT

F riday night had arrived, and Jake was arguing with Libby at Molly's entrance.

The pub's name was everywhere—in green neon with a shamrock underneath on the two windows on either side of the door, green writing on a white background on the hanging walkway sign, and gold curly writing above the entrance. It was also on the glass of the two swinging entry doors, in case you were still wondering if you had the right place.

Raucous laughter and the roar of chatter from those inside filtered out onto the street. A few patrons sat at the outside tables, watching them with amused interest.

"I said no, Libby!"

Libby folded her arms, refusing to budge. "Don't tell me what to do! I told you I was coming along. This is a public place, so you can't stop me from going in!"

"I've told you why I don't want you here." Jake could feel his frustration rising. "Stop being so difficult!"

A female voice with a broad Irish accent broke into their argument. "Excuse me, there, folks. Would you both be kind enough to move it along, please? You two fighting out the front of our pub is no good for business."

The pair turned to find a young woman with pale, freckled skin and shoulder-length, wavy red hair, dressed in a dark green top with Molly's logo and a long black skirt. She stood there, holding empty pint glasses, and although the smile was polite, Jake could tell she was forcing it. The last thing he wanted was for her to ban them from entering the pub for the night.

"Very sorry, ma'am. We'll take it down the street." Jake reached out and grabbed Libby by the arm.

"Let me go! How dare you!" She angrily slapped his hand as he dragged her away.

As soon as they turned the corner, Jake released her. "I'm sorry, but I don't want you in there. The Irishman is dangerous, and I can't, with good conscience, take you into a potentially life-threatening situation."

"Stop treating me like some porcelain doll! My life's been in danger before. I've had a heart transplant, remember!"

"It's not the same thing, and you know it."

With her hands on her hips, Libby glared at him, refusing to move. "We go in together, or I'll go alone. It's your choice, detective."

"Damn you, woman. I'll bet there are mules out there less stubborn than you!"

"You'd better believe it!"

Jake sighed in defeat. "Oh, all right! We'll go in together. But you stay close to me, okay?"

"Fine!"

Jake gestured for Libby to lead the way, and together, they walked back to the pub.

One of the older men sitting outside drinking smiled at them. "So, you're back. Is everything okay?"

"Just a silly lover's spat. You know women." Jake gave the man a wink. "We're all good now."

Not appreciating the blatant male chauvinism, Libby frowned and elbowed him hard in the ribs, causing Jake to flinch. Even though he was playing a part, Jake realized he deserved that. He gave the man a friendly nod to end the interaction, and they walked inside.

The pub's décor presented a warm, old-world feel—dark wood everywhere, including wooden stools and tables.

Jake tapped Libby on her shoulder and pointed to an empty table for two in the corner. "Let's sit over there while we scope the place out," he said.

"What?"

The pub noise made it hard to be heard, so he raised his voice and continued pointing. "Over there. Let's sit over there."

Jake dragged the stool out from under the table and gallantly gestured toward it when they arrived. However, Libby ignored the offering, chose the one on the opposite side, slid it out, and sat down.

So much for trying to be a gentleman.

Jake plopped himself down on the stool he'd just pulled out. "Look, I'm sorry, Libby. I'm not trying to be difficult here. I'm a police detective, so I'm more used to dealing with shady sorts like this. All I'm doing is looking out for you."

"I appreciate that, but I'm not a child. I can make my own decisions."

"Duly noted. Let's start again. We could be in for a long night, so how about we try to make it a bit more pleasant? Okay?"

"Agreed." Libby assessed the pub's clientele. "Hardly any women in here."

"Yeah, the ladies turn up later to these places. Most don't care about the happy hour, as the men usually buy their drinks. That's probably yet another reason I shouldn't have brought you here. You're drawing too much attention. A pretty young lady like you stands out."

Libby fluttered her lashes at him in a deliberately over-the-top, flirtatious manner. "So you think I'm '*pretty*,' detective?"

Jake rolled his eyes. "Focus, woman. We're here on a mission. But first things first. What'll you have?"

"Sorry?"

"We're in an Irish pub. If we're not drinking, it'll look suspicious. So I repeat, what would you like to drink?"

"I'm not fussed. Surprise me."

"You okay with beer?"

"Yeah, fine."

"Okay, well, you stay here. I mean it. Don't move."

Libby stared off into space, pretending not to be listening.

God, this girl is frustrating! If only she weren't so darn cute.

The young woman who had told them off earlier was bartending. "Hello again, sir. I hope you sorted everything out with your lady friend. What can I get you?"

"Some beer, I guess. What do you have on offer?"

"Well, we have a lot of excellent beers to choose from." She rattled them off. "Apart from our famous Irish Guinness, we have Murphy's Irish Stout, O'Hara's Irish Wheat, Smithwick's Irish Ale, and Kilkenny Irish Cream, just to name a few."

"So, what do you recommend?"

"If you can't decide, we have a happy hour special for the Guinness. I'm a Guinness girl myself. You really can't be going wrong there."

"Okay. Sounds good. Well, a couple of those then, thanks."

"Be right with you, sir."

When Jake finally returned to their table with the drinks, he was annoyed to discover that Libby wasn't there. He had told her to stay put.

Where is she?

He scanned the pub and almost thought she had left when a crowd of young men blocking his view parted, and he spotted her. She was talking to a man with long gray hair and a beard seated at a table near the far end of the bar. Although nothing like the man in his dreams, as soon as Jake set eyes on him, his lungs constricted severely, and he started hyperventilating, making him realize it was Sean.

Libby laughed and carried on, and then, to Jake's horror, she casually reached out and pushed the hair off the side of Sean's face as if it was the most natural thing to do in the world.

For the love of God! What is she thinking?

He slammed the beers down on the nearest table and angrily started striding toward them.

Libby noticed and cautioned him to stop with wide eyes and a slight headshake.

Jake halted in his tracks, grinding his teeth. It took everything in his power to resist the urge to go there and grab Sean by the throat. The thought of Libby being anywhere near that evil man made his skin crawl, but he knew he needed to trust her judgment. Besides, he was only a few feet away and could rescue her if need be.

He watched the pair converse for a couple more minutes until Libby said goodbye to Sean. She then walked back to him with a smug smile on her face.

Grabbing her by the arm, Jake furiously squired her away from Sean's sight. "What the hell do you think you were doing?"

"I found him—the bastard who set up my dad."

"I know! How could you tell?"

Her eyes flicked in Sean's direction. "While I was waiting for you, he walked right by me, and out of nowhere, my heart started racing so fast it was painful. It started racing even more when I looked up at him, and although he looked so different from our dreams, I could *feel* it was him. But I had to get a closer look."

"Dammit, you should have waited for me! The man's a murderer, for God's sake."

"Oh, come on! What can he do? We're in a public place. He doesn't know me. As far as he's concerned, I'm just some girl flirting with him."

"Yeah, I noticed the flirting, all right. And the playing with the hair. How could you bear to touch the bastard, knowing what he's done? What's up with that?"

"Well, he's aged a lot, and now he has that beard and the long hair, but I knew there was one thing that wouldn't have changed ..."

"Like what?"

"That ugly tattoo on his neck—the shamrock, with the skull. That would have to be the same. Unless he had it removed, of course. I had to move his hair to check."

Jake's eyes were wide. *This girl had the makings of a detective, after all.* "And?"

"To be sure, to be sure," Libby said the well-known Irish phrase in an Irish accent with a coy smile. "It was right there on his neck."

"Hate to say it because I'm still so pissed at you, but well done. I knew it was the Irishman because I could barely breathe when I set my eyes on him."

"Glad I came along now?"

Jake shrugged. "I suppose. You did a good job. And now, you need to go home."

"What? No! Why?"

"Because I'm going to call Barney to help me arrest him, and I want you safe and far from here when that happens. I don't know what Sean's likely to do when cornered. He may have a weapon." Jake rested his hand on top of Libby's. "Please. If I'm worried about you, I can't do my job properly because ..."

"Because?"

Embarrassed, he dropped his eyes. "Because I like you, okay—a lot. The thought of you potentially getting hurt in any way tears me apart. So, please, do this for me."

Myriad emotions crossed Libby's face. Finally, she agreed. "Oh, all right."

"Thank you." Jake was relieved she saw sense.

He quickly escorted her out of the building to her car. Fortunately, she had parked near the pub's door, so Sean had no chance of exiting Molly's without being seen.

Once Libby was inside her car, she started it and rolled down the window. "Promise you'll text me, at least, with an update."

"Yes, I will, as soon as I can. Now, get going. I need to call Barney for some backup. The Irishman could leave anytime, and I can't let him escape."

As soon as Libby drove away, Jake rang Barney.

On the fourth ring, he answered. "Hey, Mav. What's up?"

"Are you working?"

"Yeah. For now. I'm just finishing up for the day. Why?"

"Because I need you to help me arrest someone."

"Always the cop. What's going down?"

"I don't have the time right now to explain. Do you trust me?"

"Always, buddy."

"Did you bring civvies into work today?"

"You should know me. I always have some in the car."

"Great! Get them on and get down to Molly's on Main! How soon can you get here?"

"You'll need to give me at least ten minutes."

"Okay. Text me when you're here. We'll go with the dealer angle and the 'meet-me-out-front' trick. I'm going back into Molly's. I'll get the man outside either by tricking him or, failing that, arresting him. Whatever happens, I need you to be ready to help me with the arrest. Keep your eyes on the front door of the pub. You'll know the play when we come out."

"Yeah, yeah, no problem. Dealer angle. Got it! See you soon."

Jake hung up and set his phone to vibrate to feel the text come in. He was ready to go.

He walked back inside the pub and over to the table where he had dumped his and Libby's Guinness. Miraculously, no one had grabbed them for themselves, and the bar staff hadn't taken them away. To allow time for Barney to prepare, he sat down and sipped his beer while his eyes remained locked on Sean.

A few minutes later, Jake grabbed the two glasses and, feigning the stagger of a drunk man, meandered over to the table where Sean was sitting. He flopped down on the stool beside him and crashed the Guinness onto the table. Some spilled out, and a few drops splattered on Sean's leg.

"Watch it, boyo!" The Irishman angrily swiped the beer from his black jeans with his hand. "Don't be sloshing yer fookin' beer on me!"

As soon as those mean green eyes locked on him, it felt surreal to be physically in the presence of the evil man who had haunted his dreams for months. Jake's lungs contracted painfully, but he fought through it and gave Sean a drunken smile. "I see she blew you off as well."

"Who be that?"

"That pretty girl I saw you with earlier. I bought her a drink, and she disappeared. I'm guessing Guinness wasn't her thing. *Women!*"

Sean nodded. "Fookin' bitches be bitches. They're just here for free drinks, for sure. I know their angle. They never fool me."

"Well, I have an extra beer if you want it. I hate drinking alone." Jake pushed a beer glass toward Sean.

The Irishman eyed it suspiciously. "Why don't ye drink it yerself?"

"What, you think I've spiked it or something to have my wicked way with you?" Jake picked up the beer and sipped it. He placed it back on the table and pushed it toward Sean again. "See, there's nothing wrong with it. I feel close to the edge and won't find my way home if I have both."

Sean shrugged and nodded. "Well, if ye insist. Who am I to knock back a free drink?"

"Exactly." Jake extended his hand. "*Frankie Butler*, at your service." The latter was a favorite pseudonym when incognito. His father's name was Frank, and his mother's maiden name was Butler.

"Sean Nolan's the name. Drinking beer's ma game."

As soon as their hands touched, Jake suppressed a shudder as the breath seemed to leave his body. Regardless, he had the bastard. The stupid Irishman even gave him his full name.

A vibration in his pocket alerted him to Barney's arrival as they sat side by side, drinking their Guinness. It was now or never—get Sean out of this bar or create a scene with a public arrest. He preferred to go the former route rather than the latter, if possible.

He pulled his phone from his pocket and read the text. It was perfect—just what he ordered. He deliberately read it out loud in front of Sean. "I'm here. Meet me out front."

Sean raised a curious brow. "Who's here?"

Jake leaned his head toward Sean in a drunken, conspiratorial way. "Can you keep a secret?"

"Maybe. What secret?"

"My dealer's out front." He then put up a finger and used talk-to-text to create his message. "I'll be with you in a minute." With a wink at Sean, he added, "Mind if I bring a friend?"

It's not the first time they have tricked a subject out into the open this way. Hopefully, Barney remembered the correct reply.

A return text came promptly. Again, Jake read it out for Sean. "Sure, if you think you can trust him."

Well done, Barney.

The Irishman appeared intrigued. "What ye be setting up there, boyo?"

Jake leaned in close again. "Just the best blow *ever*! It gives you a high you'll never forget."

He flicked open his wallet and displayed what looked like a wad of cash. It was only a one-hundred-dollar note sitting on a stack of one-dollar bills. Jake had pre-prepared the ruse at home in case he needed it. He had applied this trick in many sting operations and figured if an offer of cocaine didn't tempt Sean outside, an opportunity to rob someone might. It seemed to work, as the Irishman's eyes widened as they locked onto it immediately.

"I came into a major win at a poker game tonight and feel generous." Jake gestured expansively. "Come with me if you want to score some white stuff for free. Snort it tonight, or take it away for later. I don't give a crap. Just want to share the love."

"Free, ye say?" The Irishman grinned and stood up. "Now, how can I refuse such a generous offer?"

"Well, I frickin' wouldn't. It's some good stuff."

Jake put his arm over Sean's shoulders as they stood up, pretending he felt too drunk to stand unassisted. They then staggered out of the pub together.

Out front, leaning against the wall near the corner, wearing a black shirt and jeans, was Barney.

Good boy!

"There's my dealer. Let's take this around the corner. We don't want anyone from the pub to hear us," Jake said.

"Yeah, yeah, boyo. That's fookin' understandable."

It's like shooting fish in a barrel.

Jake staggered along with Sean and Barney.

Immediately upon turning the corner, the Irishman noticed the police car. "Hang on! What the fook?"

Jake dropped, pivoted, and, in one smooth movement, grabbed Sean's right arm, then twisted it behind his back. With a smile, Barney walked over and produced handcuffs from his pocket. They synchronized perfectly, having done this many times before.

Sean soon found his hands together behind his back in cuffs, with Jake reading him his rights.

"Sean Nolan, I'm arresting you on suspicion of the murder of Ranjeet Singhe, Gladys Phillips, and Daniel Bell at Singhe's Supplies convenience store. You have the right to remain silent. Anything you say can and will be used against you in a court of law. You have the right to an attorney. If you cannot afford an attorney, one will be appointed to you ..."

The Irishman's small eyes became enormous with shock as Jake finished reading his rights. Barney also looked very surprised but went with it. Their shared history meant they trusted each other implicitly.

As they escorted him to the police car, Sean resisted and protested. "Ye got the wrong fookin' man! Let me go, ye fookers!"

Ignoring the Irishman's tirade, Barney opened the back door, and Jake pushed him inside. Five minutes later, they were standing outside of the Houston Police Station.

Now they had the Irish bastard, and it was time for the hard part.

CHAPTER 24

IRISH TEMPER

Sean Nolan had an unpleasant end to an otherwise enjoyable evening. One minute, there he was, downing a pint at his favorite Irish pub, and the next, he was being arrested and hauled down to the police station.

Ye wouldn't read about it!

To say he was unhappy about this turn of events was an understatement.

"I told ye, I don't know what the fook yer talking about." Sean glared belligerently at Jake and Barney, who stood before him. "I know fook all about a convenience store robbery, and as far as murdering three people? How can ye be accusing me of such a thing? I be a kind man who wouldn't hurt a fookin' fly."

Jake smashed his fist on the table, causing Sean to jump. "Admit it! You did it! We have evidence."

"Oh, do ye now, boyo? So, what kind of evidence would that be? Because from where I'm sitting, ye got nothing on me." Sean held his gaze without blinking until Jake turned away. The Irishman smirked. He could outstare anyone when he set his mind to it.

Sean could see Barney was uncomfortable, so he worked on him. "Are ye on board with all this, lad? I can see by yer face that yer not. Who be the one in charge? I want to see yer supervisor because ye have nothing to hold me here."

The two cops turned their backs. "Are you sure you've got something on him?" Barney asked, just loud enough to be audible. "We've just taken him in without an arrest warrant."

"Probable cause!" Jake locked eyes with his partner and nodded toward the interrogation exit.

Barney understood, and the two stepped out of the room. Fierce whispering ensued, sounding a lot like an argument. Sean couldn't understand what they were saying, but he felt confident he had them worried.

There's no way either of them had any evidence against him. How could they know what he had done? Suddenly, a name jumped into his mind.

Doyle! That fookin' little bastard! He's the only one who could have ratted me out. Dammit! I should have dealt with that loose end years ago! If they ever let me go, I'll—

Before Sean could ponder the subject further, the door banged open.

Jake folded his arms. "I think a night in lockup might make you realize it's in your best interests to confess to what you've done."

"You're holding me on what grounds?"

"As I told you—on suspicion of murdering three people."

The two cops exchanged a tacit agreement and pulled Sean out of the chair. They led him through the door and down the hallway. He deliberately dragged his feet, causing Jake to give him a firm shove in the small of his back. The Irishman wasn't happy about being pushed around, but there was little he could do about it, being handcuffed.

"Easy does it, boyo! No need to get so physical."

"Stop stalling and keep walking!" Jake said.

"I *am* walking! I'm not a young man, so I can't walk as fast as you. Give me a break. What be yer name, boyo? Yer supposed to identify yourself when I ask. I know ma rights."

"Detective Jake Masters," Jake responded, giving him another firm push in the back.

"So not Frankie Butler, then? I didn't think so." Sean turned his head toward Barney. "So, what's yer name?"

Barney raised a supercilious eyebrow. "Detective Cotter. Now, just shut up and keep walking."

Before long, they arrived at a holding cell. Barney unlocked it. Jake then uncuffed Sean and shoved him inside.

He spun around to face them immediately and angrily rubbed his sore wrists. "I demand an attorney! Ye offered me one when ye arrested me. So where is he, then? I'll be mentioning that to yer supervisor first thing when I see him."

Barney shook his head. "No public defenders were available tonight, so we must hold you until morning unless you know an attorney we could call. If you do, tell us now."

"Do I be looking like a man who can afford to have an attorney on tap? Ye bastards can provide me with one on yer dime since yer so keen to keep me here."

"I'll organize a public defender to see you first thing tomorrow," Barney said.

"Yes, ye fookin' well will."

Sean noted the looks exchanged between the two officers, and Barney appeared unhappy about the situation. The cell door slammed, and Sean ran to it, putting his face against the bars to watch them walk away.

As soon as they were gone, he turned around to inspect the tiny jail cell. The walls were light cream. In the left corner sat a single bed with a sheet, blanket, and pillow stacked on a gray mattress, and on the right was a stainless steel toilet with a hand basin above.

Fook ye, coppers!

Sean angrily swiped the linen onto the floor and plopped himself on the bare mattress. Realizing he wanted the pillow after all, he rescued it from the floor and secured it behind his head upon lying down.

For the next few hours, Sean lay there staring at the ceiling, plotting revenge against everyone involved in this process. He got very creative until finally falling into an uneasy sleep.

Early the following morning, a loud voice broke the silence of the prison cell. "Breakfast!"

Sean rubbed his tired eyes and sat up. He found that someone had pushed a food tray through the slot at the bottom of the cell door. He was starving and keen to see what was on offer, but his nose wrinkled with disgust upon inspecting the contents.

Fookin' porridge! Fookin' mushy, awful stuff!

Angrily, he snatched up the bowl and flung it at the wall as hard as he could, cracking the plastic and splattering the gooey contents everywhere before it fell to the floor. Sean smirked with satisfaction at the mess he made.

An hour later, Barney and a young female officer stared at him through the cell door bars. Barney, noticing the porridge-stained wall and overturned bowl, rolled his eyes, shook his head, and frowned at Sean. "Stand up, Nolan, and put your face against the back wall."

Grumbling to himself, the Irishman stood up and complied. He heard the cell door slam open, then felt himself being grabbed and handcuffed. The two officers spun him around, and with a firm hold on each side, they escorted him back to the interrogation room.

When they arrived, Barney dragged a chair out from under the table, led Sean to it, and placed an authoritative hand on his shoulder, pushing down to force him to sit. "Wait here."

"Like I have a fookin' choice, mate!"

A few minutes later, the door opened. A blond woman dressed in a blue suit stepped into the room. "Sean Nolan?"

"That be me, beautiful. What can I be doing for ye, ma darlin'?"

The woman frowned and flattened down her jacket with her hands. "My name's Captain Bennett. It's come to my attention that two of my officers arrested you last night, and I don't believe there's been enough probable cause to hold you." Bennett turned to Barney. "Officer, uncuff this man."

Looking none too happy, Barney complied with her order, then stepped back and hung his head.

"Oo, I love a powerful woman who knows how to take charge." Sean rubbed his wrists and treated the captain to a salacious wink. He received an icy stare in response. "Now this woman knows what's what. What she said is precisely what I was fookin' saying last night."

Bennett seemed unimpressed with the Irishman's attempts to flatter her. "The station apologizes for any inconvenience this has caused you.

If you wish to file a formal complaint regarding the officers involved, please go to our website to fill one out online, or you can get a paper copy from our front desk." She turned to Barney again. "Please escort the gentleman out, Cotter. And then I'd like you to call Masters and tell him to get him in here. We need to discuss this matter further."

"Yes, ma'am. Right away, ma'am." He then grabbed Sean's arm, helping him to his feet.

"Get yer fookin' hands off me." The Irishman snatched his arm away with a snarl.

"Apologies, sir." Barney gestured toward the door. "Walk with me, please."

"Oh, it's *'please'* and *'sir'* now, is it? We were pretty short on the word 'please' last night when yer good self and yer young mate were manhandling me."

As Sean walked out the door, he turned to Bennett. "And ye can be sure I'll be putting in that complaint. Ye need to put a leash on these officers of yers."

Minutes later, Sean and Barney stepped outside into the sunshine. The Irishman squinted in annoyance, wishing he had some sunglasses.

"You're free to go, sir." Barney pointed down the street. "It's only a short walk back to the pub unless you prefer me to give you a lift."

"Oh, that would be just fookin' lovely. Another ride in yer pretty cop car. Well, ye can shove that grand offer right up yer fookin' arse with a red hot poker."

Barney's eyebrows shot up at the verbal assault, but the Irishman knew he could do nothing about it. No witnesses.

My fookin' word against yers, copper!

"Well, toodle-oo, *Constable Plod*. I'll be off now." Loudly muttering about the Houston Police Department's incompetence, Sean turned and headed down the street.

My Baby better be okay, or someone's gonna pay!

Baby was a classic Harley-Davidson won in a poker game three years ago. The Irishman quickly fell in love with her and the whole biker vibe. He even ditched his short hair and clean-shaven face to adopt the retro biker persona of long hair and a beard. He found the updated look attracted the ladies and saved a fortune on hairdressing.

Sean was relieved to discover that Baby was fine. No one had messed with her as he feared. With a smile, he unlocked his helmet, shoved it on his head, then jumped on Baby and started her motor. Within seconds, she was purring like a kitten. That sound never got old.

The smile turned into a massive grin as he gave her a few loud revs, alerting everyone in the neighborhood that Baby was ready to roll.

The Irishman's eyes then narrowed. He knew who was likely responsible for his uncomfortable night in the holding cell, and something needed to be done about it.

Time to pay Doyle a little visit. It's well overdue, and I have no more time to waste.

CHAPTER 25

RAT TRAP

Twenty minutes later, Sean was standing in front of Lucas's house. He didn't want to alert anyone about his arrival, so he parked his Harley a block away and walked. Baby may be beautiful, but she made a grand and noisy entrance.

Sean had taken great pains to keep tabs on Lucas's whereabouts. For years after the murders, he ensured they met weekly for beers at Molly's. He liked to remind his accomplice how important it was to keep his mouth shut. However, as time passed, these catch-ups became further and further apart. When Baby came into his life, they eventually stopped altogether as Sean embraced his new biker persona, and it wasn't a good look to associate with the likes of Lucas. He realized that becoming too comfortable trusting the young man would never talk was a big mistake. Well, that was about to change.

Sean stepped up to the front door and knocked hard. His keen hearing detected movement from the inside as boots walked across wooden floorboards. He noted that someone peeked through the blinds, but the door didn't open. The man may be a flake, but he wasn't stupid.

Fookin' little shit!

Then, something occurred to Sean. He remembered Lucas kept a spare front door key under a flowerpot around the side of the house.

In the early years after the murders, the Irishman gave Lucas a lift to and from Molly's for their regular Friday night catch-up before the young man bought himself a car. When dropping Lucas home, Sean noticed that Lucas frequently forgot his house key and would fetch the spare.

"Well, I guess ma old mate isn't home. What a shame. I'll be off now," Sean said out loud as he walked away.

After waiting a few minutes, he doubled back to the side of the house. The cracked old flowerpot sat there in the same place. A quick flip on the side revealed that the key was still under it.

Old habits die hard.

Sean returned to the front door. As quietly as he could, he unlocked it and turned the handle. As the door opened, it gave a loud creak. He grimaced and cocked his head to one side. There seemed to be the sound of pots and pans, which told him that Lucas was now in the kitchen.

Can't wait to see Doyle's face. Bet the little shit soils himself.

Sean found him standing in front of the stove. "Well, hello there, Lucas, ma old mate. Long time no see."

Lucas turned in shock, almost knocking the frying pan off the stovetop. He caught it, placed it on the kitchen bench, and turned off the burner. There was terror in his eyes, but somehow, he forced a smile. "Sean! Fuck, what a surprise. How did you get in?"

The Irishman held up the front door key and smirked. "With this, boyo. I can't believe you still keep this out the front under that pot. I knocked on the front door, but ye didn't answer, and I was about to head off. But then I remembered the key and figured I would wait for ye to come home. But here ye are."

Lucas's eyes darted everywhere, and Sean realized he was scoping the exits. There was nowhere for him to go. He had him cornered.

"Sorry. I didn't hear you knocking. You must have caught me in the middle of washing up." He gestured toward the dishes in the sink. "It gets noisy. You understand."

"Of course, boyo, of course. Ye would never deliberately ignore yer old mate. Not after all we've been through together."

"No, I would never disrespect you like that."

"Of course, ye wouldn't, boyo." Sean sat himself down at the kitchen table. "But we need to have a wee chat."

Lucas became even more squirrely. "About what?"

"Has anyone been asking questions about me?"

The color drained from the younger man's already pale face, and he looked so terrified he couldn't speak.

Time for a less threatening tactic.

"Look, lad, ye been doing me a favor. So, it's all right. Just tell me."

Lucas continued to look uncertain but answered, "Okay, well, yeah. This dude came around a few days ago asking after you."

"Oh, well, did he now? So, tell me, what did this *'dude'* look like?"

Lucas frowned as he recalled. "He was a tall young guy with light brown hair. He was the type that chicks would drool over."

Sounds like that cop, Masters!

"And what would ye be telling this young man?"

"I didn't tell him anything about the *you-know-what*, I promise you. But he seemed to know all about it. So, I figured you told him."

"Now then, boyo. What did he seem to know?"

"You know," Lucas lowered his head and mumbled, "about the convenience store ..."

"About the what now?" Sean had heard but wanted to torture Lucas a little.

"He knew you shot those people. You must have told him."

"I did no such thing, boyo."

Lucas looked confused. "But you must have said something to someone. He seemed to know all about it."

"Okay. Interesting. And what did ye do then?"

"Well, he seemed to know you and said you were handy with a gun. He asked me where you hang out because he wanted to chat with you. He said something about having a job for you. So I ... er ... I told him."

"So ye *told him.*"

"Well, yeah. Sorry. I didn't think the guy meant you any harm."

"Didn't mean me any harm," Sean repeated dully.

Stupid boy!

It was time for a quick change of subject. The Irishman nodded toward the frying pan. "I see ye had some bacon and eggs going there.

Now, that's what I call a proper breakfast. How about ye cook up some of that for me?"

"Sure. No problem. I can do that. You can have these if you like."

"Nah. I prefer my eggs scrambled. You can have those. Just cook some more the way I like them. There's a good lad."

Lucas nodded. He poured the cooked bacon and eggs onto a plate. He then headed to the refrigerator to get some more.

As soon as the younger man opened the door and bent down to get what he needed, Sean quickly pulled up the leg of his jeans, revealing Reaper, his trusty knife retrieved earlier from Baby's storage compartment, attached to his boot. Sean pulled Reaper from the sheath and moved it to the inside pocket of his coat. Smirking, he leaned back in his chair.

Soon, the new batch of bacon and eggs was crackling away on the stovetop.

"That smells good, boyo. Let's sit down so we can enjoy a nice breakfast together. We can chew the fat. It's been too long."

Minutes later, the men had bacon and eggs in front of them. They tucked in.

When they finished, Sean sat back in his chair, patting his full belly. "Oh, boyo, that's the best bacon and eggs I've had for a long time."

"Thanks. Mom used to cook them for me."

"So, what's the story with yer ma? I remember ye telling she was sick the last time we spoke. Is she still with us?"

Lucas shook his head. "Lung cancer took her a few months ago. I think it was due to all those years of smoking—such a nasty habit. Anyway, I inherited the house when she died. I don't exactly have the woman's touch—certainly not with the garden. Mom used to love gardening until she got sick. It's not quite the same without her here. I miss her even though she used to drive me crazy."

Sean reached forward and patted Lucas on his hand. "Ah, boyo. That's the sad thing about parents, ay. Yer gonna lose 'em someday, God willing. Much sadder when a parent loses a child."

"Yeah, I suppose so."

"Well, she certainly taught you how to cook. That breakfast was a tribute to yer dear old ma."

"Thank you."

"Ye know what would go down well right now?"

"What?"

"I need a bit of the hair of the dog."

"The hair of the dog?"

"I need a beer, boyo. Do ye have some in the fridge?"

"I think so."

"Well, would ye be a kind lad and get me one?"

"Okay."

As Lucas turned around to walk to the refrigerator, Sean quietly stood, pulled Reaper from his coat pocket, crept up, and grabbed him from behind. As the Irishman dragged the blade across the younger man's throat, he put his mouth close to his ear. "So, ye miss yer ma, ye rat bastard. Well, ye'll be seeing her soon enough." There was no chance to scream.

Once released, Lucas turned around, eyes wide with horror. He clutched his bleeding throat with one hand, and with the other, he desperately reached out and grabbed Sean by his left arm as he collapsed against him. Nails dug in, tearing flesh, and the pair engaged in a horror dance, nose to nose, as Lucas grimly clutched on and Sean tried to escape his grasp.

"Let go of me, ye fooker!" The Irishman still had Reaper in his right hand, so he stabbed Lucas multiple times to force him to release the death grip.

After what felt like an eternity but, in reality, would have been a few seconds, Lucas submitted, his knees giving way, and he sank to the floor, leaving a blood trail down Sean's body and scratching his arm as he went.

"Oh, for fook's sake!" The Irishman glared down at his blood-soaked coat, shirt, and jeans as he kicked free his legs from the dying man's grasp. "Look at the fookin' mess ye made of me. This visit was supposed to be a quick one. But out of the kindness of ma heart, I wanted to let ye have a nice last meal and a chat. And look what ye've gone and done, ye little gobshite. Ye fooked it all up."

Sean stared with dispassionate eyes as Lucas drew his last breath.

"Now I'm truly sorry, boyo. Yer not a bad lad, and we shared some good times. I'll cherish that. But this is what ye get for being a dirty little rat bastard." He gave Lucas a hefty last kick for good measure. "Let this be a lesson to ye, boyo. No one, I repeat, no one crosses Sean Nolan."

He wiped Reaper's blade on the side of his bloodstained jeans and returned it to the sheath attached to his boot. "Now, I can't leave your fookin' house and get on my Baby looking like this. You don't mind if I use your facilities?" He cocked a hand to his ear, pretending to be waiting for a response. A manic grin followed. "No, I didn't think so."

Whistling, Sean headed to the laundry, stripped naked, and put his blood-soaked clothes in the washing machine. He inspected the brand of the laundry powder and grimaced.

Cheap, nasty, fookin' stuff! You were always such a tight arse, Doyle.

He put the clothes through the washing cycle.

While in the laundry, Sean found a bottle of bleach and a rag and took them to the kitchen. He grabbed the dishwashing gloves next to the sink, and while still whistling cheerfully, he carefully started cleaning all the surfaces he had touched—cups, plates, utensils, chairs, table, and all doorknobs.

Finally, he came to Lucas. Sean pushed him over onto his back to ensure he was dead and found his victim's eyes and mouth fixed wide open with horror.

Yep! Most definitely fooked.

Sean tipped bleach all over the front of the body, then rolled it face down and poured more on the back.

When finished, the naked Irishman stood back and inspected his work. The bleach should have destroyed his DNA on the body and anywhere near it in the kitchen. However, he couldn't be sure and decided the most intelligent move was to burn the entire house down before he left.

But first, it was time to get clean. Sean headed into the bathroom. He took a long, hot shower, ensuring he had removed every speck of blood.

Afterward, with a towel wrapped around his hips, he strolled from the bathroom to the laundry and saw that the washing machine had finished its spin cycle. Now, it was time to put his clothes in the dryer.

The load was small and completed in thirty minutes. Sean pulled out the clothes. Just as he finished doing up his jeans, there was a loud rapping on the front door.

"Open up, Doyle! I can see your car in the driveway. I know you're here," a male voice yelled.

Oh, for fook's sake! Who the fook is that?

The Irishman quickly pulled on his boots, ensuring Reaper remained attached. He grabbed the wet towel from the floor and pushed it to the bottom of the laundry basket under a pile of dirty clothes. He then peeked around the corner of the door. Suddenly, a face appeared at the side kitchen window. It was Jake.

Not that cop again!

Sean quickly pulled his head back into the laundry. The cop would have seen Lucas on the floor for sure.

Fook! Should've moved that fookin' body out of sight!

Suddenly, he heard broken glass.

Fook! The copper's seen the body and is breaking in! Fook! Fook! fook!

The laundry had an exit door to the backyard. Sean waited until Jake started climbing in, then headed for the door as quietly as possible. As he slowly opened it, a noisy creak assaulted his ears, and he froze, holding his breath. Running feet were now coming for him.

Fook!

There was no point being quiet now. Sean flung the door open, slammed it shut as he left, sprinted toward the back fence, and was about to jump over it when the words, all criminals dread, rent the air.

"Police! Don't move!"

Sean turned his head and saw Jake standing on the laundry step. Their eyes locked.

Fook! He's seen me, and he knows who I am. Who is this fookin' cop?

According to Lucas, Jake Masters somehow knew Sean was the convenience store murderer. And now, he could pin another murder on him. He needed to find out more about this copper.

Jake didn't appear to be holding a gun, so Sean ignored him and jumped the back fence. It would be easy to lose the cop if he gave chase. Ever since he was a teen, the Irishman had heavily been into Parkour. It was a handy skill for breaking into houses and getting away. It was the main reason the cops never caught him.

Even though he was in his early fifties, he still practiced the art and was fitter than most men half his age—far from the feeble old man act he pulled at the police station. After jumping multiple fences in and out of several backyards, he emerged two streets away and angrily strode back to Baby. This cop was a big problem he needed to fix.

Sean pulled on his helmet and then rode Baby down the road to observe the Doyle residence from a distance. He noticed the cop sitting on the front veranda's steps, and a young woman was beside him. Something was very familiar about her, and then it hit him. It was the girl who chatted him up at the bar last night. She must have been working with the cop.

Realizing he needed to be careful to ensure the pair didn't spot him, Sean noticed a nearby set of units. He rolled his bike down the driveway and used the visitor parking at the back. He returned to the road and hid in a nearby bush to observe the scene.

When the police finally arrived, his instincts screamed at him to run to Baby and ride away, but he resisted the self-preservation flight urge, needing to learn more about that cop. He continued watching until Jake and the girl returned to a Mustang.

Sean decided he needed to eliminate them—that cop, in particular. It wouldn't do to have a witness on the loose. He ran down the driveway, jumped on Baby, and arrived just as the Mustang pulled away.

The Irishman tailed them discretely, as far back as he could without losing them, until the police station loomed up. The pair parked out front and walked inside.

Oh, fook!

Sitting and waiting for them outside on Baby would be very conspicuous. Sean noticed a café was across the road.

Perfect.

He parked Baby down a side street, returned to the café, walked inside, and found a booth.

A young waitress who looked barely out of high school approached him. "What can I get you, sir?"

Sean picked up the menu. "I'll have the endless cup of coffee and a piece of that custard cream pie, ma darlin', that I spotted in yer display cabinet on the way in." He then pointed at the TV screen in the corner. "Also, could ye be a love and put it on the sports channel? I might be here a while if that's okay. I'm waiting for someone."

The young waitress nodded. "Certainly, sir. Stay as long as you want. We're not busy right now." She pulled a remote from her pocket, pointed it at the screen, and put it on Fox Sports.

Five hours and countless coffees later, the cop and the girl finally walked out and headed to the Mustang.

About fookin' time!

Sean threw some money on the counter. "Keep the change," he called as he ran out the door back to Baby. Before long, he was tailing the Mustang again. It was now rush hour, so the traffic was slow, making blending in and keeping a couple of cars between them a lot easier.

He followed them to a house on Chapman Street. He watched Jake park the car, and they both went inside.

Sean glanced down at his boot.

Reaper, ma good mate, I think we need to pay this pretty pair a late-night visit. We've got some more loose ends we need to tie off.

CHAPTER 26

GRUESOME DISCOVERY

Earlier that day, Jake and Barney sat in Captain Bennett's office with their heads hung low as she berated them.

"Do you realize how many protocols you broke in the last few days?"

Both men remained silent, faces grim. They felt like two naughty school kids called into the principal's office.

She pointed an accusatory finger at Barney. "As the senior detective, you should know better. D.R.D. privacy protocols are in place for a reason. I should suspend you."

"Yes, ma'am. I'm very sorry, ma'am."

Jake jumped in. "Don't blame Barney. It's my fault. I lied to him."

"Care to elaborate?"

"I told him I wanted to research our state's last execution during my time off because I was bored. He brought me the info I asked for to help me out. Detective Cotter wasn't aware that Kingsley was my donor. He didn't even read the information. He just gathered it and gave it to me."

"Just like that?"

"Yep, just like that."

"And the arrest of Sean Nolan?"

"Once again, it's all me. I asked for help to arrest a suspected felon. I took advantage of our friendship." Jake turned to Barney. "Sorry."

With a grim-faced nod, Barney silently accepted the apology.

Bennett groaned. "So, Masters, you want to take full responsibility for this breach of protocol. Am I to understand you correctly?"

"Yes, ma'am."

With a sigh, she turned to Barney. "You're dismissed. But don't think this is over, Cotter. We'll discuss this kind of information sharing and arrest protocols in the future. Now get out."

"Yes, ma'am. Once again, I'm very sorry." Barney courteously nodded to the captain and exchanged worried glances with his friend before walking out and shutting the door.

Bennett returned her attention to Jake. "What's going on with you, Masters? You've been through a lot, and I've always suspected much more psychological damage than you've led me to believe concerning your organ transplant.

"I'm sure it's not ideal to discover that you have a killer's lungs inside your body. However, that gives you no right to drag a citizen off the street without probable cause or an arrest warrant. And all this while you're supposed to be on mental health leave."

The captain raised her palms in exasperation. "With so many protocols broken, Sean Nolan has grounds to sue our department. So what makes you think that this man is a killer?"

Telling his angry captain the truth right now would not go down well. "I ... ah ... wanted to learn more about my donor. I read Kingsley filed countless appeals, protesting his innocence and saying that the convenience store murders were the work of some masked robbers.

"I also noticed that the court-appointed attorney assigned to his defense worked pro bono for Kingsley the whole time right up until his execution, so it would appear she believed in his innocence.

"Anyway, I wanted to look further into the case. While retracing the steps of my donor on the day of the murders, I came upon information leading me to Nolan and—"

Bennett put up her hand. "I'm going to stop you right there, Masters. What we need here is a little thing called evidence. Got some?"

"Well, I talked to his accomplice. He told me about Nolan and where to find him."

"His accomplice? Well, why didn't you bring this man in to testify? I assume you understand that without producing the witness, what you are telling me is all hearsay."

Jake frowned as he tried to come up with a suitable response. It would appear to be a rookie error. However, Jake knew he had tricked Lucas into confessing, and the accomplice would clam up the second he realized Jake was a cop, bringing them back to square one, regardless. But he couldn't reveal that to Captain Bennett because she would demand to know who told him about Sean in the first place, and he wasn't ready to go there yet.

Unable to think of anything to say that wasn't an outright lie, Jake shrugged and hung his head.

The captain sighed. "Well, Masters, after this, I'm afraid I will have to put your reinstatement into the police force under serious reconsideration while I get your mental health assessed. This current obsession with your donor has caused me some grave concern."

She waved a dismissive hand. "That will do, for now. I expect you to make an appointment with Helen for counseling before you leave. Now, get out."

With a curt nod, Jake stood up, spun on his heels, and walked out the door.

It had been a day when nothing was going the way Jake wanted. The plan was to organize a public defender for Nolan so that they could continue the interrogation. Jake was gulping down his morning coffee when Barney called, telling him to come to the station immediately because the captain wanted to speak to him.

By this stage, she had already ordered Barney to let Nolan go. Jake rushed to get dressed and drove to Molly's as fast as possible, hoping to catch him, but the Irishman had already gone.

It was then off to the station to sit outside the captain's office. Barney, who sat alongside him, told Jake he had confessed to the captain about sharing Jonathan Kingsley's D.R.D. file to explain the motivation behind Nolan's arrest. Barney figured they were in enough trouble already that it was best to come from him before someone else reported them. All they could do was wait for her to make the time to see them, which was the worst bit, as they both knew what was coming and wanted it to be over.

As Jake jumped in his car, contemplating his next move, his phone beeped, breaking into his thoughts. He grabbed it and saw there was a message from Libby.

Morning! Have you put away any murderers recently? ;-)

Jake sighed deeply. He wasn't looking forward to giving her the bad news. "Hey, Google, video call Libby."

Within seconds, her face popped up on the screen. "Hey there, detective. I got your text telling me you had him, and I've been dying to hear from you with another update. After all the excitement, I don't think I slept a wink last night." She self-consciously adjusted her hair. "I must look a sight."

"You look pretty beautiful to me." Jake then suppressed a groan. Why did he say that? Too many years of practice at being a schmoozer with the ladies.

Regardless, Libby seemed pleased. "I haven't even brushed my hair yet. But that's sweet of you to say. Anyway, what's happening with the Irishman?"

"I hate to be the bearer of bad news, but my captain cut Nolan loose this morning."

"No! You've got to be kidding! So what now?"

"Well, my captain's pretty pissed at me, and I guess I'll have to risk making her even more upset."

"What's the plan?"

"I want to trick Doyle into confessing again, but I'll record the conversation this time. He's the only other witness to the crime. Without him, we don't have a case."

"Isn't it illegal to record someone without them knowing?"

"No. That's the beauty of Texan law—it's a one-party consent state. Barney and I have taken down a few nasty perps that way. I should have thought about doing it the first time. But I rushed in there—adrenaline overload, brain disengaged. It was a typical dumb Maverick move."

"Maverick?"

"Barney's nickname for me because I do things my way and take risks."

"Your Barney sounds like a good friend. Is he going to help you?"

"I know he would, but I won't ask him. I risked his career enough on this, so I'll have to fly solo. It shouldn't be a problem. Lucas is a skinny and scared little dude. I've taken him down once and can do it again."

"Well, detective, it sounds like you need some backup. I'm here to assist."

Jake gave a cynical laugh.

"I'm serious. At the very least, I want to ride along like the last time we went there."

"And I suppose if I say no, you'll turn up there, anyway?"

"You've got it."

"Oh, all right. I'll pick you up in half an hour. Be ready."

Forty minutes later, the pair sat in the Mustang a few doors from Lucas Doyle's house. They saw the old Ford pickup was still out front in the drive-by, so it appeared he was home.

Before Jake jumped out of his car, he turned to Libby. "You know the drill. You stay in the car. If you see or hear anything that sounds like trouble, you call 911 straight away. Got it?"

"Yes, detective. I've got it."

Within a minute, he was at the front door, his covert recording device ready to go, knocking loudly and yelling, "Open up, Doyle! I can see your car in the driveway. I know you're here."

There was silence, and no one was peeking through the window blinds this time. It appeared that Lucas was playing hardball today, and Jake would need to break in.

Probably best to approach from the side to avoid the risk of a concerned citizen reporting it.

None of the side windows had blinds. Jake put his face up against the glass and stared into the kitchen. He thought he saw something move, but became distracted by a body lying face down on the floor. It looked like Lucas.

Speed was essential and might mean the difference between life and death. He bent down, grabbed a nearby landscape rock and threw it at the window, shattering the glass. Carefully putting his hand through, he flipped the latch, pushed up the frame, and climbed inside.

Before having time to check on Lucas, a creaking noise alerted him that someone was still in the house. Jake ran to the laundry and arrived just as the back door slammed shut. He opened it and stood back in case the assailant was waiting on the other side with a weapon. As he peered through the open door, he saw a man running away.

Jake strode outside onto the back step. "Police! Don't move!" he yelled as the man was about to jump the back fence.

The man briefly turned his head, and their eyes locked.

Nolan!

Ignoring him, the Irishman jumped the fence and was gone.

As much as Jake wanted to give chase, Lucas had to be his priority right now. The man might still be alive.

He ran back into the kitchen and squatted next to the body on the floor. Bleach fumes invaded his nostrils. Turning the body over revealed the sliced throat and multiple stab wounds. Blank eyes stared at him, and the mouth was wide open in a contorted death grimace.

Poor bastard!

He pulled his phone from his pocket to call it in when an unexpected scream caused him to jump. Jake turned and saw Libby standing on the other side of the broken window. Her eyes were wide with horror.

Damn! Forgot about her.

"Libby, please try to remain calm. The person responsible for this has gone. I'm just about to call 911."

"Don't bother. I've already made the call. The operator's still on the line and waiting for an update."

She held out her phone to Jake through the window. He strode over and took it, and after giving over his badge number, the crime details, and the address, he hung up and handed it back.

Libby looked stricken. "He's dead, isn't he?"

"Yeah, I'm afraid so."

Libby started climbing in the kitchen window to join him, but Jake put his hands out to stop her from proceeding.

"No, Libby, no! There's broken glass, and this kitchen's a crime scene. I've contaminated the evidence enough. You need to keep the fuck out!"

"Well, *excuse* me! Language!"

Mortified, Jake bit his lip. Duress had caused the f-bomb to slip out of his mouth yet again. Worse, it was in front of a lady.

Mom would turn in her grave.

"I'm sorry, Libby. Thanks for calling 911, but it would've been better if you'd stayed in the car, as I told you. You didn't need to see this."

"I know what you ordered, but I heard the broken glass and was worried. Then I heard you yell, 'police, don't move!' and got even more worried. I imagined you hurt, and I couldn't get that image out of my mind." With tears in her eyes, Libby shrugged helplessly. "I can't help caring about you."

Jake couldn't have felt more of a heel. "I care about you, too, and I feel bad that all this will scar your mind. I'm so sorry, Libby."

He climbed out the window and pulled her to him. She melted into his arms, and it felt like they were one as she buried her face in his chest. Jake's mind returned to the first time they did this in the park.

Why does hugging this girl always seem right, even when the situation is wrong?

When they released each other, the pair returned to the front veranda to sit and wait for the police to arrive.

Jake noticed Libby was shaking horribly from the shock, so he wrapped an arm around her shoulders and held her hand for moral support.

I should never have allowed her to talk me into bringing her along. Too late now.

Before long, sirens filled the air. An ambulance was first on the scene, immediately followed by the police. Barney was amongst them.

Jake squeezed Libby's hand. "I've got to go deal with this, okay?"

Libby, still trembling a bit, nodded. "I understand."

Jake dropped his arm from her shoulders and stood. Barney walked over to him, his eyes wide. "What the hell are you doing here, Mav? The captain's going to have a hissy fit!"

"She shouldn't have cut Nolan loose." Jake gestured toward the house. "In the kitchen, you'll find the body of a man called Lucas Doyle, Nolan's accomplice. The Irishman killed him for what he knows."

"How can you be so sure Nolan is responsible?"

"I saw the bastard running away from the scene. It's unlikely to have been anyone else."

As they spoke, the older of the two paramedics in attendance headed into the house to confirm Doyle was deceased. At the same time, the other, a tall, handsome young man, approached Libby, wrapped her in a blanket, put a comforting arm around her shoulders, and led her to the back of the ambulance.

Jake felt an unexpected stab of jealousy but checked himself.

He's just doing his job, you idiot!

Barney turned his eyes in the same direction and thumbed toward Libby. "Who's the babe? Doyle's girlfriend?"

Jake shook his head. "Her name's Libby. She's been helping me with my investigation. She has Kingsley's heart, and she's also his daughter."

"Wow! Seriously? That's messed up."

Jake nodded.

"I know you've been in enough trouble today, Mav, but you know we'll need a statement from you and Libby."

"Yes, of course."

Barney indicated the nearby police car. "Do you guys need a lift to the station?"

"No. My car's here."

"I'll tell the captain you're on the way. I wouldn't want to be in your shoes."

Jake couldn't resist smirking. "Your feet wouldn't fit, anyway. See you back there."

As soon as Barney left, Jake saw that the young paramedic still had his arm around Libby as they sat together at the back of the ambulance on the step. Rather than checking her vitals, he appeared to be trying to engage her with a huge smile, displaying his way-too-perfect teeth.

Step off, buddy!

With a frown, Jake walked over to them. "Thanks, but I'll take care of Ms. Davis from here."

The paramedic seemed annoyed. "And who are *you?*"

Jake pulled out his badge and thrust it into the young man's face, stopping short of whacking him on the nose. "I'm the detective investigating this matter. Ms. Davis needs to come with me."

The young man frowned at the aggressive move but reluctantly let Libby go.

Understandable. Libby is one stunning young woman.

Once back inside the Mustang, Jake put his hand on Libby's. "I know this has been a shocking day, and you will probably want to go on home, but we need to head to the station and make a report. Are you up for it?"

"Sounds like I have little choice. Okay, detective. Let's get this over with, then."

As Jake drove them back to the station, he sighed deeply, knowing what was coming, and was not looking forward to it.

The captain is going to be pissed!

CHAPTER 27

CONVINCING THE CAPTAIN

J ake and Libby, along with Barney, sat in the captain's office several hours later.

Bennett looked exasperated. "Masters, what part of *off duty* don't you understand?"

"I told you Nolan was dangerous!" Jake said as he glared at her. "You shouldn't have let him go without speaking to me first."

"Oh, not this again. Are you trying to tell me that Nolan killed this man?"

"Yes. Exactly. I saw Nolan running away from the crime scene, so it's unlikely to be anyone else. He must have gone straight there after you released him."

"You understand I had to follow protocol, Masters. Cotter told me Nolan was sitting in a bar having a drink and minding his own business until you both lured him outside. He wasn't committing any crime. You can't drag him into our station, interrogate him, and lock him up without probable cause or an arrest warrant."

"You know I had probable cause. Doyle said—"

The captain put up her hand. "Do I need to repeat myself? Until you bring a witness in to testify, it's all hearsay! Cotter told me you didn't have any other evidence. To top it off, they solved this crime twenty years ago. The attending police officers found Kingsley at the scene with the murder weapon in his hand. It seemed pretty cut and dried." The captain gestured toward Libby. "So, who's this young lady? What does she have to do with all this?"

"My name's Elizabeth Davis, ma'am. My surname used to be Kingsley, and, with due respect, this case is far from 'cut and dried.'"

"Kingsley?" Bennett frowned, and she turned to Jake. "Is this young woman related to the D.R.D.?"

"Yes, she's his daughter."

"How did you two meet up?"

"Remember that support meeting you and Helen made me attend? Well, we met there."

"And?"

"I did some sharing, we got chatting, and we realized we had some things in common, and er—" Jake hesitated. It would probably end his career if he told the captain about his dreams.

Libby had no such concern. She jumped in, and her words came out in a rush. "Like the day that we received our organs from my father. We had dreams about the convenience store robbery and knew my father was innocent. We saw who killed those people. It was Sean Nolan."

The captain blinked rapidly with eyebrows raised as she took it all in. "Dreams? And are you telling me you also have an organ from Kingsley inside you? Did I hear that right?"

Libby nodded. "Yes. I have Dad's heart. If you had read his records properly, you'd know that. You people killed my poor father for a crime he didn't commit. He only volunteered to become a death row donor because my mom told him I was dying from cardiomyopathy and needed a heart transplant."

Tears formed in Libby's eyes, and Jake automatically put his arm around her shoulders without thinking. He hated seeing her upset.

God, this girl is making me soft.

"Ma'am, without going into too much detail, there's been some bizarre stuff going down concerning our donor," Jake said. "And yes, there have been dreams. We've also been in contact with another recipient called Claudine McDonald, who received Kingsley's corneas and—"

"You've done what!" Bennett was furious. "That's an unforgivable breach of protocol! You realize you could lose your badge for this!"

"Yes, ma'am, I understand," Jake said as he defiantly held her gaze. "But it turned out to be a good thing. Ms. McDonald seemed thrilled that we reached out to her. She's an artist who's also struggled with the nightmares about the murders, causing her to feel compelled to paint images of the men responsible as a form of personal therapy."

Jake pulled his phone from his pocket and found what he sought after a few quick finger flicks. "You said you wanted evidence," he said, holding up his phone and showing a painting of Sean. "So check this out."

Bennett snatched Jake's phone from his hand and adjusted her glasses on the end of her nose. "What am I looking at here?"

"It's a painting of Nolan, but twenty years younger. He may be older and hairier these days, but his beady little eyes are unmistakable, and he still has the same neck tattoo."

The captain looked at Jake skeptically. "Are you expecting me to believe Ms. McDonald painted this because of a *dream*?"

Jake nodded. "If you don't believe me, then call her. Her details are in the D.R.D. recipient list document." He pointed at his phone. "Swipe to the next photo. You'll also find a painting of Doyle how he looked twenty years ago."

The captain did as instructed and held the image up for Jake's inspection. "Is this Doyle?"

"Yes."

"The man you found murdered today?"

"Yes."

"Was he a murderer as well?"

"No. Doyle was the accomplice."

Bennett's eyes flicked to Libby. "And you, Ms. Davis or Ms. Kingsley or whatever name you choose to call yourself—do you fully concur with this account of events?"

Libby nodded. "Yes. It's all true. Nolan's a killer, and you need to catch him and put him away."

The captain sighed as she stared hard at them both. "You realize this sounds crazy, right?"

"Look, I get it, ma'am. If I were you, I wouldn't believe us either." A glance at the expression on Barney's face told Jake that his friend was also having trouble with what he was hearing. Not surprising. "Why do you think I've been reluctant to tell you about it? But if you want more evidence, you can talk to my sister. I told her everything about my dreams. And then there's Trish from the support group. I shared my dream with her and everyone else there before I had my first proper conversation with Ms. Davis."

"And you can talk to my psychologist," Libby said. "I told him my dreams before I met Jake. I'll bet if you rang other recipients of Dad's organs, you'd find there's more of us, and—"

Bennett raised her hand, cutting her off. "All right, enough, the pair of you. I assure you I'll be ringing all the people you mentioned except the remaining recipients on the list apart from Ms. McDonald. I'll have to apologize to her on behalf of our department. You've both done enough damage there.

"But you need to be realistic. Dreams prove nothing because they're in your head, not the real world. You didn't experience any of this. It's the same issue we have when dealing with psychics. Supernatural evidence doesn't hold up in a court of law."

"But the paintings—"

"Yes, Ms. McDonald's paintings are interesting, but nothing a talented lawyer couldn't explain away."

Jake could feel his exasperation rising. "So, that's it then. We're giving up. Nolan gets away with murdering three people in cold blood."

The captain shook her head. "I didn't say that. There is something tangible we can work with regarding the case of who murdered Doyle. Masters, you say you saw Nolan running away from the scene? Well, that's enough for me to put a warrant out for his arrest, and we'll go from there."

"And what can I do to help?"

"I want nothing more from you right now, Masters. A man is dead because you went rogue and withheld this information from me until now. You need to go home and stay there. But I must warn you—if I hear of you trying to insert yourself into this investigation without my

approval, I *will* take your badge from you. If I need you, I'll call. Got it?"
Bennett pointed at the door. "Now get out, the pair of you."

Once the captain decided on something, there was no swaying her.
As instructed, Jake and Libby took their leave, headed outside to the
Mustang, and jumped in. By this stage, they had been at the station for
five hours.

First, they had to give detailed statements about Lucas Doyle's
murder and then sit around waiting to be interrogated by the captain.
By the end of it all, the pair felt drained.

"So, where to now, detective?" Libby asked.

"Well, this has been a tough day, so we need an unwind and a debrief.
I was, therefore, wondering if you'd like to accompany me back to my
place for dinner tonight. I cook a mean spaghetti Bolognese."

Libby gave a coy smile. "You mean like a date?"

Jake shrugged. "You could call it that. Or you could call it two people
getting together and having a meal. I'll let you decide what you want it
to be."

"Okay. I'd better call Mom and let her know."

"Yes, you do just that."

Seconds later, Libby was talking to Sarah. "Hi, Mom."

"Where did you rush off to this morning?" Sarah asked. "You tell me
nothing these days."

"I'm having dinner with Jake, and I just wanted to tell you not to
bother waiting up for me. I might not be home tonight at all. See ya!"
Libby hung up before her mother could ask any more questions or
protest. She then immediately turned her phone to silent.

Jake's eyes were wide, and it was hard to suppress a grin.

Don't bother waiting up! That sounds very promising.

He then started up the Mustang and headed home.

CHAPTER 28

THWARTED PASSION

Ten minutes later, they were at Jake's front door. His home was old-fashioned with a light brown clapboard exterior, white window trims, and a low-maintenance rock garden.

A green and white canopy swing seat sporting matching cushions, left behind by the previous house owner, sat on the veranda next to the front door. Jake would have put it out for curbside pickup when he moved in, but Goosy talked him into keeping it by telling him any girl he brought home would love it. It proved good advice, as he wooed many young ladies on that swing. A smile came to his lips. *It could happen again tonight if he gets lucky.*

Jake opened the door and invited Libby inside.

The living room had a single-man vibe with sturdy, dark-tone furniture. A large red brick fireplace dominated the middle of one wall, with stacked piles of chopped firewood on either side. It was minimalist, with no decorations other than a few framed photos on the mantelpiece.

A multicolored patchwork quilt draped across a dark gray suede couch was the only object that gave the room some femininity. Goosy had given him the quilt after his transplant. It didn't suit the rest of the décor, but Jake loved it. It was cozy, which came in handy most nights. Since the transplant and the accompanying nightmares, he often snuggled up in that quilt and fell asleep on the couch watching TV.

"It's not much, but I've paid it off, so it's all mine," Jake said.

"It's nice ..." Libby turned to him with a playful smile. "It's very ... you."

Unsure whether he should feel flattered or insulted by that remark, an awkward silence followed as the pair stood side by side, staring at the living room as if it were the most interesting place in the world, until Jake said, "So ... er ... would you like something to drink? A glass of water or a wine, perhaps?"

"A wine sounds lovely, thank you, but first, where's your bathroom?" She patted the handbag that hung by its strap from her shoulder and sat securely under her arm. "I'd like to freshen up."

Jake pointed. "Through that door, turn left, and it's at the end of the hall. But before you go, I need to know what wine you prefer. Red or white?"

"Either is fine. Your choice. Surprise me." Libby then disappeared for five minutes. When she returned, it was clear she had brushed her hair and applied a fresh coat of lipstick. Her full lips were redder than before, pouty and shimmery. She looked stunning.

"I've left my phone charging in your bathroom. I hope you don't mind. Don't let me leave here without it, okay? I can be forgetful sometimes."

Jake shrugged. "Well, if you do, it will mean you'll have to return for another visit, right?"

Libby smiled and batted her lashes flirtatiously.

He then picked up the two glasses of red sitting on the coffee table next to an open wine bottle and handed her one. "Enjoy."

"Thank you." She took a dainty sip of her wine, wandered over to the mantelpiece, and grabbed a photo of the twins. "So, is this your sister?"

"Yep. Sure is."

"It's hard to tell whether she's older or younger than you."

"If you asked Goosy, she would say she's my older sister because she beat me out of the womb by a whole two minutes."

Libby's eyebrows shot up. "So, she's your twin? Wow, you're nothing alike. From this photo, you look at least six inches taller than her."

"It's a common misconception that all twins should share physical similarities. But we're fraternal twins. Different eggs, different sex, and different people."

With a nod, Libby turned and returned the photograph to the mantelpiece. She reached out for the wooden-framed image of his parents.

Jake frowned. He made a habit of hiding that photo when he had women around. But having Libby come to his home had been unexpected. He realized she knew his parents had passed, but not the circumstances. The image could spark a more in-depth discussion about their unfortunate demise, which was one downer he preferred to avoid tonight at all costs—time for a distraction.

"So, are you hungry? I know I am," he asked.

"Yes. Starving. I haven't eaten since breakfast."

Jake rubbed his hands together. "I'd better head to the kitchen, then. I don't want you drinking on an empty stomach. Want to keep me company while I make us some dinner? It won't take long. We should be ready to eat in about fifteen minutes."

"Okay. Sounds good." Libby replaced the photo and followed him out of the room.

Jake pulled a stool from under the island bench for Libby and gestured for her to sit. He grabbed a pot, filled it with water, put it on the stovetop, set it to boil, and then pulled a packet of pasta from the cupboard.

Libby leaned forward as she watched him, elbows on the bench and hands under her chin. "Would you like me to help, detective? Chop some vegetables? Whatever?"

"Thanks, but there's not much prep required. I only have to boil the pasta and heat the sauce in the microwave. Just sit back, relax, and enjoy your wine. I've got this."

With a smile and a nod, Libby complied.

As promised, fifteen minutes later, the two sat at the dining table, toasting each other with their second glass of red and enjoying spaghetti Bolognese.

An hour later, they were full and mellow from their meal and wine, which Jake followed up with bowls of ice cream for dessert. It hadn't taken long for Libby to break down Jake's defenses, and before he knew it, he had shared the whole sorry tale with her about how his parents died.

By the end of another hour, they had opened another bottle of red and traded their war stories about their transplant experience. They progressed to their first love and kiss, leading to how they lost their virginity. Jake was relieved that Libby had experienced her share of wild times and promiscuity. It made it easier to tell her he'd gone off the rails and been a bit of a player since the death of his parents.

They both had one thing in common. Neither had ever been in love and couldn't grasp the concept. They agreed it was because they hadn't met the right person.

Something strange stirred within him as Jake stared deep into Libby's eyes. It was an unfamiliar feeling—a longing he had never felt before. The chat was becoming flirtatious. They even started discussing their favorite positions in bed, and Libby startled him when, at one point, she remarked, "How pedestrian."

Their heads became closer and closer across the small table. Jake felt drawn and unable to keep his eyes off her full red lips. He was sure she was pouting at him just a little. It would be easy to lean in and kiss her, but he knew they had drunk too much wine for him to go there. His police background and their recent complicated history made him cautious about crossing boundaries without consent.

Libby interrupted their flirtation and sat back in her chair with a groan, rubbing her neck.

"What's the matter?" Jake asked.

"Oh, nothing. It's just a sore neck. I told you I didn't sleep very well last night. I need a good massage."

Jake smirked at the blatant invitation for some physical intimacy. *Why not? I'll take the bait.* "If you want me to help, I have some skills in that department."

Libby smiled and nodded. "Sounds lovely. I would never refuse a free massage." Without hesitation, she undid the first few buttons of her blouse, revealing her ample cleavage, pushed it off her shoulders along with her bra straps, and dropped face down on the table, resting on her arms. She reached behind her neck and pushed her hair out of the way. It cascaded over her head and fanned out in front of her. "Go ahead."

The provocative vision transfixed Jake for a few seconds. She was playing with him. *Okay, let the games begin.* With a deep breath, he stood up and walked behind Libby. He reached out with tentative fingers, placing them onto her shoulders, and kneaded the muscles and skin. His reward was some low, seductive groans of appreciation.

After a few minutes, he leaned in and whispered in her ear. "Sit up."

Libby gave an appreciative shrug of her shoulders and complied. Jake pushed his fingers through her locks and massaged her scalp. Before long, she was leaning back toward him to increase the pressure of his fingertips.

Now, it was his turn to play. He leaned in and whispered again, "Not hard enough for you, am I?"

Yep, I'm going there.

The ploy worked spectacularly. Before Jake could say anything further, Libby twisted around and stood up. Eyes locked on his, she grabbed him by his shirt collar and pulled him in for a kiss. Her soft lips pressed against his, warm and enticing.

It would have been so easy for Jake to go with the moment, but the annoying cop in him needed to be sure. With a hand on either side of her head, he held her away and looked deep into her eyes. "Libby, look at me."

She stared at him, a tad confused.

"I need you to tell me you want this. I don't want to cross any lines here."

Libby gave him a cheeky smile. "Cross away. There are no lines." She made a wiping gesture at the air. "I rubbed them all away." She grabbed his hand and ran his fingers along the underside of her arm. "Feel that? I even have a contraceptive implant, so you don't need to worry about getting me pregnant. Now let's take this to your bedroom. Is that clear enough for you, detective, or do you require me to sign a consent document? If so, hand it over and pass me a pen."

Jake's eyes were wide with surprise. The confident directness was arousing, and the invitation couldn't have been more explicit, so he grabbed her hand and led her to his bedroom.

The pair laughed as they threw themselves onto the bed. Jake pulled Libby to him, and their lips locked once again. It turned passionate as their kiss deepened. Both starved of sexual intimacy for too long, bodies rubbed, hips ground together frantically as if they tried merging into one. Only a few layers of clothing prevented them from consummating their relationship.

And then it happened. Jake's lungs started constricting. He pulled back, clutching his chest as he gasped for air. Despite his extreme physical discomfort, he noticed from the contorted expression on Libby's face that she seemed to be in similar distress.

Instinctively, he rolled away from her, and the second he did so, his lungs started working again. His eyes flicked to Libby. From the relief on her face, she, too, had returned to normal.

Their eyes locked in confusion. The pair shrugged it off and resumed kissing. The coupling lasted mere seconds before, to Jake's horror, he found his lungs had ceased working again. Simultaneously, Libby started moaning and trying to push him away.

After rolling away from her, his lungs opened to let air in. "What the fu—" Jake stopped himself mid-rant. Despite what had happened, he was determined not to drop the dreaded f-bomb again.

Libby's eyes were wide, but it appeared her physical discomfort was gone again. She sat up with a hand flat to her heart. "Wow! That was horrible!"

Jake pretended to be offended. "Well, thanks."

"You know what I mean."

"Yes, unfortunately, I do. You don't think?"

Libby understood and nodded. "Yep." She looked up at the ceiling. "Dad! It's my life! Butt out!"

Jake couldn't help but laugh. "It appears your dad doesn't want his daughter dating a cop. Do you want to test this theory one more time?"

"I'm game if you are."

With a nod of agreement, the pair fell back on the bed. It only took a couple of deep kisses before Jake had to pull away again. He rolled onto his back, staring at the ceiling, feeling defeated as his breathing returned to normal. "This could prove problematic for a relationship in the future."

Libby rolled onto her side and propped herself, hand to head, observing him quizzically. "Relationship? I thought this was only some stress relief after an awful day."

Sadness washed over him. It's not what Jake wanted, and the thought surprised him. Having Libby in his home seemed right. It was like she belonged. For the first time since his parents had died, he contemplated settling down.

However, supernatural forces seemed to make a physical relationship between them impossible. And without physicality, there would be no passion or the chance to have kids, so how could they have a future together?

Shut up, Jake! Get a grip!

Libby ran a gentle finger down the side of his face. "You don't look happy, detective. What are you thinking?"

Jake shrugged. "I guess I was getting caught up in a romantic dream for us that can never happen. It's obvious what your dad thinks of me, and it's not very much, it seems."

Libby's face softened, and she, too, looked sad. She reached out and grabbed his hand. "I'm sure he would have liked you if he had ever met you. And I must admit you weren't alone in the romantic fantasy. We would have made a good couple."

With a sigh, Jake rolled off the bed onto his feet. Libby sat up, regarding him in a cross-legged position. He stared down at her, unable to imagine his life without her in it or finding this kind of connection with someone else. There was only one thing to do. He offered his hand. "Friends?"

With a sad smile, she reached out and shook it. "The best of friends."

Jake rolled his shoulders when they released, trying to shake it all off. "Right. Great. Now, there's only one minor issue."

"What's that?"

"I've had too much to drink, so I can't drive you home. Would you like me to send for an Uber?"

Libby fell back onto the bed and stretched. "I'm quite comfortable right here, detective. And I told Mom not to expect me home tonight, so ..."

"Okay, well, I don't want to upset your dad. Why don't you have my bed, and I'll take the couch? I'm used to sleeping there, anyway. How does that sound?"

"That's very nice of you. Thank you." Libby yawned and stretched. "I'm pretty tired."

"Yeah, you and me both. An early one?"

"Yes. An early one."

Jake pulled an oversized T-shirt from his chest of drawers and handed it to Libby. "Here. Something for you to sleep in."

"Thanks."

"Okay, I guess I'm heading off now." Jake leaned over and kissed Libby on the forehead. "Sweet dreams, *princess*."

"Sweet dreams, detective."

Jake headed into the living room, stripped to his boxers and T-shirt, and plopped on the couch. Provocative thoughts about Libby consumed his mind. His body reacted, and he moaned as he had to readjust himself. One part of him was not accepting the ghostly bedroom intervention. He briefly considered his usual nocturnal habit of pressure release but decided that would be a crass move with his new *best friend* only in the next room—time to exercise self-control and turn his thoughts elsewhere.

Flopping back against the couch, Jake pulled the quilt to his chin, grabbed the remote, turned on the television, and adjusted the volume to avoid disturbing Libby. He immersed himself in the news channel until his eyelids dropped, and sleep claimed him.

In his dreams, he found himself back in the convenience store.

Oh no, not again.

From experience, he knew he had no choice but to go with it.

The younger Sean stood in front of him, gun to his head. Jake steeled himself to replay the scene where he shot the woman on the ground.

However, for the very first time, something different happened. Jake felt compelled to turn his head and look up at the round, convex surveillance mirror in the room's corner. He'd never done that before.

Staring back at him, with his eyes wide with horror, was Jon, and then, like a camera zooming in, Jon's face filled the entire screen of Jake's mind. Lips moved with great urgency, trying to say something that wasn't quite audible until, suddenly, like someone had turned up the volume from zero to one hundred, Jon's voice blasted in his head. "Wake up! Listen to me! You need to WAKE UP!"

Jake's eyes flicked open just in time to see Sean Nolan standing above him, about to plunge Reaper into his chest. He gasped and rolled off the couch in a self-preservation reflex. A searing pain shot through him as the blade sliced the back of his left arm from shoulder to elbow. Although only a flesh wound, as he had pulled it away before Sean could do any significant damage, it was still a shock.

Holy hell! That hurt! This is no dream!

Jake clutched his bleeding arm and rolled to a standing position.

Nolan is in my house! How can this be happening?

As Jake dodged and weaved to avoid Reaper's razor-sharp edge, Sean slashed the air repeatedly.

"Oh, for fook's sake! Stand still! Ye won't be testifying against me, ye fooker! Without ye, they've got nothing."

All Jake could think about during the attack was Libby in the bedroom. He hoped she stayed there and knew there and then that he would fight to the death for that woman. But right now, he had an injured arm and no weapon handy to defend himself. It appeared the Irishman had the upper hand.

Sean stepped around the couch and lunged at him. As Jake dodged again, he lost his footing, fell backward, and struck his head against the edge of the coffee table.

All went black.

CHAPTER 29

BATHROOM BREAK

L ibby was dreaming about the convenience store again, but something was different. This time, her father was yelling at her to wake up. She sat bolt upright in bed and heard strange noises, then a distinct, angry voice that she could swear sounded like the Irishman, shortly followed by a loud crash.

What the hell was that?

Without thinking, she immediately jumped out of bed, self-consciously pulled down the oversized T-shirt, and ran into the living room. She quickly flicked on the light just in time to see Jake lying on the ground with Sean standing above him, Reaper in hand.

Libby screamed in fright. She then grabbed the heavy wooden picture frame with the photo of the twins from the mantelpiece and threw it at Sean as hard as possible. The corner hit his forehead, cut him, and bounced off. He looked dazed for a second but remained standing, glaring at her as he wiped away the blood that began to drip down his face.

"Ah, ye fookin' little bitch! Ye'll fookin' get it now!"

As the Irishman pursued her, Libby ran for her life. She headed for the bathroom at the end of the hallway. She knew the door had a bolt because she'd automatically slid it across to lock it when using it earlier. It was a force of habit from living with housemates.

A side table was in the hallway. Libby grabbed the edge, overturning it as she ran by. Unable to stop, Sean tripped over it and fell, swearing to the ground. Libby couldn't help but smirk as she ran into the bathroom and bolted the door.

With her eyes darting around the bathroom, Libby realized there was no window, just a skylight, so the only way out was the way she came in. *Trapped!* And then she spotted it. *Thank God! My phone! I forgot about that!*

Panic-stricken, she ripped the phone from the charger and, with fumbling fingers, punched 911.

Seconds later, a calm female voice replied. "911, what's your emergency?"

"My name's Libby Davis. I'm locked in the bathroom, and a man called Sean Nolan has broken into my friend's house and attacked him with a knife. I don't even know if my friend's alive, and now Nolan's coming after me. Please hurry!"

Boots stomped on the floor, coming toward her. It sounded like Sean had recovered from his fall, and it was terrifying.

"I'll get someone to you as soon as possible, Libby," the operator said. "What's the address?"

The door handle rattled as the Irishman tried to turn it. "Open up, ye fookin' little bitch! Don't make this harder on yerself."

"I'm somewhere in Chapman Street, Houston." Libby had dropped her voice to a low whisper, not wanting Sean to know she was on her phone. "I'm not sure of the exact number. It's a brown and white house with a swing seat on the veranda and a rockery out the front. Detective Jake Masters is the owner. Ask the Houston Police Department. They should have his address on file somewhere."

"Thank you. With that information, we should be able to locate you. We're also doing a trace on your phone right now."

The door handle rattled again. "This is yer last chance! If I have to break this fookin' door down, I'll make ye suffer when I get to ye. Do ye hear me, girl?!"

"Please hurry," Libby said to the operator.

"Keep the line open, Libby. My name's Amy, and I'll stay with you until the police arrive. We'll get help to you as soon as we can."

There was a thud on the other side of the door. It sounded like Sean punched it in anger.

"Fookin' stupid little bitch!"

Libby suspected the door wouldn't keep the Irishman out for long. She needed to slow him down so he wouldn't get to her before the police arrived. And then something occurred to her. She turned her back to the door and whispered, "You record these calls, right?"

"Yes, we do."

"I'm putting you on speaker. Say nothing for the next few minutes. It's vital. Do you understand me, Amy? He can't know that you're on the line."

"Okay. Understood. But know that I'm here listening if you need me. Just call out."

Suddenly, there was a crash and a slight splintering noise as Sean tried kicking the door in. A repressed groan and an angry muttering followed this. "I'm getting too old for this fookin' shite!"

The door seemed solid, and the bolt lock was large and heavy-duty. It sounded like the Irishman underestimated them when trying to break in, and he'd hurt himself.

Good! I hope you broke your foot, you evil bastard!

Libby jumped back in fright as another kick to the door resounded, not as loudly, and seemed more tentative than the first. Regardless, there was more splintering, and a crack appeared near the bolt. Sean wasn't giving up, sore foot or no sore foot. One or two more hefty kicks, and he would be in. She had to distract him before he tried again.

Here goes.

"Sean Nolan! Stop! I'm Jonathan Kingsley's daughter!" she yelled as loud as she could and then held the phone up to the door, waiting for a response.

There was a sudden silence, and then Sean finally replied. "What did ye just say there, girl?"

"I said that I'm Jonathan Kingsley's daughter. You know who he is. You set him up when you killed those three people at Singhe's Supplies. They executed my father because of you."

"Oh, yes, I well remember that handsome little black boyo. So, yer da finally got the guts to rat me out. It took long enough. At least now I know where yer cop friend got his information. So, they executed him, you say? No witnesses left now, so the cops have nothing."

"It won't bring my father back, but you owe me the truth. Admit it! You killed those three people at Singhe's Supplies and set my father up for it."

Sean gave out a sinister laugh. "Ye bet yer sweet precious little arse, I did. Stupid little fook that he was. He was well-behaved and did what I told him to do. All it took was one call from an anonymous witness to seal the deal."

"What do you mean? What call?"

"Please help! There's a black man shooting people at Singhe's Supplies! I saw everything through the glass door as I was about to enter! I must go before he comes out and shoots me, too. Please hurry! Don't let him get away." Sean was using a high-pitched voice that sounded like an old Irish woman.

It reminded Libby of the voice Brendan O'Carroll used when he played the title role of the hilarious sitcom *Mrs. Brown's Boys*, which her mother enjoyed streaming from BritBox. However, unlike that show, this was very far from funny. "You bastard!"

"I've been called worse." Sean's voice then became menacing. "So I guess I'll have to do what I threatened if he ratted me out."

"What are you talking about?" Libby held her phone closer to the door. The Irishman had no clue he was burying himself, and even if she didn't make it, the world would know the truth. "What did you threaten?"

"I promised yer da if he ever gave me up or described me to anyone that I'd slit yer throat, and yer dear ma will be next, assuming she's still alive. I'm a man of ma word."

"You leave my mother out of this, you pig!"

"Ah, so she is alive, then. Great! She'll soon learn the price of having a rat bastard for a husband." With that, Sean gave the door one last mighty kick, and it finally splintered at the lock, crashing open.

Libby dropped her phone from fright and watched in despair as it smashed onto the tile floor and bounced away. Panicked, she grabbed the air freshener from the top of the toilet cistern.

That'll have to do.

"Go to hell!" Libby stepped forward, sprayed him in the eyes, and then threw the can at him, hitting him on the bridge of his nose.

Sean howled in pain and reeled back. "Ye fookin' bitch! When I get hold of ye, ye'll wish ye didn't do that."

The Irishman stood in the doorway, blocking her from escaping. He slashed the air with Reaper as he rubbed his eyes, blinded by tears, trying to clear them.

Realizing he couldn't see, Libby dropped low, curled into a fetal position in the bathroom's corner, and trembled in terror as the deadly blade swept over her head. It was only a matter of time before Sean found his target.

God, help me!

Libby covered her face with her hands, awaiting the inevitable when the sound of breaking glass and a thud startled her. She peered through shaking fingers and saw that the Irishman was gone. As she brushed tears from her eyes in confusion, she heard Jake's voice.

"Libby! Are you all right?"

She crawled on her hands and knees, tentatively poked her head through the doorway and saw Jake crouched over a semi-conscious and groaning Sean. Beside them was a broken, empty wine bottle. It would seem Jake had smashed the Irishman on the head with it. Reaper was halfway down the hallway, and Libby realized Jake must have kicked it there.

Jake spotted her and looked relieved. "Thank God you're okay. Now stay back!"

He waved her away, and he stood with one foot on Sean's back to ensure he stayed down as he quickly pulled off his T-shirt, ripped it apart, used it to secure the dazed Irishman's wrists and ankles, and brought them together in a hogtie.

It was the first time she saw him without his shirt. He had the torso of an Adonis. Sure, scars covered his chest, as she expected, but somehow, that made him seem more manly, like some Hollywood warrior.

As soon as Sean was fully bound and unable to move, Libby launched herself at Jake, threw her arms around his neck, hugged him, and cried, "I was so worried he'd killed you."

"Just bumped my head and knocked myself out." Jake reached a hand around to the back of his head. Blood streamed from the cut on his arm.

Libby noticed. "Jake, you're bleeding."

Blood also covered the hand brought back from checking his head wound. Jake's knees suddenly buckled, and his eyes rolled upward. Libby reached out to stop him from falling, but she wasn't strong enough, so they collapsed together on the floor, on top of Sean.

"Get off me, you fookers!" the Irishman said with a moan.

Horrified, she rolled off him and, using all her strength, rolled Jake away from Sean onto his back. Libby cradled the young detective's head in her lap, not caring that he was bleeding all over her. She used her hands to press against his wounds, attempting to prevent him from losing more blood.

She stared at the evil man, groaning on the floor before her. Every impulse screamed to get as far away as possible. However, she wasn't strong enough to lift Jake and couldn't leave him. Libby felt helpless.

Her eyes flicked toward the bathroom. Hopefully, her phone was still on speaker and didn't break when she dropped it. Only one way to find out. "Amy, can you hear me?"

Please ... please still be there.

"Yes, Libby, I can hear you. Are you okay?"

"I'm fine, but you'll need to send an ambulance."

"We already have one on its way. How many people are injured?"

Libby tapped Sean with her foot.

"Fook off." The Irishman wiggled furiously but couldn't break loose. Jake must have been an excellent Boy Scout because he knew how to tie a knot.

"Only my friend. Nolan appears to be just fine, unfortunately," Libby replied.

"Fook you!" Sean retorted.

"Okay. Don't worry. Help should arrive soon."

As Amy spoke, Libby heard the front door smash open. Within seconds, cops were everywhere.

It was over.

CHAPTER 30

RUDE AWAKENING

"Mr. Masters? Can you hear me?"

An unfamiliar female voice was calling him. It seemed very far away.

Am I dreaming? What's happening?

Someone was gently rolling back Jake's left eyelid with their thumb. There was a sharp light, and he winced from the unexpected intrusion into his slumber. Then, mercifully, the mystery person let his eyelid go. It was a short-lived relief as they repeated the procedure on the right. He wanted to protest, but his lips wouldn't move, and his throat was sore.

Who is that? Why are they torturing me?

He tried to open his eyes, but his eyelids wouldn't cooperate. This won't do. He had to see what was going on.

"Shouldn't my brother be awake by now?" asked a second familiar voice.

The first voice spoke. "His pupils are reacting to light, which is a good sign. The sedation is wearing off. Give it time."

"Is he going to be okay, doctor?" Another familiar female voice, full of concern, joined the conversation.

"We'll know in a few minutes, ladies. Please be patient. I'm confident he'll be fine, although you never can be one hundred percent sure with these things."

Someone grabbed his right hand and started stroking it. "Come on, detective. Come back to us."

Within seconds, someone else took hold of his left hand and squeezed it a bit too hard. "You've got this, little bro! I believe in you."

It was two different styles of care. Jake felt he should know who these two women were. Why couldn't his stupid brain put the pieces together?

He could vaguely comprehend their concern and was determined to dig deep. Pulling on every internal resource he had, Jake willed his eyelids to open.

Squinting, he saw body shapes surrounding him, but everything seemed blurry. Wherever he was, the lighting was bright.

"Look, doctor, he's coming around. Oh, thank God!" the voice on his right said.

Jake struggled to regain his vision. He blinked rapidly, and to his relief, things started coming into focus.

Still very disoriented, he stared upward. Standing above him was a middle-aged Asian woman with a pixie bob haircut and a white coat.

She smiled at him. "Welcome back, Mr. Masters. I'm Dr. Junko Tanaka, and you're in the neuro intensive care unit at Memorial Hermann Hospital."

Before the doctor could say anything more, Goosy leaned in from the left with a massive grin. "Well, it's about time you woke up, little bro. Now speak to me. I need to make sure your brain isn't all messed up. You know I'm not equipped to deal with that crap. I'd put you in a home in a heartbeat."

"Ms. Masters!" The doctor sounded quite shocked.

Someone seemed to find Goosy's outburst hilarious, and a familiar laugh filled the air. Jake turned his head to the right and saw Libby staring at him. Tears filled her eyes.

"Nice to see you awake, detective."

"Ladies, step aside, please," the doctor said. "I want to examine Mr. Masters. I need to ensure the concussion hasn't impaired his cognitive abilities."

Goosy snorted in disgust. "Well, what do you think I was trying to do just then?"

Dr. Tanaka appeared unamused. She pointed to the chairs on the other side of the room. "Over there and sit down, please, Ms. Masters." Her head turned to Libby. "And you, too, Ms. Davis. Thank you."

Jake watched as the two girls exchanged annoyed glances, but they complied and sat watching at a distance as the doctor performed her examination.

"Mr. Masters, you sustained an injury when you fell and hit your head. The impact caused minor swelling of the brain and a slight bleed. You also suffered a cut to your left upper arm. Fortunately, it wasn't too deep, but there was significant blood loss."

Jake pulled his injured arm out from under the sheet for inspection and noticed a bandage covered it. He wiggled his fingers and was relieved to find everything seemed to work. There appeared to be no pain, so he knew he must be on some excellent drugs.

"Do you remember what happened to you?"

"Yes." Jake's voice sounded raspy. He clutched his throat and swallowed painfully. "May I have some water?"

Without another word, Dr. Tanaka picked up a nearby water jug, filled a sippy cup, and put it to Jake's lips. "Drink."

He grabbed it and gratefully gulped down all the contents.

The doctor took back the cup and placed it on the side table. "Better?"

"Yes." Jake gave her a smile and a thumbs-up. "Thanks."

"Because of your injuries, we wanted to give your brain the best chance of recovery without surgery, so we put you in a medically induced coma for a few days. Do you understand?"

Jake nodded. His mind flashed back to six months ago when he woke up in the hospital after the transplant. His sore throat suggested the medical staff had intubated him, but at least this time, they removed the tube before waking him. He shuddered as he mentally pushed the unpleasant memory away.

"I would like to perform some basic tests and ask a few questions to ensure all is well with you." Dr. Tanaka held up some fingers in front of his face. "So, Mr. Masters, how many fingers am I holding up?"

"Three."

"And what do you do for a living?"

"I'm a detective with the Houston police."

Dr. Tanaka beckoned Goosy to her side. "And who is this person to you?"

His sister couldn't resist crossing her eyes and poking out her tongue.

Jake smirked. "This is my annoying twin sister, Lucy, but everyone calls her Goosy."

Dr. Tanaka nodded. "Now, I would like to ask you a question to determine whether you lost any time from your concussion. You might find it distressing, so I must apologize in advance."

"I'm a police officer. I can handle it. Just ask me."

"Okay. Can you remember the name of the man who attacked you?"

Jake's mouth set in a straight line. "Yes. His name's Sean Nolan."

"And where did this happen?"

"In my home. It was in my living room, to be exact."

"Very good. Again, I apologize for reminding you of such a traumatic event. On the upside, your brain injury doesn't appear to have caused any short-term memory loss. You should fully recover, and if all goes well, I expect to release you in a couple of days."

"Thank you, doctor."

Dr. Tanaka turned to Libby and Goosy. "Ladies, as you can appreciate, this has been a disorienting experience for Mr. Masters, so we don't want to overwhelm him. I suggest you say your goodbyes and come back a bit later." She turned to Jake. "A nurse should be with you shortly, Mr. Masters. I'll be back to see you tomorrow." The doctor gave them a polite nod and left the room.

The second she was gone, both girls were at his side.

"Man, that bitch was intense," Goosy said. "I reckon if she smiled, her face would crack."

"She's just doing her job, sis. Have a little respect for the medical profession." Jake then looked from Goosy to Libby and back again. "So, I see you two have met?"

He was concerned. Goosy never seemed to like any of his girlfriends. If she even got a whiff of him getting serious with anyone, she was all over it with negativity and finding fault. It was a primary reason he found it challenging to consider settling down.

"Yeah. We braided each other's hair while you played *Sleeping Beauty*." Goosy gave Libby a wicked sideways glance. "She's pretty hot, so we've even been making out to pass the time. I hope you don't mind. You know we always seem to share a similar taste in women."

Jake frowned. "Goosy! Behave! God, I can't take you anywhere."

He accepted his sister's blatant bisexual lifestyle long ago, but she often used it for shock value. When they were in their teens, Goosy coming on to any girl he was dating was a mechanism she employed to scare them away, and it pissed Jake off.

However, when his police career made him decide to keep his relationships casual, he allowed this behavior if it helped detach a five-stage clinger required for a good time, not a long time. But he didn't want that happening with Libby.

Therefore, he was stunned to see her sidle up to Goosy and put an arm around her waist.

"I'm sorry, detective. But the heart wants what the heart wants." Libby lovingly rested her head on Goosy's shoulder and fluttered her lashes at him.

Jake thought his eyes were going to bug out of his head.

The two girls seemed to suppress smiles until they broke. They looked at each other and laughed. They then planted a loud *mwah* kiss on each other's lips. Both pairs of mocking eyes turned back to Jake.

Bitches!

He smirked. Finding a woman who appreciated his sister's warped humor was a relief. It appeared Goosy also liked Libby. Jake thought such a woman would never exist.

"Excuse me, ladies"—a young male nurse with buzz-cut black hair, who looked like he had stepped straight out of a fashion magazine, broke into their tomfoolery—"I need to get Mr. Masters prepped for transfer. He'll need privacy, so you both should take a break. If you want to come back, say six to seven pm this evening, I'll have him all cleaned up and well settled into his new room by then."

Goosy released Libby and threw her hands up dramatically. "Okay, okay! First the doc, and now you! We can take a hint ... er"—she leaned in and blatantly read the nurse's name tag—"*Clark*. So, where are you taking my little bro, *Clark?*"

"We'll be moving Mr. Masters to a private room."

"Second question," Goosy said, licking her lips and devouring him with her eyes. "What time do you get off?"

Jake couldn't help but smirk. *Typical Goosy. Such a flirt!*

"I get off at ten—precisely when my *boyfriend* picks me up," Clark said, not missing a beat.

Undeterred, Goosy winked, smiled coyly, held up three fingers, wiggled them suggestively, and paused as she eyeballed him.

Jake's eyes widened in horror as he got her meaning immediately.

No, Goosy! No! Too far—way too far!

Clark seemed to understand the offer and was up for the challenge. He held Goosy's gaze without blinking, hands on hips as he arched an amused, beautifully manicured eyebrow as if daring her to speak it aloud.

Jake and Libby witnessed the non-verbal exchange, enthralled with eyes wide.

Goosy looked away first and broke the uncomfortable silence by laughing. "*Third* question," she said, wiggling her fingers again as if this was her intention all along and not the threesome request Jake knew she was really offering. "What will be his room number?"

Clark shrugged. "We don't know that yet. Just call or ask reception when you come back. Will that be all?"

Goosy nodded. "Yes, *Clark*. That'll be all." She then turned to Jake. "Catch ya later, little bro. I'll be back tonight."

"Me, too," Libby said.

Goosy offered Libby her arm. "Lunch?"

Libby took it and huddled in close. "Love to. My treat!"

"No, I wouldn't think of it. I insist on paying. I asked you out first."

Jake shook his head at the performance.

Oh, for God's sake!

"Split the bill?" Libby asked.

Goosy nodded. "Okay. Let's go with that."

The girls exchanged conspiratorial winks, blew Jake kisses, and then, arm in arm, sauntered out of the room.

CHAPTER 31

DAD'S APPROVAL

By the evening, Jake was feeling more alert and human. After the medical team removed his intravenous line and condom drainage, they transferred him to a private room, where he ate his first proper meal in days. He even walked to the bathroom to enjoy a hot shower and a shave with Clark's assistance, who changed his arm wound dressing afterward.

As promised, Libby and Goosy returned to visit him just in time to interrupt his dinner. His sister plopped herself on his bed, grabbed his ice cream and jelly dessert without bothering to ask if he wanted it, and then, as she devoured it, regaled him with stories about her *awesome* day out with Libby.

Libby sat down on the other side of his bed and watched his face with ill-concealed amusement as she filled any occasional pauses Goosy left. Jake barely spoke during the exchange between the two women beyond offering an "Uh-huh" or "Okay."

The incessant chatter continued for the next hour and didn't stop even when the food services lady stepped in to take his empty meal tray away.

A polite knock on the door, followed by Barney entering the room, finally shut them down. "Well, well, well! He lives!" He gave a slow, mocking clap. "You should buy shares in this place—you're here that often. I hoped to catch you in the middle of a sponge bath with a hot nurse." The large man chuckled at his joke, and the girls joined in. Encouraged, Barney held up his phone and pointed at it. "I was even ready to take a photo to share with the guys at work."

Everyone's a comedian today. Okay, I'll play.

"You're too late," Jake said. "My nurse *was* hot but not your type. His name was Clark."

Goosy shook her head and put up her hand in disagreement. "I'll stop you right there, little bro. Clark's anyone's type. Trust me, Barney, if any guy were going to turn you, he would."

Barney's booming laugh erupted, infecting everyone in the room, but there was concern in his eyes when the laughter died. "But seriously, Mav, how are you? Brain okay and all that?"

"I'm feeling much better than when I first woke up, and today's brain scan was fine. My doc wants to monitor me for a couple more days, but I already feel good enough to go home."

"Thank God for that. I thought I'd get stuck with that rookie detective I've been training permanently." He looked over at the girls. "Sorry, I should have said hello earlier, ladies. Thanks for calling and telling me he was awake."

Goosy gave Barney a friendly punch on the arm, and Libby smiled.

Jake was losing patience with all the small talk. "Look, Barn, it's great to see you. The fun and games have been entertaining, but it's time you caught me up on what I've missed. What happened with Nolan? Is he all right? I remember clocking him pretty hard on the back of the head with a wine bottle and tying him up with my T-shirt. It went foggy after that and—"

Before he could finish, a middle-aged nurse with gray and brown hair styled in a tight bun walked in to check on him.

Dammit! It's like a revolving door with these hospital people!

The nurse smiled at them, walked over to Jake, and put a cuff on his right arm to take his blood pressure. "How are you, Mr. Masters?" she asked, waiting for the cuff inflation. "Any arm pain? Any headaches?"

"I'm fine, thanks. I just need some private time. Police business and all that."

"Understood." The nurse noted his blood pressure result and, when finished, deflated the cuff. "All good, Mr. Masters. Everything appears normal, so this will be your last check for the evening. Press the buzzer if you need anything, and we'll be right with you."

"Thank you." Jake turned back to Barney with questioning eyes.

"Don't worry. The bastard's fine. Unlike you, he has a hard head and is in jail where he belongs. The good news is that we got him. And I mean, we *really* got him, and—"

"Oh, God! Are we going to talk about this crap again?" Goosy interrupted, pulling a face. "No offense, little bro, but I'm over it. Don't get me wrong. It's great you're conscious and everything, but this evil Irishman stuff is just too negative for my psyche. I'd rather leave you guys to it. I have a gig I must prepare for tonight anyway and need to be in a positive head space, so I'm going to take off, okay?"

Jake smirked. One thing he loved about his sister was her complete lack of a filter. Goosy never left him wondering how she felt about anything. "That's fine. I know you hate any form of police business."

"Yeah, you get me, little bro." She walked over to her brother and planted a big kiss on his cheek. "Love ya. I'll drop in again tomorrow for some twin time, okay?"

"Bye, sis. And I love you, too."

Goosy winked at Libby on her way out. "If you ever want to go on another *date*, you have my number." She then performed the *call me* gesture with her pinkie and thumb as she mouthed the words, blew her a kiss, turned away, and left the room, wiggling her butt provocatively.

Classy!

"Sorry about that," Jake said, turning to the other two. "Please go on."

"Well, the good news is that pinning Nolan for Doyle's murder turned out to be relatively easy." Barney coughed. He put his finger up, showing he needed to pause for a second, grabbed Jake's empty cup, filled it with water, took a sip, and then went on. "Even though he'd tipped bleach all over the body to degrade the DNA evidence, the autopsy revealed that Doyle scratched him. Nolan's skin was under his fingernails, and the bleach had missed it. And then there was his knife—"

"You mean *Reaper*?" Jake and Libby simultaneously interrupted, followed by, "Jinx!" They then locked eyes and laughed.

Barney was confused. "Sorry, but am I missing something?"

"Private dream-related joke," Jake said. "Don't worry about it. So, what did you find?"

"Okay, well, forensics discovered that Nolan's knife, *Reaper*, or whatever you call it, had DNA from three people - Nolan, Doyle, and you, after he sliced your arm with it, of course. And there was plenty of Doyle's DNA and blood on his boots. We also found specks of Doyle's blood and Nolan's DNA in the bathroom and the laundry when he tried to clean himself up afterward. All that evidence, along with the fact that you saw him running away from the crime scene, left zero doubt he was the killer."

"But what about the convenience store murders?" Jake asked.

"Well, it's quite a girl you've got here," Barney said as he gently nudged Libby with his elbow, and she smiled. "Thanks to her, we got him for those as well. Talk about quick thinking under pressure.

"When Nolan went after Libby, she got him to confess, and the 911 operator recorded everything. Based on the conversation, it wasn't hard to put it together.

"We had two critical pieces of evidence to work with. First, we had the original 911 recording of the anonymous witness retrieved from Kingsley's audio file. The voice was very distinctive, with an Irish accent. Our experts compared it to the recent 911 recording when Nolan put on that voice for Libby. It was a match. And then there was Kingsley's driver's license and the photograph of his family that sealed the deal."

"You mean the ones Nolan took from him at the crime scene?" Jake asked.

"How could you possibly know?" Barney scratched his head, momentarily confused again, then his face lit up with understanding, and he nodded. "Oh yeah, that's right—those psychic nightmares of yours. Well, we got a search warrant for Nolan's place. The bastard kept them in a locked box like freaking trophies. It supports the theory that Kingsley deliberately failed to identify him as the shooter because of the threat to his wife and Libby.

"The Irishman also had every newspaper clipping about the murders back then. When the police put the evidence together, they determined Nolan was the killer, and Kingsley was innocent of the crime."

"So, where are we at with putting him away for good?" Jake asked.

"Job's already done. When faced with all this, Nolan's attorney cut him a deal—the death penalty was to be taken off the table and commuted to life imprisonment without parole if Nolan confessed to Doyle's murder and the other three to save the state the trouble of a trial. The prosecutor agreed, so the case was closed. That murderous bastard will never see outside a prison again."

Barney nodded toward Libby. "The captain will ensure that the state exonerates your father, and you can expect a hefty compensation for your loss to you and your mother."

Libby shook her head. "It was never about money."

"Yeah, I know, but it sure ain't gonna hurt," Barney said. He leaned forward and patted Jake on the hand. "Good work, detective. I think you'll be back on the force quicker than you thought. As soon as you're back on your feet, of course."

"And what does the captain think about all this?"

"I'm sure you'll be hearing from her soon. I wanted to be the first to tell you. Anyway, I'll leave you two to have a chat and will catch you tomorrow. Glad to see you're looking a lot better, Mav."

The two men shook hands.

"Thank you for everything you've done and for believing in me," Jake said.

"I know you would have done the same for me."

As soon as Barney left, Jake and Libby smiled at each other.

"It's over." Libby gave a deep sigh.

"Yep. All over." Jake eyed her warily. "So, what does this mean for us?"

She shrugged and edged close to him from where she sat on his bed. "You don't know how glad I am that you're okay." She threw her arms around him, hugged him hard, then sat back and stared at him longingly. The two held each other's gaze for what seemed an eternity.

Tentatively, Jake reached out and ran a gentle finger down her cheek. She cocked her head to one side, causing her long hair to fall away, exposing her neck. He wanted to kiss that neck so very much.

"Oh, to hell with it," Jake muttered. With a groan, he reached out to Libby and pulled her to him. She put up no resistance as their lips drew together.

They started with careful and gentle kisses, but their passion soon grew. Libby kicked off her shoes, climbed onto Jake, and, before long, the pair were writhing against each other.

Suddenly, Libby pulled back, hand to heart, eyes wide with fear.

Jake frowned. *Oh, no! Don't tell me it's happening again!* He reached out his hand, putting it on top of Libby's. "Are you okay?"

She gave a slow nod. "Yes, detective. I think so. And you?"

Jake took a few tentative breaths. "Yep. So far, so good."

Libby wiggled her eyebrows suggestively and, with her eyes fixed on his, unbuttoned her blouse. She parted it to reveal her black lacy bra and ample cleavage again—a memory that had burned into Jake's mind in the park. He gently ran his finger up and down her scar in wonder, and she shuddered. Her huge, brown eyes were half-closed, staring at him, filled with desire.

Libby then reached her hands under his hospital gown. Her fingertips stroked his skin, exploring the scars on his chest. Somehow, for the first time, Jake wasn't self-conscious. He realized she had already seen them, so he reveled in her loving touch on his bare flesh.

To provide better access, he pulled off the hospital gown and dropped it to the side of the bed. He was now naked, his modesty only preserved by a hospital sheet concealing his lower half.

A coy smile came to Libby's lips, showing she liked what she saw, but then worry creased her brow. "Are you sure you're up to this, detective?"

Part of Jake's body was more than ready. Throwing back the sheet and revealing this was tempting, but that would be vulgar. Instead, he answered her question by pulling her to him for another deep kiss, burying his fingers in her hair.

As they attempted to consume each other, Libby grabbed Jake's hands, directing him to unhook her bra. He was eager to comply, and his reward was the sight of the lacy undergarment falling away to expose spectacular, full, yet perky breasts.

Oh my God!

He couldn't resist cupping them and gently running his thumbs back and forth across their rosy peaks. He received a soft moan of encouragement. Jake was keen to take one of them into his mouth, but didn't get the chance.

To his surprise, Libby rolled away from him and stepped onto the floor. With a cheeky smile, she dragged the hospital curtain around his bed, enclosing them. Jake's eyes widened as he watched her peel off her jeans and lacy black panties. Once naked, she stood and presented her stunning body with a precocious twirl, much to his delight.

Libby wasted no more time. She reached out with one hand, grabbed the top of the hospital sheet, and pulled it back with a flick of her wrist, revealing his desire for her. Her eyebrows shot up as Libby ogled his body and manhood in all their naked glory and seemed impressed. She then jumped back on the hospital bed and straddled him.

Jake had planned on offering more foreplay, but it seemed Libby wasn't willing to wait. Her moist heat enveloped him as she descended. She then rode him with a rhythm as old as time. He bucked back against her as they urgently took their relationship to the next level. They knew someone could enter at any moment and catch them in the act, but neither cared. Nothing else mattered but this.

Afterward, Jake and Libby lay naked, face to face, holding each other under the hospital sheet. They locked eyes in wonder, knowing precisely what the other was thinking, but it didn't need to be said.

Jonathan Kingsley finally approved.

ACKNOWLEDGEMENTS

Thank you to Alan, who cracked the whip on me to finish writing this book because he thinks it will make a great movie. Your encouragement and feedback gave me the impetus to pull my finger out after many false starts and get it done.

Thank you to Alice and Mez for picking up those typos in my first draft and giving their feedback, making this a better book. You girls were terrific.

Thank you to fellow writer Julian, who came halfway on this journey with me some years ago before procrastination caused me to set it aside again.

Thank you to my cover critics, Claudine (for the bleeding-heart idea) and Shane, who pushed me to improve it. Also, thank you to my hubby, Ray, who inspected every version presented to him with good grace and to various board gaming, trivia, and tennis buddies, of whom there are too many to mention.

Special thanks to Sparky (Clark), who not only assisted with proofreading and providing medical knowledge and feedback but was also a constant source of encouragement and support with the time-consuming cover creation process and the countless variations when I had well and truly worn my other friends out.

Additional thanks to my beta reader, Peter, who, after the first small print run, gave excellent recommendations that were implemented in this book.

Notwithstanding the great help from these contributors, I own any errors that remain.

Finally, thank you to my dear readers whom I haven't met but decided my book looked worth reading. I would appreciate your feedback, so please take a few moments to write a review.

You can also contact me at info@vikkimount.com.

Thank you one and all!

About the Author

Vikki Mount is an Australian writer of thriller and romantic fiction.

Vikki completed the beginners and advanced courses with The Writing School in the early '90s. This led to a career as a commercial copywriter for radio from 1995 to 2006. During that time, she published two short stories and created two Australian romance novels, "Love Child" (published 2024) and the yet-to-be-published "Halfway Hearts." The latter is coming soon.

"An Innocent Heart" is Vikki's first thriller.

For more up-to-date information, visit Vikki's website at: -
www.vikkimount.com